STOLEN TWILIGHT

Book 3 of the Gypsy Notes Series

S. DALAMBAKIS

COPYRIGHT

AUTHOR NOTE

Trigger Warning

This book touches on themes of abuse, both mentally and physically. If you struggle with these issues, this book may not be for you. If you do decide to continue reading, proceed with caution.

If you or someone you know is a victim of abuse, please call:
    The National Domestic Violence and Abuse Hotline: 1-800-799-SAFE (7233)

Remember you are strong, you are fierce, and you got this.

Much Love,
    S. Dalambakis

QUOTE

Moonlight is the proof that there
will always be light in the darkness.
-Unknown

THE POEM

In the human realm is the first piece of the puzzle that you
seek,
In a house of white, hidden in plain sight.
Adventure and treasure await those brave enough to look,
But be careful for danger lurks.
For one to succeed all she would need,
Is the help and love in the form of her mates, which are three.
Together they will change the realms for all to see.

From the human realm you must go,
To a place covered in ice and snow.
Dance with the king and you will see,
Not all appears as it seems.
To get the treasure that you seek,
You must show that you are not weak.
For you may take a life, but do it with strife,
And save more than just your pride.

For the next piece that you seek,
you go down, down, far beneath the trees.

Fire and brimstone are what you'll find,
But be wary of deceit and webs of lies.
A date with the devil is what you'll get,
But you'll have to be quick.
For your gift will only get you so far,
And you'll have to rely more on your wit.

The last piece of the puzzle you will find
in a place where only the moon shines.
A party in the moonlight will be quite a sight,
but be prepared to fight.
Assemble the pieces and follow the trail,
you'll end up in a distant land.
A throne is what they sought,
now go and take back what they took.

PROLOGUE

UNKNOWN PERSON

"I need you to check something for me," Finley's mother says as she whirls into my living space. I gently place the book I was reading down.

"And what would that be?" I question. I watch as she walks over to the Fountain of Reflection.

"I need you to show me Finley's father." She runs a hand through her pale blonde hair. "I need to see where he is and what he's doing. I need to know if he's looking for her."

"You're finally going to tell me who he is?" I can't keep the hint of surprise out of my voice.

"I don't have a choice. This whole situation is forcing my hand. Finley and her guys are one piece of the map away from having the whole thing. Word is going to get out, if it hasn't already. I never once thought he wasn't looking for her. With all of this happening, it makes it easier for him to find her." Finley's mother starts pacing and running her fingers through her.

"Do you really think he is still looking after all these years?"

I stand, moving around the coffee table. Finley's mother stops and stares me right in my eyes. Her gray ones meeting my blue.

"I don't think he ever stopped," she whispers. There is concern etched on her face. "They have three pieces already. Word has to be getting out." She's right. There has to be whispers, or rumors, circulating by now. Something like this can't stay secret.

"Even so, the Realms hardly interact with each other. Do you honestly think they would let it be known that they were stolen from? No, that is something that they would keep to themselves. The only two realms I'm sure know that Finley took the map are the Earth and the Faerie. Winter Court isn't looking for her though. After Kellan died and Cirro took over, he willingly let them keep the piece of the map hidden there. The Earth Realm is, but they think she lives there. They haven't begun looking in the other realms for her. As for Lucifer, the last time I checked, he hadn't realized what she took. He's pissed, but mostly because she one-upped him. He's more curious about what and who she is."

"Does Lucifer have anyone looking for her?" She places her hands on the edge of the fountain, gripping it tightly.

"I thought you wanted me to check in on Finley's father?"

"I do, but..." she trails off.

"But you're just stalling." I wave my hand over the water. An image of Lucifer appears. He's pacing his office as a demon is relaying information.

"That's all well and good, but what about the other thing I asked of you?" Lucifer voices.

"As of right now, we haven't had any luck finding her."

"What do you mean you haven't found her?" he bellows. "I told you she lives in the Magic Realm. How hard could it be to find one pink-haired woman?" Lucifer's voice booms. The demon takes a step back, lowering his head.

"The Magic Realm is vast, and we don't know exactly which

part she lives in. They also aren't welcoming to our kind there. It's been hard gathering information when no one will talk to us." Lucifer lets out a roar. The demon falls to his knees.

"Keep looking for her."

"Yes, my Lord." The demon scrambles to his feet and out the door.

"Where are you my little muse?" he runs his fingers through his black hair. He walks over to the shelving on the right side of the room. Gently, he runs his fingers over a violin. "You can run little muse, but I will find you. I know you took the map, and I want to know why."

I wave my hand over the water and the image disappears. Finley's mother can't put this off any longer.

"I need his name," I say softly.

"Orson...Orson Acker," she chokes out.

My head whips up at the name. Orson is well-known in certain circles. He has his fingers in everything, and none of it legal. He has dealings with every realm.

"H-How? W-why?" I stammer.

Finley's mother looks up from the fountain, fresh tears falling down her cheeks.

"I was young and stupid." She hangs her head before continuing. "We met during one of the times my family was visiting the Earth Realm. We went to one of those State Fairs and I was having the time of my life." Finley's mother lifts her head, meeting my eyes. "He was there with a group of his friends. I was waiting in line to ride the Ferris Wheel, picking at my cotton candy, when I glanced around me and saw him. Orson was in line for the bumper cars; our eyes met. I smiled at him and he smiled back. He said something to his friends and walked over to me. We must have rode the Ferris Wheel at least six times. We joked and laughed. It was perfect. We kept in touch."

"What happened?" I question.

"We were twenty and had been together for a few years. I thought we were going to be together forever. I was so naive. I told him about me, about who and what I am. I told him everything about the realms. I knew he would be curious. At first it was the usual questions... Does this exist? Is this real? What would happen if this happened?"

"But then?"

"But then questions changed when he learned of my background... when he learned of the treasure and that I was a descendant. His kind and calm demeanor changed into someone I didn't recognize. He became greedy and hell bent on finding the map. Then I found out I was pregnant, and..."

"And I know the rest. I know how that turns out."

She wipes the tears from her face. "You do, but there is so much more that happened. I don't know when the change in him happened. Maybe it was there the whole time and I was too blind to see it." I walk over to her, wrapping her up into my arms.

"You don't have to say anything else," I whisper into her hair as I stroke her back. It doesn't take a genius to piece together what happened. We stay like that until she's ready. "Are you sure you want to do this?"

She pulls away, using the sleeve of her robe to wipe her face. "I have to." I give her a few more moments to gather herself. I move back over the fountain and wave my hand over the water. A tall man with light brown and graying hair appears.

"Any news on my daughter?" Orson asks another man standing across the desk from him.

"No, Sir."

"I have to give her mother credit. She has hidden her well. It also doesn't help that I don't know exactly when she was born or where she's hidden her." He drums his fingers on the desk. "What about the other thing?"

"There has been chatter that someone is finding the pieces

4

of the map." Orson stops drumming his fingers and sits straighter in his chair.

"Have they been successful?"

"Yes." A grin spreads across his face.

"I think I just found a way to find my daughter."

"Sir?" The man standing slightly tilts his head.

"Take a seat and let me tell you a story about a prophecy." I wave my hand over the water, clearing the image.

"No, no, no," Finley's mother starts shaking her head. "He can't find her. We have to stop him." She starts pacing. "I was afraid of this happening. I always knew he would never give up on finding her. He's too greedy and selfish."

"Would he hurt her?"

"Maybe not at first, because right now she would be useful to him, but the second she's no longer needed..." she trails off. She doesn't need to finish because I know what she's implying. Her eyes well up with tears. I walk around the Fountain of Reflection, pulling Finley's mother back into my arms, hugging her tightly.

"We'll make sure it doesn't come to that." I pull back, cupping her face. "He'll never lay a hand on her." I pull her back into my arms and let her cry. "I promise.

CHAPTER 1

FINLEY

"Come on, Obsidian. You can't keep putting this off and making excuses. We've given you a month."

I follow Obsidian as he stomps through the living room and into the kitchen. Stolas is leaning against the counter with a cup of coffee in his hands and a smirk on his face. He's enjoying this a little too much. His black hair is perfectly tousled, and his silver eyes sparkle with amusement. Verkor is sitting at the kitchen table eating a bowl of cereal. His shoulder length, blonde hair is pulled back into a man bun, and as much as I thought I would hate it, I have to admit it looks good on him. I meet his blue eyes. He raises an eyebrow at me, silently questioning if everything is alright. I give him a slight nod. Obsidian whirls, blocking my view of Verkor. He faces me with his ever-present scowl on his face.

"I don't want you there," he growls.

"Yeah, well you don't have a choice," I growl back. Having taken on some hellhound traits since becoming pregnant has really helped me. I can growl and bellow right back at any of them.

"You don't know what it's like there. You don't know those shifters like I do." He runs his hands through his auburn hair, giving it a tug.

"You haven't been back there in years." I point a finger at him. "You don't even know what it's like there anymore. Things could be different." Obsidian laughs, and not in a happy way. More as if, he thinks I'm crazy. He narrows his amber eyes at me.

"And you don't know if it is different. For all we know it could be worse. Do you really think I want to take you there and put you and our baby in danger?"

I sigh. This is a repeat of every conversation we've had since returning from the Hell Realm and learning we need to go to the Shifter Realm for the last piece of the map. Obsidian is from the Shifter Realm, and he hasn't been back since he left. I know he had a horrible past, but every time I've tried to bring it up in the past month, he's refused to talk about it. He either changes the subject or just walks out of the room. How can I help him if he won't let me? I hate to see him hurting.

I can't say I know what he's going through because I have no idea. I know his kind are hunted. Hamrammrs are rare. I'm sure more than one of the scars I've seen hidden in his tattoos come from having to defend himself. But, he refuses to talk about it.

"You don't get it. You don't understand. None of you do." Siddy's eyes bounce back and forth between all of us.

"Then help us to," I say.

"It's not that easy. I just can't open up and pour my heart out to you, as much as I know you want me to." His hands fist his hair again.

"You don't have to tell me everything. You don't have to tell me the worst of what happened to you, just tell me something so that I can understand... so we can understand," I say, pointing at myself, Verkor, and Stolas.

Obsidian starts pacing the small confines of the kitchen. He glances over his shoulder at me and starts muttering under his breath. We all let him go, allowing him to work out whatever he needs to. It doesn't take long for Siddy to release a shuddering breath before turning and facing all of us.

"It's not just that I was hunted or bullied as a kid for what I am. I've had horrible things happen to me that I don't think I'll ever be able to talk about. What I can say is that the Pack-master is a vicious, cruel man. He condones and participates in as much of the torture and punishment as his loyal followers. You can't say or do anything against what he wants or you'll pay for it later." Obsidian's eyes glass over, and he starts to rub at a spot on his forearm, and I know he's thinking of something from his past.

"Obsidian," I say softly. I need him to bring him back to the present. "You have stopped every bad thing that has come our way. In case you've forgotten, I'm pretty handy with a pair of blades myself. As much as I know you want to protect us," I place a hand over my rounded belly, "...is it really us you're trying to protect, or yourself?" Obsidian jerks back like I slapped him. There it is, the real reason he doesn't want to go home. Yes, he wants to protect us, but he's always protecting himself and I can't say that I fault him for that. "You know you're not going alone. I'll be there, and so will Stolas and Verkor. You keep telling me that I'm not alone anymore and that you'll always be there for me. Now it's my turn to tell you the same thing." I take a step closer to him and then another when he doesn't back away. "We'll fight your demons together." I reach a hand out, placing it over his heart. I feel the erratic beating under my palm. He's more terrified than I thought.

"She's right, bro," Stolas says, setting his mug on the counter before walking the few steps toward us. He places a comforting hand on Obsidian's shoulder. Verkor stands, moving over to us, placing his hand on Obsidian's other shoulder.

"You've held this in for too long. It's time you face it and deal with it. Then you can truly be free," Verkor says. I see Obsidian clench and unclench his fists.

"None of you know what you're talking about." He shoves all of our hands off him. He steps around me. "None of you know what I've been through. None of you know what it was like." He turns to walk out of the kitchen.

"Then tell us. Help us understand," I call after him. Obsidian stops and looks over his shoulder.

"You don't need the nightmares my past will bring." He doesn't say another word before he turns and stomps away. A few seconds later, we hear the door to his bedroom close.

"At least he didn't leave the house this time," Stolas states. I turn, facing them.

"What the hell are we going to do?" I cross my arms over my chest. "We can't wait any longer."

"I know, baby. But you have to understand, there are things about Obsidian's past that he hasn't even told us," Verkor says. "You're going to have to go about this a different way." I snort.

"You think. We end up yelling at each other every time I bring it up." I let my arms fall to my sides. "I think I have an idea." I turn to step out of the kitchen but stop. I glance over my shoulder meeting both Stolas' and Verkor's eyes. "If you don't hear any screaming in thirty minutes, send out a search party." Stolas chuckles, and Verkor rolls his eyes. Yeah, he's been spending way too much time around me.

I stroll out of the kitchen, through the living room, and down the hallway, stopping right outside of Obsidian's bedroom door. I hesitate for a moment. I should let him calm down, before needling him again. Fuck it; he's already pissed. I don't even knock. Instead, I grip his door handle and shove the door open. I'm only slightly surprised that he didn't try to lock the door. Then again, I'd do what I did last time, pound on it until he opened it. That was a fun day for me, but no one else.

I find Obsidian sitting on the side of his bed with his back to me. His arms are at his sides, gripping the edge of the mattress.

"What do you want Finley?" There's a little bite in his voice. He doesn't want me here, yet he's not going to tell me to leave.

"I want to talk to you," I say, entering his bedroom and closing the door behind me.

"I have nothing to say," he clips out.

"Fine." I walk over, taking a seat next to him. "You don't have to talk. You can sit there and listen." I see Obsidian's muscles tense in his arms. His knuckles turn white from how tight he's gripping the mattress. "I want to say I'm sorry." Obsidian's head whips in my direction. I chuckle. "Not what you thought I was going to say, huh." I nudge him with my shoulder.

"No," he replies.

"Yeah, well, clearly the way we've been going isn't the way to go about this." We both sigh. I chuckle while he shakes his head. "I know I shouldn't push you, and you're right, I don't know what you went through or what the Shifter Realm is like. But I'll help you if you let me."

"I want to shield you from all of that. It's not pretty. I've spent my whole life running from it." He looks over at me.

"But don't you think it's time to stop?"

He shrugs his shoulders. "I don't know any other way."

"I meant what I said; I'll help you. We all will; you just have to be willing." I lean against his shoulder, resting my head. He sighs.

"I know you guys will. It's just not something I thought I was ever going to have to face. I avoid taking jobs in the Shifter Realm because I don't want to confront my past."

"Maybe that is exactly why you should. If you don't want to go, you don't have to. I'm sure Verkor, Stolas, and I will be fine going on our own."

Obsidian growls and quickly has me pinned beneath him. He clasps both of my wrists above my head in one of his hands. His other hand grabs my chin, making me meet his gaze. There's a fire in his amber eyes, and a scowl on his face, but his touch is gentle.

"There is no way in hell I will ever let you step foot in that realm without me."

"Then you need to get your shit together because we can't wait any longer. Do you remember what Abaddon said? He said if you confront your demons then the violence level will no longer affect you. Don't you want that?" He growls again and pushes away from me. He stands and starts pacing his room. I move myself so I'm sitting on the side of his bed once again.

"I told you it's not that easy," he runs his fingers through his hair, making it stand up.

"I never said it was. Do you think I find any of this easy? I don't. I know that when we're done with finding this map and treasure that we're going to try to find my parents. Do you think it's easy to know that if we find them that I'm going to have to face the people that didn't want me? Hell, there's even a chance they could reject me all over again. How do you think that makes me feel? How do you think Verkor felt going back to the Winter Court? Do you think he wanted to go back to the place that his mother died? No, he didn't, but he did it anyway." I stand, walking over until I stop right in front of him. "You know what..." I stare Obsidian dead in the eyes. "...we all have to do things we don't want. Now it's your turn." I don't say another word. I pivot and stride right out of his bedroom.

OBSIDIAN

I watch Finley walk away, knowing she's right. There are things in my past that I want to shield her from, things I don't ever want her to know. It's the same things that I refuse to tell

Verkor and Stolas. I clench my fists wanting to punch the wall. Hell, it's my house I'll fucking fix it. I turn and punch a hole in the plaster. I do it a few more times. I'm not angry at Finley. I'm angry at myself. When Finley accused me of trying to protect myself, it felt like a punch to the gut. She's not wrong. Who in their right mind would want to relive their horrible past? I left it behind a long time ago. Never looking back, never thinking about it.

I'm being a coward, and that's not who I am. I know Finley will keep her word and go without me. I know Verkor and Stolas will protect her the best that they can, but they don't know those people like I do. They're conniving, deceitful people, who take joy in harm and mutilating others. I rub at a particularly thick scar on my forearm. I can still remember how it felt to have a burning hot poker pressed into my flesh. I tried not to scream but the pain was too much. The scent of my flesh burning stuck in my nose for days afterward. My hand drifts up and I touch the scar on the back of my bicep. It's a nasty jagged looking one. My arms were tied above my head. I was hanging from some rope in the middle of the Packmaster's torture room for defying him. I can still feel the tip of the blade digging in my arm and being dragged down. I shiver as my finger traces the line. How can I send them into that unprepared? I shake my head, before dropping it back. I can't.

"*We must protect her,*" my shifter essence whispers in my mind.

That is something that I'm still getting used to. It's weird hearing another voice in your head. But according to it, I wasn't strong enough until after Finley claimed me as her mate. It's only because she ended up pregnant and taking on hellhound traits that this even happened. But my essence is right, we must protect her. In this moment, I made my decision. I sigh, looking over to my bedroom door. I guess I should go and tell her.

I square my shoulders and march out into the hallway. Their

voices drift to me from the kitchen. I pause right outside the doorway.

"He'll pull his head out of his ass sooner or later," Stolas states.

"I know. I feel bad for pushing him, but how else is he going to face this? It's not like we'd let him do this on his own. I didn't let Verkor go through it alone; why would he think I would let him?" Finley questions. There's a note of sadness in her voice.

"I don't think he thinks that. There are true horrors in his past, and I can't blame him for putting this off. The only reason I went back to the Winter Court was because of you, Fin. I don't think I would have ever returned otherwise. I think Obsidian feels the same. He just needs a little more time coming to terms with it," Verkor says.

"No, I don't," I say, striding into the kitchen. I meet Finley's stormy gray eyes. She quirks an eyebrow at me.

"Are you saying that you're going to go with us, because I was going to make plans to go without you," she says, holding her arms over her chest.

"I know you would, and I know those two stooges..."

"Hey," Stolas says as if he's offended.

"... would blindly follow you. No one here knows that realm like I do. No one here knows those shifters like I do. I can't let you walk into that knowing what I do."

"You've decided to come, but how long will you keep stalling before we go?" Finley questions. I want to say as long as I can, but I know that I can't. I already put it off this long, and I'm surprised she waited.

"We'll need a few days to pack and get ready." I meet all of their eyes, and they nod. "I do have one condition though."

"Of course, you do," Finley says with a roll of her eyes.

"This is one I will not budge on. You have to listen to me and do what I say." Finley opens her mouth like she wants to argue, but I cut her off with a shake of my head. "No. Like I said, you don't know these people like I do. I *need* you to listen to me. This will be the way that I make sure that you're safe. I can't let them sink their claws into you." I see Finley deflate in her seat.

"Okay," she whispers. I give her a sharp nod of my head.

I walk over to her, lean down, and whisper in her. "If you have to, pretend that we're in the bedroom. You have no problem following my orders in there."

She sucks in a breath. I pull back meeting her eyes. Lust fills them. I inhale deeply, smelling her arousal. A growl rumbles through my chest. I want her. I scoop her up into my arms, bridal style, and turn, heading back to my room when Stolas whoops out a cheer. I look down at Finley; she smiles and rolls her eyes. I use my foot to close the door. I walk over to the bed, sitting her down on the edge.

"I bought something for you that I think you're going to like." Heat blazes in her eyes.

"Oh?"

I nod, walking over to my closet. Finley knows what I keep hanging on the back wall behind my clothes. I was browsing through my favorite sex shop when I saw this harness. My mind and vision blurred imagining Finley's luscious body in it. There was no way I was leaving the store without it. I bought it and hung it up with the other toys that I keep in here. I grab the harness and close the closet door. I turn back toward Finley, dangling the harness in front of me.

"How would you feel being strapped in this?" Finley stands, moving over to me. She reaches her hand out feeling the leather and metal.

"How does it work?" I love the huskiness of her voice. My mate is never shy about trying something new.

"Let me show you." She nods.

I toss the harness onto my bed before turning my attention back on Finley. I reach out, trailing my knuckles down the side of her face. She leans into my touch. My fingers continue their path down her neck, across her collarbone, and down between the valley of her plump breasts. Her breathing picks up, and I smile. I'm barely touching her, but she knows what's coming. I place a hand over her rounded belly, stroking it. Grabbing the hem of her shirt and lifting it over her head, I toss it to the floor.

I walk behind her, caressing the soft skin of her back. I stop at her bra, flicking the clasp open. Using both hands, I pull the strap off her shoulders, letting the bra fall to the floor in front of us. I press my front to her back. Bringing my arm around her, I cup her neck with my hand and place my mouth right next to her ear.

"Take off the rest of your clothes."

I take a step back and watch as she hooks her thumbs into the waistband of her yoga pants and pulls them down. She takes her panties with them. I growl at the sight of the rounded globes of her ass sticking up in the air. In quick succession, I land a smack on each cheek, before running a soothing hand over the red handprints. Finley straightens, glancing over her shoulder at me. Her eyes are dripping with desire. I step forward, closing the little bit of space between us. My hand goes back around her throat, keeping her head tilted to the side. I squeeze it gently. Her lips open and I dive in, plunging my tongue into her open and waiting mouth. She moans as our tongues dance together. I pull back, nipping at her bottom lip as I go. I release her and walk over to my bed, sitting on the edge.

"Come," I say. Finley doesn't hesitate. She immediately moves until she's standing before me. "Good girl."

I grab the harness from beside me, releasing the buckles. Finley's eyes watch my every move. I know she's putting it together on how this will fit her. Her pupils dilate, and I grin. She's excited, my kinky little mate. She really is perfect for me.

I don't mind arguing with her outside of the bedroom. I love her fire and determination, but there is something so beautiful about the way she submits to me behind closed doors.

Reaching around her, I start fastening the harness in place. There's a buckle around her neck that is attached to a single length of leather that runs down the spine of her back and a buckle for the strap of leather that sits around her hips. I make sure to keep that one loose. Then I secure the ones that go around her thighs. At her hips are leather straps for her wrists, which I quickly put on her. What I love about this harness is I can unhook her wrist from her hips and clamp them to any round metal loop that runs the length of the strap along her spine. Oh, the positions I can put her in.

"Step back for me." Finley does as she's told. "Stop." I growl at the sight of her. "Turn. Slowly." I clench my fists to keep from reaching out and pulling her back to me. I lick my lips. She's my every desire and temptation strapped in leather.

FINLEY

I try to clench my thighs together to alleviate the throbbing I feel in my pussy. I feel my wetness pooling between my thighs, all from the look on Obsidian's face. I want him to touch me. I *need* him too. I don't move a muscle as I watch Obsidian strip. With every article of clothing he removes, more of his muscular, tattooed body appears. As much as I love his body and almost everything about him, I'm impatiently waiting for my prize. It doesn't take long for Obsidian to take off his pants and boxers. When he's done, he stands before me, utterly naked with his Prince Albert piercing winking at me. This time it's me that licks my lips.

Obsidian takes a step to the side then points to the place he just vacated. He doesn't need words to tell me where he wants me. Over the last couple of months, I've become well versed in

Obsidian talk, especially when we're in the bedroom. I hate taking orders. I don't like when others try to tell me what to do, but in here, with Obsidian, now that is a different story.

He has a need for control. The old Icelandic proverb written in Old Norse down his spine is a testament to that. *He who lives without discipline dies without honor*. I asked him once what it meant and he told me he would tell me one day, but so far that day hasn't come. I'm now convinced it has something to with his past, and whether he likes it or not, the past always has a way of resurfacing, especially when you try to keep it hidden.

"Finley, come, doll." The sound of desire in Obsidian's voice breaks through my thoughts. Honestly, I don't even know how my mind wandered that far when I have such a delicious piece of man candy standing before me. I do as he says, and I move to the spot where he's pointing, right next to him. "Face the bed." I do.

Obsidian walks behind me, pushing my pink hair to the side, giving him access to his mark on my shoulder. He kisses the spot then nips at it, sending a shiver down my spine.

"I should punish you for all the arguing you've been doing with me lately, all the back talk." My skin tingles at his words. A chill of anticipation rushing through me as my heart beats erratically in my chest. I love Obsidian's punishments. "But not this time." His arms come around me, his hands cup my breasts, squeezing. He places more kisses along my neck and shoulder. He pinches my nipples, hard, giving me a little pain with my pleasure. "I've come to the conclusion that arguing is our type of foreplay." Obsidian trails his hand down my stomach, stopping at the top of my mound. "Will I find you wet and ready for me, doll?" he whispers against my ear, then nips at the lobe. I suck in a breath and nod. "Mm, I think I should find out," he growls low.

He slides a finger through my folds, and he growls. He's kissing my neck and shoulder, while one of his hands is playing with my breast, and his other with my clit. Lord can this man multitask. There is so much stimulation going on that I don't know where to focus. I lose all train of thought as he pushes a finger inside me. I get lost in the sensation of Obsidian and what he's doing to me. I try to lift my arms, but I can't. It's then that I remember they are clipped to my sides. Obsidian chuckles. He knows how much I love touching and marking him.

He picks up his pace plunging his fingers in and out of me faster. He bites my shoulder and pinches my nipple at the same time, and I almost fall over the cliff. I'm so close to my release, but Obsidian stops, removing his hands and mouth from my body. I groan in frustration. Obsidian just chuckles again. I'm glad he finds this funny.

"Did you really think I would let you come that easily?"

"I thought you said no punishments," I say breathlessly.

"This isn't a punishment."

"It feels like one."

"Oh, no. It's not. Trust me, you'll see stars by the time I let you come, and when I do, it'll be on my cock while I look into your eyes." Well, shit.

I feel his hand on my back, pushing me forward. I bend at the waist, laying the top half of my body across his bed. He nudges my feet open more. I realize this helps balance me out more. I sink a little more into the black comforter. Obsidian runs his hands up and down my sides and back. He unclips my wrist at my sides but brings them back and clips to one of the metal loops at my lower back. There's a small tug at the leather strap laying along my spine. I wait. The anticipation is killing me. The only sound in the room is my heavy breathing.

That quickly changes when a sharp smack lands on my ass cheek. I don't cry out. No, I gasp from the suddenness. I wasn't expecting it. Another smack follows on the other cheek. Obsidian does this a few more times, before he starts to caress my heated skin. I feel him rub his cock along the seam of my ass. I wiggle it, wanting him inside me, fucking me.

"Please," I beg.

Obsidian leans over me, pushing some of my hair from my face. "Just because you beg so pretty." He kisses my lips, before thrusting inside me.

"Fuck!" I cry out. He feels so good, so thick and full. And fuck me that damn piercing hits all the right spots.

Obsidian grips the leather above where my wrists are hooked, and his other hand goes to the back of my neck. I'm completely at his mercy, and I love every second of it. Obsidian's thrusts become faster and harder. I feel myself climbing that precipice again.

"Yes, more!" I'm so close. I'm right there, but Obsidian stops yet again. I cry out my frustration. The bastard just chuckles again.

"I'm going to help you stand." He does. "Take a step back." I obey. Obsidian moves, sitting in front of me. His hands go to my waist. "Climb up into my lap and sit that pretty pussy on my dick." Why do his filthy words turn me on so much?

Obsidian helps me climb on the bed. I place a knee on either side of his hips, lowering myself down onto his cock. I moan, closing my eyes. I focus on the feeling of the piercing rubbing along my insides.

"Look at me, doll." I open my eyes, meeting his lust-filled gaze. "Don't break eye contact." Obsidian helps me move, keeping me steady with his hands. "That's it, doll. Just like that. Let me see those perfect tits bounce while you ride my cock." Fuck me and his dirty mouth. Obsidian leans forward, taking a nipple in his mouth, and sucking on it. He does the same to other. "Come for me, doll." And I do. I scream my release as Obsidian grunts, coming with me.

I lean forward, placing my head on his shoulder, as he slows my movement. Both of us are breathing heavily. I don't know how long we stay like that, but it was long enough for both of us to get our breathing under control. Obsidian rubs my hips, before moving his hand to my back. He unclips my wrists. I bring them forward, and Obsidian starts to rub my arms.

"Are you okay?" he asks.

"I'm perfect." I answer.

"Are your arms tingly? Do your hips hurt? What about your belly?" he rattles off his questions.

"I'm fine, Siddy. I promise. Nothing hurts." I reach up, running my fingers through his sweat slicked hair. He pulls me flush against his body. I smile at him. "You were right about one thing."

"What was that?" he raises an eyebrow, but there's a small smirk on his face.

"I did see stars."

CHAPTER 2

VERKOR

I'm just finishing up making dinner by the time Obsidian and Finley emerge from his bedroom. Finley has a smile on her face, and Obsidian looks like he usually does. Grumpy. But I see he's more relaxed. He's been carrying a lot of tension over the past month. I don't know why he was surprised that we had to go to the Shifter Realm. It should have been obvious that eventually we had to go there. Hell, we went to the Winter Court and then to Hell. There weren't many options on where the last piece of the map or the treasure could be hidden. Process of elimination.

We know the last piece of the map is in Shifter Realm, which leaves only the Magic and Heaven Realms on where the treasure may be hidden. Could we really have been that close to the treasure this whole time? Could it really be hidden in the Magic Realm? What about Heaven? If it's there, why?

"Oh, thank God. That smells amazing," Finley says as she comes over to stand next to me. "What is it?"

"Cajun chicken pasta," I answer and lean down, kissing the top of her head. Her stomach growls loudly. All of us laugh.

"Worked up quite the appetite I see," Stolas says cheekily. Finley glances over to him, winks, and shrugs her shoulders.

"Damn right I did," she replies with a smile on her face. Stolas grins back and shakes his head. Obsidian grabs some plates and utensils and starts setting the table.

"It's got about another minute or two before it's done." I nudge Finley with my shoulder. "Go take a seat. We have to start making plans for our trip." Finley nods, goes up on the tips of her toes, and places a kiss on my cheek.

"Thanks for making dinner."

"Anytime, baby." She gives my ass a quick pat before taking up her usual seat at the head of the table.

It's where she belongs, because whether it's stated or not, this family centers around her. I don't think she and the others really see that. Finley is the heart of us because without her, we would be nothing. Sure, we'd still have each other, but she's showing us just how lonely we truly were. All of us were just going through the motions. But Finley has brought so much love and joy into our lives.

Stolas laughs and jokes around more. He found a partner in crime with Finley. Obsidian is still grumpy and an asshole on his best days, but Finley calms him down. He smiles now, which is something he never did before. He found a perfect match in her because she's not afraid to go toe-to-toe with him and call him out on his bullshit. He won't admit it but he loves it. As for me, she's bringing me out of my shell. I'm usually the quiet one. Only speaking out when I have too. I'm the one that comes up with plans, the brains so to speak. Finley is quick witted and easily follows along with my ideas. She makes suggestions on how we can change something, and it'll make the plan easier. She doesn't let any of us take advantage of her. Finley's perfect for us.

We all seemed to easily fall into this relationship too. I thought there would be more jealousy and fighting, but there isn't. Finley's been great when dividing her time among us. If she senses one us needs her more than the others, she lets us know and does what she needs to. I suspect she'll be sticking close to Obsidian during this journey. We're all going to be there for him.

"So," Finley says as she claps her hands once. "There are a few things we need to talk about. One is obviously our trip to the Shifter Realm. Another is our housing situation, and last Izzy."

"What's wrong with Izzy?" I question. I turn off the oven and bring the pan with dinner it over to the table. I carefully set it down on the potholder in the center. Stolas grabs the salad and some drinks from the refrigerator.

Finley sighs. "Nothing, yet."

"Okay," I draw out the word.

"It's just that I feel bad. I spend the majority of my time over here, leaving her alone in that shitty house in that shitty neighborhood."

I take the seat to her right. "Has she said anything about it?"

Finley shakes her head. "No, but she doesn't have to." She sighs. "I feel like I've abandoned her."

"You want to help her. It's understandable. You've lived together for years and she's your best friend. It's only natural that you would want to do something to help her out," I state. I grab the bowl of salad, placing some on the corner of Finley's plate before putting some on my own.

"What do you want to do to help?" Obsidian asks. Finely shrugs her shoulders.

"Honestly, I don't know. I thought about buying her a house after we found the treasure, but then I thought, what if it's gone? I can't make plans for the money if we don't know if it's still there." Obsidian serves Finely and himself some of the pasta dish then hands it pan off to Stolas, who took the seat next to him.

"Well, how about we sell her this place." Obsidian states. Finley whips her gaze in his direction.

"Wh-what?" she stammers.

"It makes sense to me. We're going to have to sell the place when we move out anyway. I'll sell it to Izzy for a reasonable price. She'll be in a good part of the neighborhood, and we can install some form of security. We'll make sure she's safe," Obsidian responds.

"Really? You would do that?" Her eyes widen. Obsidian shrugs.

"Of course, I would. I'd do anything to make you happy." Finley doesn't say anything. Instead, she stands then launches herself at Obsidian. He wraps his arms around her waist as she peppers his face with kisses.

"You're the best." Obsidian chuckles.

"Remember you said that the next time we argue." Finley laughs. Obsidian pats her ass. "Now, sit back down and eat." She does as he says.

"I can't wait to tell her. Actually, I think I should wait, at least until we find a house first. Her birthday is coming up. I think it'll be a nice surprise," Finley says before shoving a bite of food in her mouth.

"Whatever you want, love," Stolas says while shaking his head and smiling.

"Where would you like to look for our future home?" I question. "We can stay close to here if you want. You'll be closer to Izzy that way."

"I don't know where I want to look. I wanted to wait to see all the realms before deciding. I mean, we don't have to stay in the Magic Realm, do we?" Her eyes flit between all of us.

"I guess we don't have to," I say.

"I would prefer if we did," Obsidian states. I turn my attention to him.

"Why?"

"It's the best place for us. The Earth Realm would flip their shit seeing real magic and shifters. I can imagine that they would try to capture us. I really don't want to be killed, or experimented on. The fucking lunatics. Hell wouldn't be too bad, but we don't know how pissed off Lucifer is, and I would like to limit going there anytime soon. Winter Court is nice, but then we'd have to stay in the castle because of the royal over there." Obsidian points to me. "Is that something you want to do?" Obsidian directs his question at me. I shake my head.

"No."

I'm okay going back to visit once and awhile, but I don't think I could ever live there again. Yes, I confronted the things from my past surrounding my mother's death, but some things are just too strong to fully get over. I know Obsidian has to feel the same way.

"There's no way in any realm that I would live in the Shifter Realm again. I would rather live in Finley's broken down home first."

"Hey," Finley says as if she's offended, but there's a smirk on her face. She knows her house is one good storm away from crumbling down.

"Heaven Realm is out too," Stolas states.

"What? Why?" Finley moves her gaze over to Stolas. "I haven't even been there yet and you're saying no." She waves a hand in Obsidian's direction. "Him I understand, even if I don't know what happened to him there." Finely waves a hand in my direction. "I also understand why Verkor wouldn't want to stay in the castle in the Winter Court. But what the hell do you have against the Heaven Realm?"

Stolas sits back in his chair, crossing his arms over his chest. "Well, the first reason should be obvious. I'm a being from Hell. Do you really think that I would be welcome there, even if I could get in?" There's no snark in the question. It's more curiosity than anything.

"I never thought about that," Finley whispers.

"Don't be sad, love. For centuries the Heaven and Hell Realms have fought against each other. The Gods and Goddesses think they are above all beings. They believe that they can do no wrong. The other realms, besides Earth, caught on to their ways. They no longer have such a strong hold over them. But, Earth..." Stolas shakes his head. He leans forward in his chair, placing his forearms on the table. "Earth is different. I know you've been there, but have you stayed there? Have you looked at their past, their history?"

"No." Finley sits a little straighter in her chair. All of her focus is on Stolas. She's interested in what he has to say.

"You should, when you get the chance. But the short story is that there are multiple religions and variations of the Gods on the Earth Realm. Not everyone who lives there is accepting of others and their differences. It's just like Obsidian said; they fear things that they don't understand."

"Okay, but what does that have to do with the Gods?" Finley asks. Stolas looks over at me. I nod. I'm better at explaining things than either him or Obsidian. I shift in my chair to face Finley, getting her attention.

"The Earth Realm has seen many wars, and some of them were done in the name of their Gods. Some use their Gods as the reason they are hateful. They use it as their excuse for the things that they have done instead of taking the blame for their own thoughts and actions."

"But don't their Gods enjoy that?" Finley frowns.

"I can't say for sure if they do." Stolas answers. "All I know is people think by doing something in the name of their God it will give them easy passage into their version of heaven."

"But that's not what happens. I think you said something on that once before," Finley says. Stolas nods.

"I did. They don't go to Heaven because what they did is a sin and they end up in Hell."

"I understand that, but why don't you like it?" Finley asks Stolas.

"Like I said, the first reason is because I'm a being from Hell and we naturally oppose each other. The second reason is they're the worst beings in all the realms and yet people think they can do no wrong. Why do you think they outsource their jobs to people like us?" He gestures to everyone at the table. "You may not have done jobs for them but count yourself lucky. They're horrible to work for and they get to keep their hands clean by making others do their dirty work for them. The entitled bastards. If we ever have to go there, you'll see."

"No one but Gods and Goddesses get to live in their realm anyways," Obsidian interjects. Finley slumps in her seat.

"Man, we're a bunch of fucked up people. I mean, mentally." We laugh, because she's not wrong. "Okay, so we find a house here."

"It's going to have to be a decent sized house too," Stolas says.

"How big are we talking?" Obsidian asks. All of us go back to eating, answering each other between bites. Stolas shrugs.

"I don't know. Do we each want our own room? Are we going to share a bedroom? Then we have to factor in a room for the pup and any additional kids we have in the future."

Everyone is quiet after that. I wait until we finish eating before voicing my thoughts. "So, at a minimum we're looking at five bedrooms. One for each of us guys, with Finley flitting between the rooms like she does here. The other two rooms would be for the kids. If we have boys, they can share a room, and the same goes for if we have girls." I look around the table seeing everyone is deep in thought. I continue on. "At the most, we'd need a seven-bedroom house. Each of us would have our own room, and then each child would have their own. That is if each of us only have one child with Finley, which I'm fine with. I think three children is a good number."

"Good Lord, that house would be huge. Seven bedrooms, plus a kitchen, living room, bathrooms, and laundry room. Who the hell is going to clean that? When the hell would I have time if we have three kids to look after?" Finley says, scooting her chair back, and standing. She starts to gather the dishes from the table. Obsidian stands to help her.

"If we decided that route, we would all pitch in and help. You wouldn't be doing anything alone," I say. I look over to Stolas trying to gauge his reaction, but I don't see anything on his face.

"Five bedrooms is all we'd need," Obsidian interjects. "All of us can share a room. We'd all sleep in there together. But there would be a separate bedroom for sex. I don't mind sharing a bed or space with all of you, but I don't want to see you guys having sex with Finley. That is one area where I can't share. I like my alone time with her. I want Finley to be comfortable in that space and time with whoever she's with. I know there are things that she does with me that she doesn't do with either of you, and I don't want you judging her for enjoying the things that she does."

"Now that sounds like an interesting story, but we already know you like control Obsidian. Or have you forgotten we've seen you go into BDSM clubs, like the one in Hell," Stolas says cheekily. Finley just rolls her eyes. She turns, meeting Obsidian's eyes.

"First, I'm not ashamed of anything that we do together, but I understand where you're coming from. I vote that if this is the route, we're making our sex bedroom be like one in the lust level. You never know what Verkor or Stolas might be into until given the opportunity to explore." Finley turns back to us and winks.

"Now, I'm really intrigued. You know I would try just about

anything with you, love," Stolas says. Finley smiles at him and winks again.

"Anyway, two bedrooms for us. A spare room for any guest, like Stolas' family, or Izzy, or even Cirro, Verkor's cousin. Then two bedrooms for the kids. Obviously same sex kids can share a room," Obsidian says walking back over to the table and gathering more dishes.

"Sounds good to me," I state. Though I'm partially surprised it was Obsidian who suggested we even share a bedroom. It's one of the things he hates the most. He's of the, what's mine is mine mentality. Maybe having him share a mate is helping him with that issue and he doesn't even realize it.

"Same," Stolas says.

"I'm in," Finley voices.

"Great, I'll start looking and show you guys what I find."

"Awesome, two topics down one to go," Finley says, bouncing on her toes. "Now, we get to talk about the Shifter Realm." The only sound heard is Obsidian's groan.

STOLAS

I watch the smile come across Finley's face at Obsidian's groan. But that's not what keeps my attention. It's the fact that Finley is showing. Her belly is growing with my pup inside it. It just does something to me deep inside. I'm quite pleased with myself. My hellhound preens in my mind. He's quite pleased with himself as well. Finley was right. It's definitely a male virility thing.

"What do you want to know?" he begrudgingly asks.

"Uh, everything," she answers. I chuckle. Like Obsidian should expect anything different. He sighs. "How about you tell me what it's like. What it looks like."

"The area where I'm from is close to the beach. There's lots of dense forest, which is nice. Before I left, there were very few humans in the realm. The ones that were there were mates of the shifters." Obsidian reclaims his seat at the table. "All manner of creatures gravitate toward the Shifter Realm. There are more hours of twilight than sunlight."

Finley stops loading the dishwasher and turns her attention to Obsidian. I see the sparkle in her eyes. She's interested in what he has to say. "What kind of creatures, and how much twilight are we talking?" she asks.

"There's only four hours of sunlight in a twenty-eight-hour day. As for the creatures, there's hamrammrs, not many, but a few. There's wolf, bear, coyote, hyena, rabbit, bird, pretty much any kind of animal you can think of. When you see any animals, don't treat them like a pet. Don't start cooing and baby talking to it, none of that cute shit you females do whenever you see any animals. It's degrading to us shifters. Don't approach any of the animals unless they come to you or initiate the contact. The last thing we need is for a pissed off mate coming our way." Obsidian leans back in his chair, rubbing his hands down his face. Finley walks over to him, placing her hands on his shoulder and starts to massage them. Obsidian's head falls forward giving Finley better access.

"Okay, so no petting the animals. No cutesy shit. What else?" she asks. Obsidian groans.

"More pressure right there." I see Finley squeezing a little harder. "Yeah," Obsidian moans. He doesn't answer her for a moment, just letting her work her magic. Slowly, the tension leaves Obsidian and he relaxes in his chair. "Thank you," he whispers.

"No problem." Finley kisses him on the top of his head, before taking her seat at the head of the table.

"The biggest thing would have to be when you meet the Packmaster," Obsidian states. "You have the Packmaster who oversees all of the shifters in a certain region. He's area only extends so far. If he has a mate, you would treat them the same as you do the Packmaster. They're mates are an extension of them. After the Packmaster would be his Beta and his Omega, in that order. They help deal with minor issues and keeping the Packmaster abreast of any issues or situations that he may need to step in and evaluate. Then there are the Enforcers. They pretty much do all the Packmaster's dirty work. Strength wise they are up there with the Beta, but don't want the responsibility the position brings. After that, it's just the regular pack members.

"The region where I'm from is different from the regions around it. Their Packmasters' aren't as strict as mine. There are a few rules you'll have to follow, and I mean follow. You *have* to do these. There are no exceptions. Do you understand?" Finley nods her head. Obsidian nods back before continuing. "*Never* directly look him in the eye, unless he is speaking to you. Keep your head cast downward; it's a sign of submission. You are deferring your power. If you don't, he'll see it as a challenge and that is something you never want."

"Challenge?" Finley questions.

"It's a fight to the death," I interject, saying it in an ominous voice.

"Could you not," Obsidian growls. "It's hard enough that she needs to remember everything I'm telling her. I don't need you trying to scare her."

I laugh, because what he just said is ridiculous. "Do you even know our mate? The chances of her pissing someone off is high."

"Hey," Finley scoffs. My gaze turns to her.

"Don't *hey* me. You know that I'm right." I point a finger at her. She crosses her arms, and my eyes immediately go to her breasts. They look amazing with the way they're pushed up from the motion.

"You might be, but I still listen, and I'll try my best not to piss someone off. I know this trip is going to be hard enough on

Obsidian. I don't want to cause more problems." Obsidian sighs. He reaches over and unhooks her arms, grabbing her hand.

"Shit seems to follow us no matter where we go and how hard we plan. We'll deal with whatever comes our way like we have been. I'm just trying to limit the damage we do. Our trip should go better with you knowing the basic rules of engagement." Finley nods and squeezes his hand.

"Okay, but is what he said about the challenge true, because if so, that's something I definitely want to avoid doing." This time it's Obsidian that nods.

"Stolas is right. Challenges are to the death. The reason being that one shifter feels like the current Packmaster isn't doing his job and they feel like they can do better. So, they issue a challenge to prove their strength. If they win, then they are the new Packmaster. They will oversee every shifter in that region."

"So each region within the Shifter Realm has their own Packmaster?" Finley asks.

"Yes," Obsidian answers.

"Who is the Packmaster for your region?"

"Axel," Obsidian replies with a growl. I can tell Finley wants to question him more about Axel but doesn't.

"So if they lose, they really are killed?" she inquires.

"Yes," Obsidian responds.

"Okay, so no challenges. All of us are coming home." Finley meets each of us in the eyes.

"Of course, baby," Verkor says. It's the first time he has said something in a while.

"Good. Now, finish telling me about the Packmaster. Anything else I need to know?" Finley's gaze settles back on Obsidian.

"Mostly, just be respectful."

"I think I manage that."

"I know you can, doll. But it'll be harder than you think. Packmasters are cocky, sons-of-bitches and not running your mouth back to them will be almost impossible. I know. I have a few scars on my body from one." Finley sucks in a breath. It's the first time he's said anything to her about what his past was like. Usually, he says he'll tell her later or brushes it off. He simply told her his past wasn't good, but this is her first real insight into it. I see the concern and the million questions she has for him but doesn't voice them. Finley clears her throat and glances at me from the corner of her eye. She bites her lip. It's killing her not knowing, but it's up to Obsidian on when and what he wants to tell her. It's his past after all. I give her a nod, showing she did the right thing by not pushing for more. She slumps a little bit in her chair.

"If you point them out the important shifters to me, I'll make sure to be on my best behavior."

"If you don't mind, can we take a break from talking about this?"

"Of course," Finley says quickly.

I'm shocked he lasted this long without flipping his shit. Obsidian stands and leaves the kitchen without another word or a glance back. Finley peers at me with worry clouding her gray eyes. I shake my head.

"Leave him be for the time being. Let him process everything and then go and check on him," I say. Finley doesn't respond; she just glances back in the direction that Obsidian left.

"Finley," she turns back toward me. "He's going to be fine, love."

"I know. I just wish he would let me in more so I can help." She twists her hands together in her lap.

"He will, when he's ready. Forcing anything will only make him pull away and clam up more. I know from experience."

"Have you either of you been to the Shifter Realm?" Finley asks. Both Verkor and I nod our heads. "What was it like?"

"The region I was in was amazing. There were shops everywhere, shifters of all kinds milling about." A smile crosses my face. "There were baby shifters, in their shifted form, running in out of peoples legs, chasing each other. It was lively. Everyone was having a good time."

Finley directs her attention to Verkor. "What was it like when you were there?"

"The region I went to wasn't in the best conditions; it could have been worse. The shifters there were struggling. Buildings were starting to look run down, with chipped paint, missing shingles on the roofs. There were people out-and-about, but not many. Honestly, it looked like the area had fallen into some hard times," Verkor replies.

"Have either of you been to Obsidian's region?" We both shake our heads.

"No. We both were in the Shifter Realm before we became a trio team. Once we teamed up with Obsidian, who refused to take jobs in the Shifter Realm, even if it was nowhere near the region he is from," I answer.

"So basically, the Shifter Realm is like any other realm. They have good and bad areas, as well as good and bad people."

"Yup," I say, popping the 'p'.

"Ugh," she groans. I chuckle. She looks so cute when she's frustrated. I turn to Verkor.

"You should go get it. It'll take her mind off of Obsidian for a bit." Verkor nods and goes to retrieve the present we have for Finley.

"What are you talking about? What is he getting?" Her eyebrows furrow.

"We got you a little present," I say smiling.

"What is it?" she asks, sitting up straighter in her chair.

"You'll just have to wait and see."

I see Verkor getting ready to enter the kitchen, but I hold my hand up to him and he pauses just out of the doorway. I quickly move to Finley and cover her eyes with my hands. I look over at Verkor and nod. He sets the violin case down on the table, opens it, and turns it to face Finley.

"One... two... three..." I say then lift my hands from her face. She gasps. Her reaction is everything I was hoping for.

I step to the side so I can see her face. Her eyes are wide, and her mouth is slightly agape. Her hand tentatively reaches out to touch the violin but stops just before. Her gaze flits back and forth between me and Verkor.

"You got me a new violin?" she asks with awe in her voice.

"Yup. We all did."

Her attention goes back to the violin. Her fingers ghost over the strings, the body, the neck, and even the bow. After admiring it in the case, she finally takes it out.

"You don't even have to worry about getting it spelled, because we did that for you as well," I state.

"You did?" she questions. I nod my head. "Who did you use?"

"Izzy. Like we would trust anyone else to spell that for you." Finley gives me this huge smile.

"Thank you." Her voice is soft, and you can see the tears welling up in her eyes.

"Will you play something?" Verkor asks.

"Hell, yeah. I haven't been able to play since I left my other violin in the Hell Realm." Finley pushes back her chair, walks over to us, and gives both me and Verkor a hug. "You guys are the best." She turns and saunters into the living room. "Can you move the coffee table?" Verkor immediately pushes it to the side. Both of us sit on the couch in front of her.

Finley places the violin under her chin and the bow on the strings. One minute the house is quiet and the next it's filled with the sound of Finley playing. She is breathtaking to watch.

The way her body moves to match the flow of the music. I don't think she realizes that she closes her eyes, and a soft smile graces her lips as she plays. It's like she's letting the music fill and flow through her. Like she feels it on a deep level in her soul. I hear the sound of feet shuffling down the hall and Obsidian appears. He makes his way over to us and takes a seat next to Verkor. I don't blame him for coming out here to watch her. It's one of my favorite pastimes.

The song comes to an end, and before she can rest her arms at her sides, Obsidian says, "Play another."

She smiles over at him, winks, then goes right into playing another song. That's how we end the night, with Finley playing for us.

CHAPTER 3

FINLEY

I made it a point to stop by and see Izzy. I wanted to check on her and to let her know that we were going to be leaving in a few days.

"Izzy," I yell as I open the door.

My beautiful, mocha colored friend appears from down the hallway. Her long dreadlocks swinging behind her. I love the way her green eyes stand out against her skin tone. Her long skirt swishes around her ankles as she walks toward me. She throws her arms around me, when she's close enough, giving me a hug.

"Hey, what are you doing here? Not that I'm not happy you're here."

We walk over to the couch and sit. Each of us curling up in a corner.

"I just wanted to let you know that I finally got Obsidian to agree to go to the Shifter Realm. We'll be leaving in a few days."

"I didn't think he would ever agree to go," she states.

"You're telling me. The only reason he agreed to go is because I forced his hand. I told him that I was going to start making plans to go without him. He refused the idea, saying that he would never let me step foot in that realm without him."

Izzy smiles and shakes her head. "You know just how to push that man's buttons."

I shrug my shoulders and look away from her. I feel guilty about it, but if I didn't push him a little, he never would have gone. We didn't get this far to stop now. We're so close I can taste it. The last piece of the map and the treasure are hovering right at our fingertips.

"Hey," Izzy says, nudging me with her foot. "Have you heard anything I just said?"

I wince. "Sorry, I kind of spaced out."

"Yeah, no kidding. You were thinking about what you did to Obsidian?" I don't have to say anything, because she knows she's right. This is why we're best friends. Sometimes I think she knows me better than I know myself. "If he truly didn't want to go, he would still be fighting with you over it. I think you're giving him what he needs to finally face whatever he's been through."

"Yeah, maybe. Doesn't mean that I don't feel horrible about it."

Izzy shifts in her seat. She reaches over, placing her hand on my arm, giving it a squeeze. "It'll be okay. I bet you any money he's not mad at you." I know she's right. I nod my head at her, placing my hand on hers. I sigh.

"I know, I know." I want to change the topic. "So, what were you telling me?" I pull my hand away. She does the same, settling back on her side of the couch.

"I think I found a spell to help protect us."

I sit up straighter in my seat. "Really?"

She nods and smiles. "Yup. It's a disorientation spell. Anyone who is looking to do harm or find you or any of us will get confused once they get within so many feet of this place.

They'll turn around and walk away. If you want, I can put the spell up around Obsidian's place when you're gone."

"That would be great. I owe you." She waves a hand at me.

"No, you don't. I know you would do the same." She's right, I would.

The rest of the time we joke around, eat, relax, and talk about the baby. I didn't realize how much I missed Izzy, and how much I needed this time with her. I don't know what I'd do without her.

~

OVER THE LAST FEW DAYS, OBSIDIAN MADE SURE WE HAD everything that we needed for this journey. He checked and doubled checked everyone's bags. I think it was mostly to occupy himself, so he wasn't thinking about the fact we're returning to the Shifter Realm; the place he said he would never go back to. He will never know how much it means to me that he's willing to do this for me. It really shows me how deep his love for me goes. I would do the same for him in a heartbeat. These guys mean everything to me.

"Is everyone ready?" Obsidian questions all of us as we stand in front of a slight shimmer that designates where the gateway sits. There is a round of yeses from all of us. Obsidian squares his shoulders. He reaches over, interlaces our fingers, and glances down at me. I give him a reassuring smile and gentle squeeze to his hand, before nodding.

"You got this," I whisper to him. He nods, looking back to the gateway.

"Here goes nothing." Obsidian takes a step forward. "Shifter Realm," he says right before we walk through.

The second we step foot in the Shifter Realm, a shiver rakes through Obsidian's body. I've never seen him react to something the way he has about coming here, but to see him now physically react to having to be in the realm... I feel like an asshole because I know the only reason he's here is because of me.

"It's not too late to change your mind. You can still go back." I nod toward the gateway that Verkor and Stolas just walked through.

"No, I won't leave you here. A strange feeling washed over me the moment we walked through the gateway. You have to remember it's been years since I've been back here. This place doesn't hold a lot of good memories for me."

"What was the feeling?" I ask.

"It's hard to describe. It's not one of home or belonging. It feels more alien. If that makes sense." I just stare at Obsidian, because to me, it doesn't make sense. He continues, "This place never really felt like home to me. Hell, even my house in the Magic Realm didn't feel like that, until..." he looks down at me, "you." My brows furrow.

"Me?" I question, not understanding where he's going with this.

"*You* are my home. You are where I feel safest, where I feel loved. I was a shell of broken pieces, but you are slowly putting those pieces back together, making me whole. You fill me with so much light, love, and happiness. You fill me with hope." My vision starts to blur from the tears welling up in my eyes. Obsidian doesn't stop there. He keeps going. "You have given me all the things that I was too scared to dream of for fear it would be taken away. I'll be damned if I let this place try to do that now that I know what I was missing out on."

Well hell, what do I say to that? So, I don't say anything. Instead, I go up on the tips of my toes, grip the front of Obsidian's shirt, and tug him down until he meets my lips. He growls, wrapping an arm around my body, pulling it flush against his. His hard cock is nestled against the swell of my belly. I try to take control of the kiss, but Obsidian doesn't let me. He nips at my bottom lip, tugging on it with his teeth, before diving his tongue back in my mouth. I moan, as our tongues dance together. Everything around us is forgotten. I revel in the feeling of being in Obsidian's arms. Now, I think I understand what he means of me being his home, because nothing feels as right, as good, as them. A throat clears behind us.

"We should get moving. We look weird standing here, watching those two practically dry hump each other out in the open where everyone can see," Stolas says, but humor laces his voice. Obsidian places another kiss to my lips before pulling away.

If Obsidian ever gave the okay, Stolas would be the first to jump into the mix. My hamrammr is too dominating in the bedroom to be willing to share. Though I could probably talk Verkor and Stolas into sharing. My mind fills with images of being in the middle of a winter fae and hellhound sandwich.

"There used to be a bed and breakfast not far from here," Obsidian states, breaking me from all my naughty thoughts. "Let's go see if it's still there."

"You don't want to stay with your parents?" Verkor asks. I jerk my gaze to Obsidian. He won't meet my eyes. He simply shakes his head.

"No," he sighs. "I don't know if they're still in the same house. They could have moved, or they might not even be in the Shifter Realm anymore. Hell, as far as I know, they could be dead."

"Wh-what?" I stutter. How can he be so blasé about this? Obsidian finally looks at me. He shrugs his shoulders.

"There's a lot of things you don't know about my past and being here will probably drudge it all up. To put it simply, my father was an asshole and my mother let him do whatever the hell he pleased when it came to me. She didn't stop a damn thing from happening," he growls the last part. I can see the anger in his eyes. I can't say that I blame him. I read between the not so inconspicuous lines. His father abused him, and his mother let it happen.

"Did he do the same to her?" I question. Usually if one person in the household is being abused, chances are there are more.

"I don't know. I never saw him hit her, but then I didn't see or hear anything behind closed doors. If my father did abuse my mother, it was when I wasn't around." His brows furrow, he's thinking about something from his past.

"Let's go and get settled, then figure out what we're going to do," Verkor states. He walks over to Obsidian and pats him on the shoulder. Obsidian glances at him. "Don't forget, we're all here for you. Whatever you need." Obsidian nods and lets out a breath. He reaches for my hand again, intertwines our fingers, and starts heading down the asphalt road.

I take in everything that I see as we make our way down the street. It's brighter here than I thought. Obsidian said there is only four hours of sunlight in the twenty-eight-hour day. I expected it to be dark, but the moonlight is illuminating here. I tilt my head back to look at the sky, and I gasp. The moon is huge. It's bigger than anything I've seen in the Earth and Magic Realms.

"Holy shit, it's so big," I whisper to no one in particular.

There's a snicker, followed by Stolas saying, "That's what she said." I just roll my eyes.

I bring my attention back to my surroundings. With the moonlight, I can see pretty damn good. There's a lot of people shuffling about, and thankfully no one seems to have noticed us yet. Looking past the buildings, I see that Obsidian wasn't kidding when he said there's a lot of dense forest. The trees here are similar to those found in the Earth and Magic Realms. The one difference between those trees and the ones here are the size. These trees are huge, bigger than anything I've seen in either of those realms. The leaves on the trees are just starting to change color from green to rich autumn colors of red, brown, and gold. It's beautiful. Too bad its beauty masks the ugliness it brought to Obsidian. I inhale deeply taking in all the scents. There's a woodsy smell that tickles my nose, and something vaguely familiar about it. Taking in another deep inhale, it clicks. The smell is familiar to me because it's Obsidian's natural scent.

The sounds of yipping draw my eyes further up the road. There are a few smaller shifters playing at the feet of a woman. She's just smiling down at them. The further we move into this part of the realm; buildings start to take shape. There's grocery, clothing, and furniture stores. There's a multitude of restaurants. The smells emanating from them has my stomach growling. We're stopping somewhere once we drop our bags off.

Ever since I became pregnant, with Stolas' baby, I've taken on traits of a hellhound shifter. I can hear, see, and smell better. I also growl, and when I'm really pissed off, smoke plumes from my nose. It's cool actually. I think the only thing I can't do is shift into a hellhound, which is bullshit if you ask me. Stolas says the reason I took on some of the traits is because it's a way for me to protect the baby, and to help me carry the baby as well, since I'm not a hellhound shifter. Come to think of it... maybe the reason why everything looks so bright here is because I have enhanced sight for the time being.

A sharp gasp grabs my attention. I look in front of me and see a pretty, blonde petite woman a few yards down the road. She's staring right at Obsidian with wide eyes. She blinks a couple of times like she can't believe what she's seeing, and I'm sure he's going to be getting a lot of that look.

"Five bucks says everyone is going to know about Obsidian's return by the time we check into the bed and breakfast and drop off our stuff," Stolas stage whispers to me.

I snort and shake my head. "I'm not dumb enough to take that bet."

My gaze never leaves the blonde woman. With one last blink she turns and high tails it out of there. Obsidian doesn't react to the woman. Nope, he keeps his grip on my hand and continues down the street, ignoring every double take glance in our direction.

OBSIDIAN

I fucking hate this place. I hate everything about it. The shifters, the smells, how it looks, the sounds. Being here is making my skin crawl. What I want to do is turn around and walk me and Finley back through the gateway. The only reason I'm not is because she would return with or without me. The goddamn stubborn woman.

I'm choosing to ignore everyone around me. I focus on the feel of Finley's hand in mine and placing one foot in front of the other. I knew it was going to be hard coming back here, and I fought and delayed for as long as I could. I tried to mentally prepare myself for this, but nothing worked. It was even worse than I imagined. Revulsion claws at my gut as I see the faces of people who knew what was happening to me and did nothing to help, even when I begged. They can't even look me in the eyes now. Good, I hope their lives have been hell since I left.

I push forward, heading straight where the bed and breakfast used to be. I just need to get behind closed doors. I need to not have so many eyes on me. I can't take them looking at me. My anger starts to rise and all I want to do is take it out on them. I want to make them suffer like I did, like I still do. It's been years since I've been here, but the nightmares I get keeps everything fresh in my mind. It doesn't help that I was the one to leave. I never got to confront or do anything about my tormentors, my bullies, my abusers. Things will be different this time. I won't let them get to me like they did back then.

Luckily, the bed and breakfast is still there and only a few

45

feet in front of me. I feel bad because Finley is practically running to keep up with my long strides and fast pace. I push open the door and sigh with relief that there's nobody in here.

"Good Lord, you would have thought the hounds of hell were nipping at your heels with how fast you were walking." Finley glances over her shoulder to Stolas. "No offense," she offers him a wink.

"None taken, love. I agree with you." He smiles back. I don't say anything. I stride over to the counter and hit the bell.

The door behind the counter opens and out pops a familiar face, but not one I like. He wasn't one of the ones that hurt me, but he did know about it and turned the other way when I asked for help. I squeeze Finley's hand. I can feel her eyes on me, searching for an answer, but instead of looking at her, I don't take my eyes off the shifter in front of us.

He's aged since I've been here and not well at that. His once brown hair is now gray, and there are age lines around his eyes and mouth. His brown eyes are dull and filled with despair.

"Obsidian," he says, his voice soft.

"Maxwell," I say in a clipped tone. "Where is Gemma?"

"She moved to the region next to us years ago."

"That's a shame," I reply. She used to run this bed and breakfast and I was hoping that she would still be here. She's the only person from this realm that gave a shit about me. The only person who tried to help me. It would have been nice to see her again.

"I took over this place when she left," he states. I shrug my shoulders. I don't really care about him. Maxwell sighs, his shoulders slumping. "What can I do for you? I didn't think you would ever come back here."

"I never planned on coming back to this hellhole, but never say never right." There's no way I'll ever tell him why we're here. It's none of his damn business. "We need to book a room for at least a week, maybe more," I respond. Maxwell's eyes widen.

"You're staying?"

I nod. "Yeah, there are some things I need to do here." He nods in reply.

Maxwell turns his attention to the computer on the counter and starts clicking away at the keyboard. I catch him peeking over at us from the corner of his eye, like he's waiting for something to happen. Unlike the shifters that live here, I don't get off on hurting and scaring others into doing what I want.

"When we're settled, can we get food? I'm starving." To punctuate Finley's statement, her stomach growls loudly. Everyone chuckles.

"Almost done here," Maxwell says. He pulls out the device that will read the credit chip in my titanium ring. "Alright, I have you in for one room with two beds for a week. If it looks like you'll be staying longer, let me know and I can go in and add the days." He scoots a tablet in my direction. "I just need you to sign, and your price is listed at the bottom of the document."

I quickly scan it, sign my name, and hold out my hand. Maxwell places the credit reader against my ring, and a few seconds later the transaction is complete. Maxwell takes a couple of steps to the side, over to the cabinet by the doors he walked through earlier. He opens it and grabs a set of keys off one of the hooks. After closing the cabinet doors, Maxwell steps from behind the counter and toward us.

"Follow me. I'll show you to your room and then you can take your mate out for dinner."

Silently, we all follow behind him. There's a set of stairs off to the right that I didn't see when we first came in. The stairs creak under my feet. We turn left at the top of the landing. Maxwell walks all the way down the hall and turns to the last door on the right, room number two-three-one. He uses the keys to unlock the door, pushing it open. He motions for us to enter the room first then follows after.

"It's not much, but it's the biggest room we have." He walks over to me, extending his arm out with the keys to the room dangling between his fingers. "Here are the keys to the room, return them when you check out." He drops them into my waiting hand. "Breakfast is free and ready at seven and available until nine." I nod.

"Thank you," Finley says, giving him a small smile, which he returns.

"Let me know if you need anything," Maxwell states.

"The Packmaster house still where it was?" I question. Maxwell nods. "I'll have to make it a point to see Axel if word hasn't spread already that I'm here." Maxwell flinches at my words.

"Axel isn't the Packmaster anymore."

"Wh-what?" I stammer, surprised. "Who the hell took him on and won?" Axel was Packmaster for so long that I didn't think anyone would have challenged him, especially because of the brand of torture he liked to administer when you defied him. "Who's the Packmaster now?"

"Breaker," he says, not meeting my eyes. A chill courses through my body.

"How the hell did that happen?" I clench my fists at my sides. One of my tormentors as a child is now the Packmaster.

"The circumstances surrounding that challenge are mysterious to say the least." Maxwell shifts from foot to foot.

"What do you mean?"

Maxwell sighs. "You know what Axel was like." I nod, because I have scars on my body from him. "You also know Breaker." I have scars on my body from him as well. "He's not muscular, or particularly large, or even strong. Under normal circumstances there's no way that Breaker should have beat Axel in the challenge. But something was off about Axel that night. He didn't look or act like his normal self. Breaker took him down pretty quickly."

"How is Breaker still Packmaster?" I question. Maxwell shrugs and refuses to look me in the eyes.

"That's the real question, isn't it?" he whispers, not elaborating on his cryptic reply. "I'll let you get settled." He leaves, closing the door behind him.

"So, we're totally going to help figure this out, right?" Finley voices. I groan.

"Of course, you would want to help. We have enough to worry about by me just being here, and the fact that we need to find the last piece of the map. Now, you want to add this on us too?" I growl. "I don't know how things will play out now that I'm back and Breaker is the Packmaster. With Axel as Packmaster I had a better understanding of what we were walking into, but this throws everything out the window because I have no idea what Breaker is like as a Packmaster. If he's anything like he was when we were kids, things didn't get better for this region... they're probably worse."

"What harm can it do just to ask around about it? We have to ask about the map anyways. We can kill two birds with one stone. I won't force you, but from the sound of it, Breaker is worse than Axel. Don't you think it's time to end the cycle of abuse? If we can help and get someone worthy as a Packmaster, just think of all the good that could come from that."

I sigh because I know she's right, but why does it have to be us? Why me? Why now?

"Fine, but we have to do this discreetly. You have to listen to me. No questions. Do you understand?" I glare at Finley. She rapidly nods her head.

"I will. I promise." She smiles. She claps her hands. "Okay, let's get settled and get the food. We can talk about everything else later."

Getting settled doesn't take us long because we all shove our bags in the closet. We never unpack, in case we have to make a quick exit.

"Well, that was easy," Stolas says as he flops on the bed closest to the bathroom.

"No resting yet. I need food first," Finley says, pushing at Stolas' legs.

"I can give you something to put in your mouth, love," he says, winking at her.

"Your dick is not going to feed this baby." Stolas jumps up off the bed, grabs Finley's hand, and tugs her out of the bedroom. Verkor and I follow behind them.

When we reach the first floor, I look around and see that no one else seems to be here. Fine by me. The less people I have to see, the better.

"Where should we go and eat?" Finley asks. "Let's make it somewhere close by so we don't have far to walk back. We can start looking around and asking questions tomorrow. I just want to rest for today."

I move forward, reaching the front door before Finley. I push open the door and gesture for her to go ahead of me, quickly following. The second I step outside, I run smack into someone I was hoping was dead.

CHAPTER 4

OBSIDIAN

"So, the rumor is true. The great hamrammr Obsidian has finally returned home to the Shifter Realm," Cain says with disdain. "I'm surprised that you're still alive. How'd you manage that?" There's an evil glint in his eyes.

He eyes me up and down the same way I do him. There's a difference this time. I'm bigger and badder than I was twenty years ago. If he thinks he can get to me, he has another thing coming.

"Cain," I say.

"What are you doing back?" he asks, crossing his arms over his chest and glaring at me. I smirk. He's trying to intimidate me, like he did when we were little. I'm bigger than him now.

"Why do you care?" I ask, glaring right back at him.

"It's my business to know who is coming and going, seeing as how I'm the Beta." This time it's him that smirks at me. I try to play it off like him being in a position of power doesn't affect me, but it does. It's always the cruelest beings that get to hold positions of power when they shouldn't. I simply shrug my shoulders.

"Well, you know I'm here and you'll know when I leave. Consider your job complete."

I move around him and start walking down the road toward the nearest restaurant. I don't get far. Cain grabs my shoulders and tries to spin me around. I grab his wrist, twist, and shove him against the side of the nearest building. My other hand goes to this throat, squeezing it.

"Let's get something straight," I growl. I get close to his face. Barely an inch separates us. "I'm not that little kid anymore, and Beta or not, I will fucking end you if try coming for me." Cain tries to growl at me, but I squeeze his throat tighter, cutting off some of his air. "That goes for anyone that came here with me today. Go be a good lap dog and run and tell your master that." I give his throat one final squeeze before letting go and taking a step back. Cain stumbles forward a step and reaches for his throat as he takes in big gulps of air.

"This isn't over," he hisses. He glares at me before taking off.

I scan the crowd that has stopped to stare, looking for Finley and the others. I spot them a few feet in front of me but off to the side, standing out of the way. I head in their direction but stop abruptly at the glint in Finley's eyes. Her gaze is narrowed at me, arms are crossed under her chest, a hip cocked out to the side, and her foot is tapping the concrete. Fuck, she's pissed, and that anger is definitely coming my way. I steel myself as I start walking toward her, knowing she's going to yell at me. I brace myself as I stop in front of her, waiting for the tongue-lashing.

Finley sighs, before launching herself at me. She wraps her arms around my waist, nuzzling her face against my chest, and I relax. I bury my nose in her hair, taking in a deep breath as I hug her back.

"Are you okay?" she asks softly.

"I am now," I reply. Finley pulls back, searching my eyes. I don't know what she sees but she's okay with it, because she nods before dropping her arms and taking a step back from me.

"Good," she says as she swats at my chest. I jump back from the hit, not expecting it. But Finley doesn't give me any space. She closes the few inches that separate us and gets right in my face, well the best that she can anyways. "What the fuck was that?" she growls. She jabs her finger into my chest. "You tell me not to go pissing people off, especially anyone of importance, and we're here, what an hour maybe two and you go and do the exact thing you tell me not to."

I open and close my mouth, because I don't know what to tell her. She's right. I did ask her to be on her best behavior. How can I ask that of her and not do the same in return?

"You're right. I'm sorry."

Finely huffs, taking a step back. "How am I supposed to be mad at you when you go and apologize?" I shrug my shoulders and smirk a little.

"I don't want you mad at me. Well, I do, because I love the sex afterward, but I would prefer it if you weren't mad at me here." There's too much going on inside of me right now. Too many feelings that I'm trying to suppress.

"I guess I'm not really mad at you, more like I'm worried," she says. "I'm going to be here for you in any way that I can." She reaches her hand out, palm up, waiting for me. I know she's going to drop the subject, for now. "Come on, let's go eat. I'm sure we'll feel better after that." I place my big hand in her small one, and she starts tugging me down the road. Stolas and Verkor follow behind.

Finley's getting ready to open the door of an Italian restaurant when I hear something that sounds vaguely familiar. I turn, scanning my surroundings, not spotting anything out of the ordinary. I'm about to brush it off, when I hear the sound again. I narrow my eyes and slightly cock my head to the side, trying to pinpoint where the noise is coming from.

"Obsidian?" Finley says my name more like a question.

I place a finger to my lips and then point to my ear. She goes quiet. I hear the sound again, and I realize that it's coming from the alley between the bar and the drug store across the street. I don't waste any time. I jog to the alley stopping at the entrance and I freeze.

The sight before me is too reminiscent of my past. Instead of the kid that's being held by his arms and is on his knees, it's me. Instead of this kid being beaten by his tormentor, it's me. I can hardly breathe as my chest restricts. The sounds from the alley start to fade, replaced with the rapid beat of my heart. My vision starts to dim as the blackness encroaches the edges. I close my eyes trying to fend off the images of my past, but it doesn't work, and I'm pulled back to one of my many horrible nights.

"Did you get him?" Breaker asks. I struggle against the hold Cain and Jett have on my arms. There's a kick to the back of my leg and my knees land hard on the pavement.

"Yeah, but you need to hurry up," Jett says. "He's strong." With those words, I struggle against their hold more.

"He may be getting stronger, but he'll never be better than me... than us. He'll be dead before long," Breaker states.

I follow Breaker as he circles around me. I hear the click of the switchblade that he keeps on him. I struggle harder and a punch lands in the center of my back. I hiss and bow backward.

"I say we give a little preview of what his life will be like. What do you say Obsidian?" Breaker leans down and gets in my face. He trails the tip of his knife down the side of my face. He doesn't break the skin, but I know it's coming. It wouldn't be the first time he's drawn my blood, and it probably won't be the last. "Do you want to know what it feels like to be hunted, to be prey? I heard hamrammrs are supposed to be feared because of what they can do, but here I am staring one in the face, and he's nothing but an unimpressive, weak bitch." Breaker sneers the last word. I narrow my eyes at him and spit right in his face.

"Do your worst little hyena, but remember, one day I will come for you, and when I do, you pray to whatever god you believe in because I can promise you, you'll die at my hands. I will have my revenge, and vengeance will be mine," I growl.

Breaker loses his shit and punches me repeatedly in the face. I smile through the blood running down my face and over my mouth. I can barely see out of my left eye, but I still look him in his eyes. "Is that all you got?" I sneer then I laugh.

I know I shouldn't egg him on, but he's just drawing out the inevitable and the faster we get this over with, the sooner he'll leave me alone. Just as I thought, my words do exactly what I thought they would. Breaker grabs me by the throat, forcing my head back.

"You want more, then that's what I'll give you," he curls up the corner of his lips.

I feel the blade of his knife against my upper arm as he drags it across my flesh. I hiss at the pain. The evil smile that comes across his lips makes me realize that I made a mistake in making that sound. After that first cut, Breaker quickly follows with one on my other arm and a few on my stomach. I don't make a sound after that first cut and that pisses him off more. He presses his knife hard on my chest, making a deeper gash than the others. It hurts, but I refuse to give him a reaction.

My vision is starting to waver, probably from all the blood I'm losing, and I feel my body slump in Cain and Jett's hold. I'm trying to hold out; I can't show them any more weakness. A sound comes from nearby; shifters are coming out of the bar. They'll smell my blood.

"Looks like time's up, boys. Drop him and let's go," Breaker states forcefully.

They do as he says, and I barely catch myself from smashing my face off the ground. The feeling is short lived when there's a kick to my ribs, causing me to fall. Another kick hits my back, and one last one to the side of my head. I fight the blackness trying to consume me. My eyes are barely open, but I watch their feet pound against the pavement, running away from me. The sound of their laughter echoes in the alley.

As I lay there, bloody and bruised, I make a promise to myself, that

one day I will repay them for everything that they have done to me.
And when I do, I'll make sure it's me laughing in the end, with them
dead at my feet. With that final thought, I succumb to the blackness.

FINLEY

"Obsidian!" I scream over and over.

No matter what I do, he's not snapping out of it. He's trapped in some nightmare and I can't wake him up. I feel the tears streaming down my face. I turn to look at Verkor and Stolas for help, but they're down further in the alley stopping some kids from bullying another. I don't know what to do. I run my fingers through my hair, tugging on the strands. I look back to Obsidian, who is literally scared stiff. I walk back over to him and wrap my arms around his waist, squeezing him tight.

"You're okay, Siddy," I whisper between hiccups. "You're safe now. I'm here. I promise I won't leave you alone. Whatever you're seeing isn't real." I rub my hands up and down his back as I nuzzle his chest, trying to comfort him in any way that I can. "Please, come back to me." I repeat this over and over again, until I feel a hand on my back. At first, I think it's Stolas or Verkor, until I hear the deep timbre of Obsidian's voice.

"Doll," he whispers. I pull back and look into his haunted amber eyes. He cups my face, using his thumbs to wipe the tears from my face. "I'm back." I blink at him a couple of times. My shoulders sag in relief and I start sobbing all over again.

Obsidian pulls me back into his body. One of his hands cups the back of my head and the other rubs my back. I feel him lay his head on top of mine and take a deep inhale. I don't know how long we stand there, but Obsidian lets me cry for as long as I need to.

I pull back when I have my emotions under control. I look up to Obsidian and cup his face. He closes his eyes and sinks into my touch. I pull him down and kiss him, then place my forehead against his.

"I'm sorry," he whispers. I'm taken back by his apology.

"Why are you sorry? You've done nothing wrong." I search his eyes, trying to understand.

"I hate making you cry. I hate feeling weak," he says.

"I was crying because I couldn't help you. I don't know what just happened..."

"Flashback," Obsidian says, cutting me off.

"Do you get them often? I don't remember seeing you have one," I ask.

Obsidian shakes his head. "I haven't had one in years. Being here, where it happened, is making all of my old feelings resurface."

"Something triggered it," I say. He looks away briefly before settling his gaze back on me. He nods his head. "What?" Obsidian's eyes go to the back of the alley. I turn to see Verkor and Stolas have the three kids lined up against the brick wall. I glance back up at Obsidian then back to the kids, and it clicks. "It was those kids wasn't it?" I ask softly, not really expecting him to answer, and I'm surprised when he does.

"Yes. It was the sound at first, and then when I saw what was happening, I froze. Old memories started to surface of when I was held and beaten in this same alley."

"That guy back there, the blonde..."

"Cain," Obsidian says.

"Cain was one of them, wasn't he?"

Obsidian looks down at me, and there's a fire in his eyes. I see his fists clench at his sides.

"Yes," he clips out.

"Did I hear correctly when he said he was the Beta?" Obsidian nods, and I sigh. "Of course, he is. I take it the new Packmaster, Breaker, was one of them as well?" Obsidian nods again. "Is there anymore?"

"A few. Jett, he's friends with Breaker and Cain. If Breaker is Packmaster, and Cain is the Beta, I'm going to assume that Jett is the Omega. There was Axel, the old Packmaster, but he's dead. The only other person left is my father."

I reach out and grab his hand. "Okay, so we only have to avoid four assholes for as long as possible."

"That'll be easier said than done. I didn't help matters when I yoked up Cain. I know the first thing he's going to do is run and tell the others. I'm guessing we're going to be seeing them sooner than I hoped," he states.

"Well, you won't be seeing them alone. Let's go help Verkor and Stolas and get some food, because I think you're a little hangry." Obsidian shakes his head but smirks.

"But I'm always angry," he says.

"Not always," I reply, giving him a wink. "Come on." I start tugging him down the alley toward the others.

"Everything okay?" Verkor questions, eyeing Obsidian.

"For now," Obsidian responds. Verkor nods his head. "What was going on here?"

"These two," he points to a brown haired boy, then to a blonde one, "decided that they were going to hold down that one," he points behind him to a red haired boy, "and let that one," he points to a black haired boy, "beat him."

"Why?" I ask, narrowing my eyes at the kids. The black-haired boy sneers at me.

"I don't have to tell you anything," he spits.

"You're right you don't." I turn and face the red-haired boy. "What's your name?" I ask softly.

"Fin," he whispers, not quite meeting my eyes.

"That's a wonderful name," I say. "My name is Finley." The boy looks up at me then. His hazel eyes growing wide, and I smile. "So, Fin, can you tell me why they were bullying you?"

"They don't need a reason," he replies, shrugging his shoulders at the same time.

"What do you mean?"

Fin sighs. He uses the back of his hand and wipes at his mouth. I see then that his lip is split open.

"They get away with a lot. They're cousins to the Packmaster, Beta, and Omega. They think it's fun to torment other kids, especially ones weaker and smaller than them."

"You better shut your mouth," the blonde-haired boy growls. Obsidian growls back at the kid. He ducks his head.

"Do you know why they picked you this time?" Verkor asks Fin.

Fin glances at Verkor before settling his gaze back on me. "Yeah." He drops his head, looking at the pavement. "I'm a rabbit shifter." He doesn't need to elaborate. They treat him like prey. "I'm one of the few shifters that have red hair; it's different, it makes me stand out."

I take a step closer to Fin, placing a finger under his chin, making him look me in the eyes. "First, I happen to like red hair," I give him a wink. I hear Obsidian snort behind me. The poor kid blushes and it's cute. "Second, just because you're a rabbit shifter doesn't mean you are weaker. Learn to use it to your advantage."

I look over my shoulder to Obsidian to make sure I'm not screwing this up, because I have no clue what I'm doing. I'm going with my gut. But, he nods in agreement, and I let out a breath. I turn my attention back to Fin.

"Normally, when someone bullies you, they're jealous."

"I'm not jealous of him," one of the kids sneers behind me. All of us ignore him.

"All of this won't matter when you're older. Don't let this define who you are or what you'll become. In the end, karma always comes back around. Use this to better yourself. Fight back. Don't let them win." I see tears welling up in his eyes. He nods once, before throwing his arms around my waist. I glance over to my guys and they're all smiling at me, even Obsidian. I wrap my arms around Fin, hugging him back.

"Thank you," Fin whispers as he pulls back.

"Anytime kid." I smile and ruffle his hair.

"Hey," he says, pushing his hair back into place, but there's a smile on his face, and I chuckle.

"Go on home. We'll deal with them." Fin nods, he starts walking out of the alley, but suddenly stops. He turns back, walks right up to the three kids, and punches all of them in the face. Fin looks at me, smiles, then walks right out of the alley.

"Well then," I chuckle. I walk closer to the guys.

"I think you just lit a fire in that kid," Stolas says, throwing his arm over my shoulder, pulling me closer to his body. "You did good, love."

"I'm just hoping I didn't cause more problems." I lean into him, resting my head on his shoulder.

"Nah. If anything, it'll teach these three a lesson. I have a feeling they're going to get a taste of their own medicine." He kisses the top of my head.

"What are we going to do with them?" I ask.

"Not much we can do," Obsidian states. "Fin said they're related to the Packmaster, and his Beta and Omega. The first thing they're going to do is run and tell them. They've been getting away with shit, and I have a feeling the Breaker and his posse are encouraging it."

"We let them go," Verkor states.

The kids don't need any prompting and take off down the alley. Right before the black-haired kid leaves, he looks back at us like he's going to say something but changes his mind and runs after his friends.

"You know, we're not doing that great of a job not pissing people off," I say, as we head out of the alley. The guys just shrug.

"We were crazy for thinking we wouldn't," Stolas says. He's got a point. It seems to be our thing.

"We'll worry about that later. Let's get something to eat," Verkor voices. That's an idea I can get behind.

CHAPTER 5

OBSIDIAN

As we walk back to the bed and breakfast, Finley leans heavily into Verkor's side and groans. "Are food comas a real thing, because I'm sure I'm headed for one." She rubs her belly. "That food was soooo good." He chuckles and I smirk at her statement. I pick up my pace to walk on her other side.

"I can carry you back if you'd like," I say, smiling down at her.

"Don't tempt me. I would let you, but I think I need to walk some of this off," she says.

She interlaces our fingers together, giving them a gentle squeeze. We leisurely continue our path down the street, heading back toward the bed and breakfast. For a brief moment, I think I can breathe and relax, but I should have known better. I can't do that here. At first, I don't see him. It's his scent that reaches me first. My body grows cold and tense. I release Finley's hand, stepping in front of her. I spot him a few feet ahead of us. I walk closer to him, trying to keep him away from Finley. He doesn't need to know who she is just yet. A growl escapes my lips even though I'm trying to hold it in. I don't want him to see how much he affects me... still.

"Breaker," I growl.

He looks the same as he did when we were younger, just an older version of the same piece of shit. His short black hair is cut and styled the same way, but his brown eyes are different. They're still cold, but there is a craziness, a maliciousness in them. He's still gangly looking with no real muscle on him. Cain is standing behind him off to the left and Jett is off to the right. Both Cain and Jett have packed on some muscle, but they are still smaller than me in height, weight, and muscle mass. Behind them are three more guys with their arms crossed over their chest, glaring in our direction. These must be his Enforcers.

I feel a small hand on my back, Finley. She tries to stand in front of me, but I block her and push her behind my back. I feel the brush of an arm on my right... Stolas. Verkor quickly fills my left side.

"Now, now, Obsidian. Is that any way to talk to your Pack-master?" Breaker laughs. The sound coming out is loud, high-pitched, and rapid. "I almost thought Cain was seeing things when he came to tell me that you returned. I dismissed the thought until my little cousin came to tell me about his encounter with three men and a pink haired woman. Naturally, I became curious. I set off to find you, which turned out to be easier than I thought. People are whispering about your return. So, tell me Obsidian, just why are you here?"

"I don't need to tell you," I split out.

"See, that is where you're wrong. I know everything about everyone within my region. Tell me why you are here. I won't ask again." The Enforcers behind him move forward. This time it's me that laughs.

"Things have changed since the last time you saw me, Breaker. I'm not that same little kid anymore. You can't intimi-date me any longer." I see Breaker's jaw tick. He's not happy.

"The past is in the past Obsidian. We're all adults. I think we can put that all behind us," Breaker grits out.

"Not likely," I state. I know the moment I say those two words that I fucked up. It gave away my feelings towards him, but the things that I went through as not easily forgotten or forgiven. I'd rip his face off for just suggesting something so stupid. The only reason I'm not attacking him is because Finley has gripped the back of my shirt, digging her knuckles into my back. That little bit of pain, from her, grounds me enough to keep a clear mind. A slimy smile crosses Breaker's face.

"So, where is this mysterious pink haired female? I heard a rumor that she's your mate."

I growl at Breaker. I don't want him anywhere near Finley. Even with her shielded behind me, it's too close for comfort. There was always something off about him... about all of them. I see movement from the corner of my eye. I don't want to break my eye contact with Breaker, but the flash of pink I see has me turning my head in Finley's direction, to see her step from behind Verkor. *When the hell did she let go of my shirt? Why couldn't she just stay behind me?* She steps in front of me, placing her back against my front.

"I *am* his mate," she glares at Breaker.

"Well, well, well. Aren't you a pretty little thing?" Breaker licks his lips as his gaze travels up and down her body.

"We should break his body into pieces for daring to look at our mate in such a manner," my essence voices in my mind.

A growl comes from my right, along with a strong whiff of sulfur. I feel Verkor tense on my left. None of us are happy with the way that Breaker is looking at our mate.

"Hey, buddy. My eyes are up here," she points to them before crossing her arms over her chest and narrowing her eyes at Breaker. He lets out another high-pitched laugh. Finley winces, putting a finger in her ear, shaking it.

"Hot and feisty. Just how I like them," he winks at her.

Breaker is playing with fire. Finley will chew him up and spit him out, but she won't have to because there will be nothing left of him by the time me and others get done with him.

"I like guys who aren't trying to make me go deaf with the sound of their laugh," she states, and I groan. She's going to get us all killed. "Besides, I have enough men in my life. I don't need another." A salacious smile crosses Breakers lips.

"You just keep on getting better. I need a strong woman who can handle my appetite, as well as my Beta's and Omega's."

I roar before launching himself at Breaker, wrapping a hand around his throat. I hear a commotion going on around me, but I only have eyes for Breaker. It doesn't take long before I hear the click of a gun from beside me. I glance out of the corner of my eyes and see that Cain and Jett have drawn weapons and are pointing them right at me. I settle my gaze back on Breaker's face, trying my damnedest not to kill him right here and now. I squeeze his throat at the sick smile on his face. He loves that he can still get to me, and that pisses me off more. So, I squeeze his throat a little tighter. I get as close up in his face, to the point where my nose is almost touching his.

"You lay a hand on my mate and I'll kill you," I growl lowly.

"Obsidian, you need to think about this. Think about Finley, about..." Verkor stops himself, but I know what he was going to say... the baby. "There will be a time in a place for this, but now isn't it." Verkor places a hand on my shoulder. I let out a growl.

"Siddy," Finley's voice drifts over to us. "Listen to Verkor. I need you to come back to me." I glance back at Finley and see that she's stepped a little closer to us. Stolas is at her side in his hellhound form; her fingers are gripping his fur.

"I'm doing what's in my right as your mate," I respond to Finley. "It's death to any shifter who tries to take a claimed mate from another." I turn my attention back to Breaker.

"Is that true?" Finley questions. I nod not taking my eyes off him. "No one is going to take me from you Obsidian. Verkor and Stolas would never let that happen. Hell, *I* wouldn't let it happen. Let him go, he's not worth the risk." I notice the infliction that she put on the word risk, putting more behind the meaning.

Some of the tension in my body easies. It takes a few more minutes before I let go of Breaker's neck. I take a step back, but never take my eyes off him. I watch as Cain and Jett slowly put their weapons away. Just when I think the situation is defusing and everyone is going to walk away without something catastrophic happening, Breaker goes and fucks it up. I know the moment I see the sly grin spread across his face that none of us are going to like what comes out of his mouth.

"Claimed or not, I will make her mine, because once I set my mind to something, I won't stop until I get it. I'll let your little mishap go this time, but you better watch yourself, berserker," Breaker taunts. I snarl at him and move forward to strike him, for calling me a derogatory name. Breaker really just fucked up. I'm going to kill him.

In a move too fast for Breaker or anyone to stop, I haul back my fist and punch Breaker in the face. He stumbles back a step. His Enforcers growl and move forward. Cain and Jett each have a hand on their weapons. Breaker lifts a hand in the air, and everyone stops moving. He wipes at his bottom lip with his thumb, coming away with a drop of blood. He licks the spot where his lip busted open. He nods his head then narrows his eyes at me.

"That's the only hit I'm going to allow you to have. Touch me again, and I won't stop them..." he waves at Cain, Jett, and his Enforcers, "...from tearing you apart." Breaker moves to step around me, hitting my shoulder as he walks past. He stops next to Finley. He leans in inhaling her scent, and picks up a lock of her hair, rubbing the strands between his fingers. "I'll be seeing you around, Finley," he says in her ear. Stolas growls a warning at him that Breaker doesn't heed. He pushes further the second he kisses Finley's cheek before stalking off down the street with his entourage following behind him.

My attention and gaze never leave Breaker if it weren't for Verkor stepping in front of me, I would have chased after Breaker. My essence is urging me to do so. He knows that we are stronger and can easily defeat any of them. I clench and unclench my fist. I can feel my body vibrating with tension and anger. I quickly glance at Finley and see that she is shocked still. Her eyes are wide and her mouth is slightly agape. I glance over to Verkor and see a murderous rage on his face. Stolas, in his hellhound form, has the flames of hell at his feet, indicating how pissed he is. I throw back my head and let out a loud roar. It's the only way I know to release some of my rage. One thing is for sure... Breaker is a dead man walking.

FINLEY

I don't know what to do. A part of me wants to go back to the bed and breakfast and shower Breaker's scent off me. The other part of me wants to go to Obsidian and try to calm him down. We don't need him stalking off after Breaker. I make up my mind; Obsidian needs to be calmed first then I can take a shower. I take a step toward Obsidian when he lets out the loudest roar I've ever heard.

"Holy shit," I exclaim.

What the hell do I do now? Obsidian makes that decision for me. He walks right up to me, picks me up bridal style and heads towards the bed and breakfast. The few shifters who popped their heads out to watch the show, scurry back into the buildings. The ones who are walking down the street turn and head back in the direction they came from. Everyone is moving out of the range of this pissed off shifter. I can't say that I blame them. I would be scared too if I didn't know Obsidian.

"Should we be worried?" I hear Stolas ask Verkor. *When did he shift back?*

"Not yet," Verkor replies. "Just keep a watchful eye on him. Finley," Verkor calls out. I try to look over Obsidian's shoulder, but he growls, and I stay in place.

"Yeah," I call back.

"Let us know if we have to step in. We've never seen him act this way, so we don't know what to expect," Verkor responds. Obsidian huffs like he's offended that Verkor would dare suggest that he would harm me.

"I think we'll be okay, but I'll let you know."

It doesn't take us long before we're back inside the bed and breakfast. Maxwell is standing behind the counter. He takes one look at Obsidian and runs. I look up at him and sigh. I can see why he did. He looks like he'll rip anyone's head off if they get in his way. Stolas runs in front of us, making it to our room door first. He unlocks and pushes the door open. Obsidian walks in and right to the bathroom. He sits me down on the counter.

I watch as he grabs the rag from the holder by the sink. He wets and lathers it with soap. He gently moves my head to the side and starts to wash the area where Breaker kissed. Obsidian takes the piece of my hair that he touched and washes that too. Just when I think he's done; he runs the rag over my arm on the same side. I roll my eyes.

"He didn't touch my arm," I say softly. Obsidian shrugs his shoulders.

"I don't care. He was too close. I don't like his scent on you."

When he's done, he sniffs at me seemingly pleased. He tosses the rag on the counter and rubs his cheek on mine. I chuckle, because his beard tickles.

"Better?" I ask. He nods his head. He places a hand on either side of me; his palms are flat on the counter. Obsidian leans forward placing his forehead on mine.

"I'm sorry," he says.

"Why?" I ask.

"I should know better. I know how they are, and I played right into their hands. I gave him what he wanted. I can't do that. I can't lose my mind whenever he's near. I'll never forgive myself if I put you or our baby in danger." He pulls back looking me in the eyes, pleading.

"Oh, Siddy," I say before throwing my arms around his neck. I see how much he's blaming himself for the possibility of what could have happened back on the street. "You're being too hard on yourself. You weren't alone on that street. Verkor and Stolas were there, and you know they have your back. Hell, even I do. Nothing is going to happen to any of us. We just have to be more careful. We'll try to avoid Breaker and the others as much as possible."

"I don't think he's going to give us that option," Stolas states. Both Obsidian and I turn our heads his way. He's standing in the doorway of the bathroom with a white envelope in his hands.

"Why do you say that?" I question.

"Because this just came for us." Stolas takes a step forward, handing me the envelope. I didn't hear a knock on the door. I take it, quickly reading it. I let out a sigh as I look at Obsidian.

"What does it say?" he asks through gritted teeth.

"We have been summoned to dinner at the Packmaster's house tomorrow night," I reply. Obsidian growls, turns, and punches a hole in the bathroom door.

"He's doing this on purpose," he says.

"You know we're going to have to pay for that," Verkor voices.

Obsidian rounds to Verkor who's standing just behind Stolas. "I don't care. Breaker is doing this on purpose. I showed too much. I reacted too much. He's doing this to push my buttons, and it's fucking working." Obsidian starts to pace the small confines of the bathroom. He runs his fingers through his auburn hair and down his face and his beard.

"Is there any way to get out of going?" I inquire. Obsidian shakes his head.

"Once you're summoned by the Packmaster, you have to go; otherwise, you're punished. At least, that's what happened when I was younger." Obsidian absentmindedly rubs at a spot of his chest, and he stares off as if he's reliving something from his past. But just as quickly as it comes, he's shaking it off. "I doubt anything has changed."

I wish I could wrap Obsidian up in a bubble. I wish I could take away all his pain and hurt, but I know he wouldn't be the man he is today if those horrible things didn't happen to him. I want to ask him what the punishment would be, but I don't think he'd tell me. I sigh.

"Can we get out of the bathroom? It's getting hot in here with everyone blowing around their hot air," I say, trying to lighten the mood, but also because I'm getting uncomfortable sitting on this counter.

Obsidian lifts me but doesn't put me down. He waits until he's near the bed and sits me on the edge. I smile at him and pat the bed next to me. He takes the hint and sits. I lean into his side, and he wraps his arm around me, kissing the top of my head. I look over and see that Stolas and Verkor are sitting on the other bed, facing us.

"Okay, so I take it we're going to have to come up with some sort of plan for tomorrow?" I ask.

"I don't know if we can," Verkor states. "We don't know what could happen. It could simply be just a dinner. A way to make Obsidian angry by having Finley back in his presence."

"Are we going to kid ourselves into thinking that there's another reason," Stolas asks, but it comes out more as a statement rather than a question.

"He's right," I say. "When we go there, we have to show a

united front." I turn my gaze to Obsidian, who looks down at me. "You can't let him get to you anymore. No more doing stupid shit."

"Fine, I'll try, but you can't go anywhere here by yourself. Don't trust anyone here except the people in this room."

"Obviously." Obsidian relaxes a little bit.

"You know what I don't understand, is why Breaker would continue to go after Finley after you told him she was your claimed mate?" Verkor questions. I shift my gaze to him and see that he's frowning.

"He could just be pushing it because of how Obsidian reacted. What's the fastest way to get under a shifter's skin..." all of us are looking at Stolas, waiting. "By going after his mate."

"You didn't seem to mind him touching her," Obsidian growls. Stolas narrows his eyes at him.

"Oh, I did. I just had better self-control. I was the one at her side protecting her and our pup. I would have jumped in if he tried to harm her," Stolas growls back.

I stand up from the bed, placing myself between Stolas and Obsidian. I hold my hands up, palms out. "That's enough," I say with a little growl. "This is exactly what Breaker wants. He wants us fighting each other, and I'll be damned if we give him that." I sigh. "Look at it this way, when we go to the Packmaster's house, it'll give us a chance to snoop around. That's where the last piece of the map has to be hidden, right?"

"The chances are high," Verkor replies.

"Well, let's use this unwelcome dinner to our advantage." I smile, meeting each of them in the eye.

"What are you thinking?" Stolas questions.

"Well..."

STOLAS

I have a love-hate relationship when Finley gets that twinkle in her eyes. I love it because it causes Obsidian to lose his shit sometimes. He's far too controlled in almost every aspect of his life. Finley is the one thing he can't control, and she would never let him, well, outside of the bedroom that is. Oh, I know the kind of things Obsidian's into. You don't live and work with someone without learning some of their deep dark secrets, even if they try to hide it. I'm not judging him, to each your own. I know he would never do anything to hurt Finley. Besides, I think she'd kick his ass if he tried to do something she didn't want, and that is something I'd pay to see. Anyways, I also love the look because I know I'll be down to help her cause mischief. I like having a little fun here and there. You can't be serious all the time. All work and no play makes for a very dull existence.

On the other hand, I hate the twinkle because I know even if we don't agree with her idea, she's still going to try to do it anyway. Once Finley sets her mind to something, it's hard to change it. The best option then is to just go with it and be by her side to protect her, even from herself. I have a feeling that we're not going to like this idea.

"Well," Finley says, drawing out the word. "I was going to ask for a tour of the house. What better way to scope out the property than to be willingly led around and shown it? We can get a few ideas on where the map might be hidden."

Okay, that idea is better than I thought. So, I voice it. "That's not a bad idea."

"How are you sure it's even in this part of the Shifter Realm?" Obsidian questions. "This is just one region, and there is more than one Packmaster in this realm." Obsidian crosses his arms over his chest, glaring at all of us.

"Have you noticed that we're intertwined with the poem as well?" Verkor asks. All of us look at him. "In the second verse, we travelled to my home. At first, I thought it was you," he nods towards Finley, "...who needed to kill to show you weren't weak, but it ended up being me. The third verse we ended in Hell, Stolas' home. All of our gifts only got us so far, and we had to figure out how to get the map without using them. Now, the fourth verse has us here in the Shifter Realm, your home Obsidian." None of us speak as Verkor continues.

"The second piece of the map was in the Winter Court, specifically where I'm from, hidden in my childhood home. That could only be because I'm from the royal bloodline and my home was the castle. The third piece," he shrugs, "it could only be with Lucifer because he's the strongest being there and rules over all of Hell and not just a portion. But, Stolas' family is known for guarding the gate that leads to Lucifer's castle. His family would have access to the castle to leave reports with the King of Hell. If we go by everything that has happened, the fourth piece would have to be where Obsidian is from. It's the only thing that would make sense." All of us stew on Verkor's sentiment.

"Fine," Obsidian says, finally breaking the silence. "If that's the case, the Packmaster is the strongest being in the region. It would have to be hidden in the pack house." Obsidian turns to look at Finley. "Ask for the tour, but all of us are going with you." Finley smiles and rapidly nods her head.

"Like there was any other option. I don't like Breaker, and I definitely don't want to be alone with him."

"Never," Obsidian growls.

"I do have one question," Finley states. We all turn our attention to her. "There is a line in the last stanza of the poem... A party in the moonlight will be quite the sight, but be prepared to fight. My question is what is the party?" Finley directs her attention to Obsidian, waiting on his answer. He shrugs his shoulders.

"I don't know. There was never any party in the moonlight that I can remember. It has to be a fairly recent thing that they are doing."

"Just another thing we can add to our growing list of things to figure out," Finley says with a sigh.

"Wait," I say, and all heads and eyes turn towards me. "I know I'm backtracking, but why would we need a tour? Obsidian is from here, haven't you been inside the pack house?"

Obsidian shakes his head. "Not all of it. There were a handful of times that I was inside, but I never made it past the room to the left when you first walk in."

"Do I want to know what's in that room?" Finley asks softly. Obsidian meets her eyes.

"No, but I need to warn all of you." He rises from the edge of the bed, grips the hem of his shirt, and whips it off. He turns his back to us. "You'll need to get close to see the scars. I've hidden a lot of them in my tattoos."

Finley is the first one to really see the marks because she was already standing close enough to him. I stand, moving on one side of her, and Verkor moves to her other side. We lean in, and when I do, because I'm looking for them, the scars seem to jump out at me. There are dozens of them, in every direction, from his shoulder blades down to the waistline of his pants. Finley gasps next to me.

"What the hell happened?" Her voice is a mix of anger and sorrow. She tentatively lifts her hand but thinks better of it and lets it fall back down to her side. We take a step back and Obsidian turns back around, facing us.

"That is what happens when you disobey the Packmaster's orders. That is what happens when you fight back. That is what happens when you're different." The grip Obsidian has on his shirt tightens. He puts the shirt back on and pushes his way past us. He doesn't say another word as he leaves the bedroom.

"Should one of us go after him?" Finley asks.

"Normally, I would say no, but given where we are and what happened earlier, I'm going to say, yes," Verkor states. "I'll follow behind him. Just close enough to watch and to help if he

needs it, but far enough to make it look like he's by himself."
Verkor leans down and gives Finley a brief kiss on the lips
before leaving.

"It's down to just two. Whatever are we going to do to pass
the time?" I say cheekily.

"I don't know if now is the right time for that," Finley
states.

"Oh, love, it's always the right time. Plus, Obsidian will be
fine with Verkor following him." I know that's the real reason
she's worried. She sighs.

"You're right. Though I could use a shower first," she states
wrinkling her nose.

"Well, let's go conserve water." I place my hands on her hips,
lifting her. Finley automatically wraps her legs around my waist
and her arms around my neck. She smiles at me before nuzzling
her face in my neck.

"Mm, lets," she says, then nips at my neck.

"Fuck," I groan.

CHAPTER 6

FINLEY

I don't let up on my nipping, licking, sucking, and kissing of Stolas' neck. His grip tightens on my hips, but he walks us into the bathroom. He sits me on the counter, the one I was just sitting on with Obsidian. His hands go from my waist to cupping my face. Stolas doesn't say anything before he starts to devour my mouth with his. He angles his head, deepening the kiss. I open my mouth, moving with his and he dives his tongue inside. I move my hands to the waistband of his jeans, sticking my fingers through the loops, pulling him closer. Stolas pulls back, and I take in a much-needed breath of air.

"Fuck, Finley," he growls.

He kisses a path down my neck, pulling my shirt to the side to expose my shoulder. He continues his path, using his teeth to scrape across his mating mark. I shiver from the contact and moan. I want to feel him inside of me.

"Stolas." His name comes out in a breathless whisper, and this time it's him who shivers.

"I want to be inside of you in the worst way," Stolas says, taking a step back.

"Then what's stopping you?" I lick my lips.

"You're right," he says.

His silver eyes heat up with desire. He grips the hem of his shirt and pulls it up and off his body, dropping the material to the ground. My eyes trail over every inch of exposed, tan, muscular skin. I follow his hands as they unbutton and unzip his pants. He hooks his thumbs in the waistband and pulls them down, along with his boxers. His hard cock bobs as it's released from its confines. I watch as the items of clothing pool at his feet. He steps out of them, pushing them off to the side. God, his body is a work of art, and it's all mine.

Stolas takes a step, but it's not toward me. No, I watch his ass cheeks flex as he walks over to the shower and turns it on. I quickly take my shirt and bra off, throwing them on top of Stolas' discarded clothes. I'm just about to hop down from the counter when Stolas turns around. Heat blazes in his eye as he takes in my half-naked body. He grips his cock, giving it a long, slow stroke. I feel my panties dampen from my wetness. Sliding from the counter until my feet hit the floor, I turn, showing Stolas my back. I look over my shoulder. He's still gripping his cock, but he looks up, meeting my gaze. I smile and wink at him, before facing forward.

I put my thumbs in the waistband of my yoga pants, slowly dragging them and my panties down my legs, presenting myself to Stolas. A low, sexy growl, almost like a purr, erupts from him, and I smile to myself. He's not the only one who can tease. I don't get a chance to fully take my pants off, before Stolas steps up behind me, rubbing his cock between my cheeks.

"Do you know how much you're turning me on right now, love? The way you're presenting yourself so nicely." Stolas runs his hands up and down my back, then over my ass, squeezing the rounded globes. "Do you know how much I want to take you right here, right now?"

I wiggle my ass against him, because I don't know why he's

not. I'm not going to stop him. Stolas groans from my movement. I see his foot step on my pants, and I feel his hands on my hips.

"Step out of them, love." I do as he says. He keeps me steady the whole time. I watch his foot push my clothes over the side. "I want you to go over to the tub and brace your hands on the rim."

I stand, looking over to the mirror, which I know is fogged from the hot water. I glance over at Stolas, he's biting his lower lip, while stroking his cock, and I wish it was me doing those things to him. I want my hands and mouth on every inch of his body. But I do as he says and lean over, gripping the rim of the tub. The position lowers my chest and makes my ass higher. A soft growl comes from behind me and I growl in response. Stolas isn't the only one turned on by this. I wiggle my ass, enticing him to come over and finally give me what I want, his cock. Luckily, it works because I feel Stolas' hands on my hips.

"Are you ready for me, love?" His voice is deep and raspy, and I moan at the sound.

"Yes," I reply, a little breathlessly.

"Mm, I think I should check for myself." His hand moves from my hips, over my belly, and down to my mound. I buck my hips forward trying to get his fingers right where I want them. He chuckles. "Eager, are we?"

"Yes, please. Just touch me." Because at this point, I'm not above begging. Stolas' fingers slide lower, right between my folds. "Finally." Stolas chuckles again. I want more, so much more.

His fingers continue to travel down, and he pushes them inside my pussy, pumping it a few times before pulling back and running it up the length of my seam. I drop my head, getting lost in the feel of his fingers on and in me. Stolas does this over and over, and I can feel my orgasm building. Just a few more strokes, that's all I need. Right before I fall over that precipice,

Stolas pulls his hand back. I'm about to voice my frustration at him stopping, but I don't get a chance to. He replaces his fingers with his cock, surging forward. The second he thrust inside me, I fall over that cliff, and scream my release.

STOLAS

There's nothing that feels as good as my mate's pussy squeezing around my cock as she comes. Nothing sounds as good as her screaming my name. I still the moment I thrust inside her, just to enjoy the feeling and the sensations coursing through my body. A shiver runs up my spine. I lean forward resting my forehead between her shoulder blades. It's then that I feel her arms shaking and I smile. I'm not even done yet. Finley's going to be jello in my arms by the time we're done. I wait until her breathing slows before I start thrusting inside her.

"So warm." Thrust. "So tight." Thrust. "So wet," I say and thrust again. "You feel so good wrapped around me."

I lean forward and clamp my teeth down on my mating mark and a violent shudder runs through Finley's body. I wrap my arms around her and keep my teeth on my mark, as I pick up my pace, trusting into harder and faster. I'm getting close, but I need her to come again before I do. I trail my fingers down her stomach, to her pussy. I stop when I reach her clit, rubbing it in time with my thrust. Her pussy starts to flutter and squeeze my cock and I know she's close. I pick up the pace and bite down a little on my mating mark, and it pushes her over the edge. Finley screams my name, as I empty myself inside her.

I release my teeth from her shoulder, moving to rest my head between her shoulder blades. I don't know how long we both stand there, but it was long enough that our breathing returns to normal. I kiss her back, and rub her hips, before rising. I don't want to leave the warmth of her pussy, but we can't stay like this forever. Reluctantly, I pull out of her and watch as my seed drips down her inner thigh, and I start to get hard all over again. Finley straightens and on shaky legs turns to face me. I want her again, but I need to let her rest. I can never get enough of her. The urge to have her gets more intense as I watch her swell with my pup.

Finley smiles at me. She's so damn beautiful. I close the little bit of space between us. Placing my hands on her hips, I tug her forward until her body is flush with mine. I lean down and kiss her. Finley sighs against my lips and melts into my touch. I want to pick her up and bounce her on my already hardened cock, but I don't. Instead, I kiss her deeply and thoroughly. When I pull back, I look down at her, moving some of her hair behind her ears. Finley smiles, then shakes her head.

"Why does it seem like we always have sex in the bathroom?" There's a teasing note in her voice. I laugh, because she's right. We do seem to have sex in the bathroom more than any other place.

"I don't know, love. But one of these days we'll make it to the bed." I wink at her. We aren't going to be doing that any time soon. I plan on having sex with her on every available surface I can. You can't let things get boring. Finley glances over her shoulder to the shower and sighs. Her gray eyes meet my silver ones.

"We probably should have turned the water off. It has to be cold, lukewarm at best." She glances back to the shower, and sighs.

"Sorry, love. I got a little carried away."

"Eh, don't worry about it. I enjoyed every minute of it. We'll just get in and have the fastest shower known to man." Finley pulls back the shower curtain and steps in. I wait a moment waiting for her to squeal or make some kind of noise at the cold water, but she doesn't make a sound. "It's not so bad," she says. "You coming in or what?" she calls out.

I sigh. I can't very well let her take a cold shower alone, because she'd never let me live it down. I pull back the curtain. *Here goes nothing.* I step in to take a freezing cold shower.

CHAPTER 7

OBSIDIAN

I didn't mean to storm out on Finley and the guys, but I just need a minute to myself. I knew coming back here was a bad idea. Seeing the faces of Breaker, Cain, and Jett, my first day back hasn't helped matters. I clench my fists at my sides. Breaker is lucky that Verkor and Finley talked me down off my ledge. I wanted to rip his throat out. I could have and there's nothing he could have done to stop me. Oh, the pleasure I would have gotten from finally being able to put one of my tormentors down. It would have been short lived, because I know Cain and Jett would have attacked me, not to mention the three enforcers he had with him. Besides, there's no way in any realm that I want to be Packmaster. That's what would have happened if I killed Breaker and somehow managed to survive.

My thoughts filter to when Breaker touched Finley, and rage so strong pulses through me. I've felt rage before; I'm no stranger to it. We're best friends at this point. But I've never felt rage quite like what I did in that moment. The voice I now hear from my shifting essence is urging me to kill the male for daring to touch what is ours. Oh, how I wanted to. I pictured

82

the way I would rip him apart limb from limb. We would bathe in his blood as a sign to any shifter who thought they could take our mate.

A prickling sensation crawls along the back of my neck and I know I'm being followed. I stop and look over my shoulder. I don't see anyone. I take a deep inhale and faintly pick up the scent of winter. *Verkor*. I sigh.

"You might as well come out. I know you're here somewhere, Verkor." It doesn't take him long to emerge from the shadows. There's plenty here for him to hide in. "So, you drew the short end of the stick and had to come follow me." I see Verkor shrug his shoulders from the corner of my eye as we walk down the sidewalk.

"It was either me or Finley, and we both know what would have happened if I let her come." A growl escapes my lips at the thought of her walking around, out here by herself. I don't trust anyone in this realm. "Exactly. She was going to come after you, but I convinced her to let me." I nod my head. That was smart of him. "Do you want to talk about it?" he questions. I don't really, but there's so much anger pent up inside of me, and I don't know how to release it. Verkor doesn't push me; he waits until I'm ready, silently walking beside me.

"I hate being here," I say. "I knew I would run into people from my past, and a small part of me hoped that things would be different, but they're not."

"Sometimes people change, like you, and sometimes they don't," Verkor says. "But I've come to realize that those who cause the most difficulty in our lives will always get what's coming to them. Karma has a way of showing up." I snort.

"Breaker and his lackeys are in the highest positions in this region. Karma's doing a fine job at making them pay," I growl.

"I didn't say when karma would happen, but it will eventually. Someone stronger than him will show up and take him down." Too bad it hasn't happened yet. "What do you make of the dinner invitation?" I growl.

"I know he's only doing it to see Finley. I let him see too much earlier in the way I reacted when it came to her. But I couldn't tell you if his reaction would have been the same if I tried to downplay who she is to me. Plus, there's the whole reason I came back in the first place. Saying that I'm showing my mate where I'm from seems like a logical explanation. Either way, we need to keep a close eye on him when he's around her."

"Of course, we will," Verkor responds. I stop walking and run my fingers through my hair. Verkor stops and looks at me. "What is it?"

"There has to be another reason he wants this dinner. I just can't figure it out, and it's driving me insane. I know we can't decline the invitation. How I wish I could, but I won't subject Finley to any form of punishment here, especially since I don't know what brand of torture Breaker's favorite is now."

"Do you think he wants to rub it in your face, so to speak, that he's the Packmaster, and if you return, you'd have to listen to him?" I shake my head.

"I don't know, maybe." I shove my hands in the pockets of my jeans.

"Well, we aren't getting anywhere with this tonight. Let's head back. I know Finley has to be worried about you. Like Finley said, we'll use tomorrow as a way to snoop around and figure out just what Breaker has in store for us." I nod at Verkor. We both turn and head back in the direction of the bed and breakfast.

I can't help feeling that something more is going on here. And as much as I hate being home, I need to find out what it is.

The walk back to the bed and breakfast is quiet. Verkor and I are both lost in our thoughts, and before I know it, we're back in front of our room door. Verkor reaches out and turns the knob, opening the door. The second I step foot inside, I'm attacked by my pink haired, pregnant mate. She throws her arms around my waist, squeezing me tight.

"Oh my God, Obsidian. I was so worried about you. Are you okay?" she asks, nuzzling her face against my chest, and I relax. I wrap my arms around her and bury my nose in her hair.

"I'm fine, doll. I just needed to get out and clear my head."

She pulls back but doesn't let go. I look into her gray eyes and see the love and concern in them. I lean down, placing a gentle kiss on her lips. Finley takes my hand and drags me over to one of the beds. I sit next to her, while Verkor and Stolas sit on the other bed facing us. This is very reminiscent of how we were before I walked out. I'm hoping she doesn't want to talk more about Breaker and what happened; I don't think I have it in me.

I don't even want to think about him until we have to go to this farce of a dinner, because if we're being honest, that's exactly what this is. It's just another ploy to get under my skin, which I've been letting him do too easily. I need to take a step back and remember that this place and these people can no longer hurt me. Finley squeezes my hand, bringing my attention to her. She smiles softly but doesn't say anything. She leans her head on my shoulder and sighs.

"I'm tired," she says with a yawn.

"I think we all are," I say with a smile. Verkor and Stolas gaze at Finley with love in their eyes.

At this point, I think we're all in a state of permanent exhaustion. The last couple of months have been crazy, and even though we've been giving ourselves down time in between retrieving the pieces of the map, the journey is still taxing mentally, physically, and emotionally. I can't wait for this mission to be done.

I kiss the top of Finley's head. "Come on, doll. Let's get some sleep. Tomorrow is going to be another long day."

She nods her head against my shoulder before rising and crawling under the covers. I glance over at Verkor and Stolas, silently asking if I can sleep with her tonight. They both nod. I just need the comfort of my mate being in my arms. I need her near, to breathe in her scent, to feel her warm body against mine.

I climb in on the other side of the bed, pulling her close. Finley snuggles into my side, placing her head on my chest, and a hand over my heart. She throws her leg over one of mine. I put my hand on top of the one on my chest, and my other arm wraps around her body, rubbing her hip up and down. She breathes out a sigh of contentment, and I know exactly how she feels.

One of the guys turns the lights off, but with my enhanced vision, I still see everything clearly. Everyone is silent and settled, and just when I close my eyes and start to drift off, Finley's soft voice breaks through the silence.

"Hey, Siddy," she says. There's a sleepy quality to her voice. It's cute.

"Yeah, doll?"

"Didn't you say your parents lived here?"

I tense under her question. If I had it my way, she would never meet them, but I know Finley and I know where this is going. "Yeah, they do."

"Are you going to see them?"

The question is innocent enough, but I don't know how to answer her. "I don't know, doll," I say honestly.

"Well, before we leave, if you want, we could go and visit. I'll be... we'll be with you the whole time. It might give you some closure to tell them how you feel."

"We'll see." It's the last thing that I want to do.

Finley's breathing evens out and I know she's sleeping.

"There's a chance something happened to them, isn't there?" Stolas questions.

86

"Yeah." I didn't really expect them to seek me out. Part of me knew that, but there was still a part that's sad that they didn't come looking for me.

"Are you going to find out?" Verkor asks.

"I do and don't want to. A part of me doesn't care what the hell happened to them, but a part of me does. I don't think that Finley will give the option not to anyway," I reply. Verkor and Stolas chuckle.

"Yeah, you're right about that. But we'll go when you're ready. You'll just have to tell that to Finley. She'll understand," Verkor says.

I know she will, but I struggled for a long time trying to push back all the memories of being here. The last thing I want to do is face them. In this moment, I realize I never dealt with them, and it's probably why I'm reacting the way I am. But the things that were done to me I can never forget or forgive. I just hope that Finley and the others will be able to understand that.

CHAPTER 8

FINLEY

We got a little bit of a late start to the day, but luckily, we just made it in time for the breakfast buffet. We were the only ones there. I'm not sure if it's because we were late or if we're the only ones here. I haven't seen or heard anyone else in the hallways. After breakfast, we took a walk, looking at all the shops and buildings. Every once in a while, Obsidian would point out something that changed or was added in the years since he's been absent.

Speaking of Obsidian, he seems more reserved today. I wonder if it has anything to do with what happened yesterday, or if it's because we'll be heading to the Packmaster's house shortly. Either way, I wish I could help him. I want to take away his pain, but I can't begin to help him until he's ready to help himself first. So, I try to be good all day, by not asking the million questions that I have, by not picking a fight with him. Though, I only do that because I like getting a rise out of him, in more ways than one. The best part is the angry, make-up sex that we have. Obsidian is so lost in his own thoughts for most of the day that I don't think he noticed.

I can't begin to imagine what it's like being here. After his flashback yesterday, more of the pieces fell into place. I realized that Obsidian may not have any good memories of being here. Not a single person genuinely happy to see him. I don't understand. What did Siddy ever do to these people? From the little bit about his past that I've gathered, Obsidian was never cruel to anyone. He was the one that was beat and abused. For what? Being different? For not being a sheep and blindly following orders? It isn't right, and I get angry for him. But I can't fight his battles. I can stand by his side and support him. And if I have to jump in and help him, I will.

After our walk, we returned to the bed and breakfast and are currently lounging around the room, even though we should be getting ready for the dinner that no one wants to go to. I would pass, if I could, because Breaker and his goons are just downright creepy and pathetic. Unfortunately, we need to go because one: I don't want to be punished by Breaker or any of his thugs. Obsidian said that's what happens when you disobey the Packmaster and I don't want to experience that. Plus, I don't want to put Obsidian through more shit. And two: the house is probably where the last piece of the map is hidden, and we need to scope out the house for where it could possibly be at. So, all of us are going to suck it up and attend and hate every minute of it.

I turn my head, which is laying on a pillow, in Obsidian's direction. He's been standing by the window between the two beds since we came back.

"So, what the hell are we supposed to wear to this dinner?" I ask. "Is it fancy, dress casual, what?"

Obsidian turns his gaze on me. "I'm not dressing up to please that asshole. I'm going with what I have on." I sit up on the bed, dangling my feet off the side.

"Is that wise? Are we going to anger him by not dressing up?"

89

"I don't know, and I don't care. If he wanted us to look fancy, he should have said something on the invitation."

Obsidian turns his head and looks back out the window. I glance over at Stolas and Verkor. Stolas is laying down on the other bed, while Verkor is digging through our bags. He stops since Obsidian quit speaking. Verkor looks over at me and I see the question in his blue eyes. *What are we going to do?* I shrug my shoulders at him. I look down at what I'm wearing.

Honestly, it's not bad. A pair of black yoga pants and a soft pink t-shirt. It's nice and comfortable. I'm not going to bother to change either. I glance around the room, looking at the guys. They each have on jeans, but Verkor is wearing a blue button-up that makes his eyes pop. Obsidian is wearing a black Henley t-shirt, and Stolas is wearing the same style as Obsidian, but in gray. Eh, we all look fine.

"Well, that solves that," I say. I smile as I see Obsidian glance at me from the corner of his eye.

"We should get going," Verkor states. "If we're not going to change, then we have to at least show up on time."

Obsidian grumbles but nods. Verkor stands, bringing me my favorite pair of black boots. They have a low heel, plenty of straps with chains and studs that crisscross over the top. They zip up on the side even though there are laces. The best part of the boots are the Chinese throwing stars that are hidden in the heels. Those have come in handy quite a bit. I smile at Verkor.

"Thanks." He nods and I quickly put them on. I go to the bathroom, checking my hair. I look presentable and that's all that matters. We all file out the door.

The walk to the Packmaster's house took longer than I thought it would. It's a beautiful two-story log cabin that sits back in the woods. There are no other houses nearby. It's a little too secluded for my taste, but then I remember what Obsidian said about a torture room and suddenly it all makes since. The house is set so far from the others so no one can hear the screams. I shiver at the thought. It's not like the shifters don't know what's going on. People talk, rumors start. Nothing stays hidden forever.

My steps get slower the closer to the porch steps we get. I'm not the only one; Obsidian has practically halted in his steps. I stop beside him, as Verkor and Stolas move forward, giving us some space. I reach over and lace my fingers through his. Obsidian looks down at me, and I see the haunted look in his eyes. I bet he's remembering things from his past. I give his hand a reassuring squeeze.

"You aren't going in there alone. We'll be with you the whole way. If it becomes too much, let us know and we'll leave," I say softly to him.

Obsidian nods but doesn't move forward. I let him take his time. I notice when the change comes over him. Instead of being scared, he squares his shoulders and his face gets a look of determination. I'm proud of him, because as much as this must be affecting him, he's not letting his fear, his memories, his past, rule him.

We stride forward and up the wooden steps. The second we step onto the porch, the front door swings open, and Breaker is standing there, filling up the doorway. I'm glad we didn't change because Breaker is dressed casually in jeans and plain white t-shirt. His short black hair is styled with some sort of product, giving it that perfect messy look. He has a strong nose and jaw line. His pink lips look firm. It's the twinkle in his brown eyes that I'm not sure is good. Breaker is nice to look at, but that pretty packaging is hiding an evil disposition and a horrible laugh.

"Took you long enough. I thought you were just going to stand out there all night, staring." Breaker lets loose one of his high-pitched laughs, and I cringe. His laugh sounds like nails on a chalkboard. I'm not going to be able to deal with that all night. I kind of want to punch him in the throat just so I don't have to hear him at all. "Please, come in." He gestures for me to go in before him. I let Obsidian's hand go and enter the house. My guys are quick to follow.

When you walk inside there's a small foyer with a door off to the left, and I shiver as I remember what Obsidian said goes on behind that closed door. There's no way I want to experience that firsthand. I push the thought away and walk forward. The foyer gives way to the living room. I swear if my jaw was able to actually drop to the floor, it would have. The inside of the house is gorgeous.

A massive, stone fireplace takes up the right side of the room. The fire's lit and there's a cozy looking black rocking chair placed in front. I bet that makes for a great reading spot. The ceiling is high, and a metal orb chandelier hangs from the center. I step further into the room and notice the glass top coffee table with beautiful, what looks like, hand carved legs. I run hands along the back of the tan couch, feeling the softness under my fingers. I turn slowly in a circle taking in the rest of the room. There are two doors. One off to the left and the other to the right. Above the door on the right is a set of stairs that leads to the second floor. Overall, the cabin has a rustic feel to it.

"What do you think?" Breaker asks, stepping right in front of me and stopping my perusal of his home. I take a step back because he's a little too close for comfort.

"It's beautiful," I say. I almost wish I could take the words back, once I see the slimy smile that crosses his face. I can tell he's happy that I like it; though, I'm not quite sure why.

"How about we go on a little tour?" Breaker holds his elbow out to me. "There's still a few minutes before dinner is done."

I glance over at my guys, who are only a few steps behind Breaker. All of them are frowning, with Obsidian being the worst. He looks like he's ready to rip Breaker to shreds and he hasn't done anything... yet. I hook my arm around Breaker's, trying to hide my shiver of revulsion at having to touch him. I paste a smile on my face when I meet his eyes.

"I would love that."

Breaker's smile gets wider. "Excellent." He guides me over to the bottom of the stairs. My guys are only a step behind us. I feel safer knowing that they're close. "I'll save you from having to walk up there. There's nothing but bedrooms and a bathroom." We step over to the door that's below the stairs. I snort, which causes Breaker to look down at me, cocking his head to the side.

"Sorry, I don't know if you've seen the old Earth Realm *Harry Potter* movies," I say. Breaker shakes his head.

"Can't say that I have," he replies.

"Oh, well, he lived in the cupboard under the stairs." I pointed to the door. "Seeing that reminded me of it." He smiles but has that look on his face. The one that says I have no clue what you're talking about, but I'm going to go with it anyway.

"Well, I definitely don't live under here; it's my office." With his free hand, he reaches out to the doorknob, turning it, and pushes the door open.

When I look inside, I see Cain sitting in the chair behind the desk with Jett hovering over his shoulder as they look at an image being projected by the Holographic Optic Virtual Assistant, or H.O.V.A. The second they see me, the image before them disappears, and I'm pissed at myself for not getting a better look at it.

"Cain, Jett," Breaker nods to both.

"Packmaster," they say unison, before lowering their heads. Shit, I haven't been keeping to the rules that Obsidian told me. Though, Breaker hasn't reacted to my indifference to the rules. That could come back to bite me in the ass, but let's hope not.

"I'm just giving the lovely Finley a quick tour of the house."

As Breaker talks to his Beta and Omega, I take the chance to look at the office. It seems ordinary with bookcases on either side of the room, a desk and a chair behind it. There are a few chairs in front of the desk. The painting behind the desk grabs my attention. It depicts a forest scene with different types of animals that you normally wouldn't see together. At the front, is a hyena followed by wolves and bears. Scattered throughout the background are deer, bunnies, foxes, various types of birds, and other small woodland creatures. The painting is beautifully done. It's then that I see it isn't lying completely flat against the wall. How cliché would it be if there was some sort of safe behind the painting? It's not like it would be the first time. That's where the second piece of the map was hidden in the Winter Court of the Faerie Realm. I make a note to tell the guys about it later.

"Let's continue the tour. Cain and Jett have some business to finish before joining us for dinner," Breaker says, breaking my thoughts. I nod and let him guide me through the rest of the house.

The kitchen is behind the other door. It's spacious with high-end, state-of-the-art appliances. There are a couple of cooks flitting around the room. They stop when they notice Breaker has entered the room.

"Packmaster," they say, and lower their heads.

"Continue what you're doing," he tells them. "Don't mind me." The cooks give each other weary looks. This is out of the ordinary for him. Their looks say it all. "I'm just giving a tour of the house." They nod and go back to their business.

So, we continue this farce of a tour. Off from the kitchen is the laundry room and the master bedroom. Breaker doesn't take us in either of those rooms. Instead, he opens the sliding glass doors that take up one side of the kitchen. I follow him out on the porch. The view is breathtaking. I've never been more thankful for the slight improvement of my vision. A happy side effect of being pregnant. Without it, I wouldn't have been able to see that the leaves on the trees are starting to change colors. It's not as vibrant as it must look in the daylight, but there are so few hours of it. I would love to see this view then. I glance around the rest of the yard, and see a pool and basketball court, which is well lit.

"Two questions," I say. Breaker looks down at me.

"I'll answer them if I can," he says with a smile.

"What's that?" I ask as I point to a building off to the left. "And does it suck living where there are hardly any sunlight hours?" Breaker throws his head back and laughs. I cringe at the sound. I'm curious as to why he's laughing. I don't find the questions I asked to be particularly funny.

"Those are not what I was expecting you to ask," he says. I arch my eyebrow at him. His laugh was one of relief. Now, I really want to know what he thought I was going to ask. I voice the question, seeing if he will answer me.

"What did you think I was going to ask?" He shrugs his shoulders.

"I guess more hard-hitting questions. I was expecting you to ask about pack life. Though, I could tell you some things, but not everything."

"Why?"

"One, because you're human." I almost roll my eyes at this. Is speciesism a thing? You know, discriminated against because you're not the right species. Because if so, that's what this is.

"What's the second reason?" I prompt, wanting to move this along.

"Even though you are mated to Obsidian," he sneers that sentence. "You are not a shifter yourself and neither of you are a member of this pack." I nod my head. It's a logical reason. You don't want outsiders to know how you operate. And I don't want to be a part of his pack anyways, the psycho.

"That's understandable," I reply, trying to be nice and not voice my actual opinions.

"But I can answer your questions. The building is the

95

garage, nothing fancy. As for living somewhere with only a few hours of sunlight, well, I don't know any different. This is my home. I grew up here. Though, I suppose it would be different and maybe hard to handle if it's something you aren't used to." I nod; it's a reasonable explanation.

"Okay, one more thing," I say. Breaker laughs.

"What's that?"

"You've shown me everything, but you didn't mention the door when you first walk in," I state. I'm trying to see if he'll actually tell me what's behind there.

"Oh, that," Breaker waves his hand dismissively. "That's nothing for you to worry that pretty little head about. It's pack business. How about we go and see if dinner is ready?" He effectively dismisses the topic. I don't say anything not wanting to push.

When we turn to walk back inside, I almost bump into Obsidian. Verkor and Stolas are only a step behind him.

"Protective lot, aren't they?" Breaker says, but there's something in the way he says it. It's in annoyance and frustration. I try to hold back my grin, but I can't, especially when I meet Stolas' eyes and he winks at me. I look over to Breaker and shrug.

"Eh, I kind of like it." I look back over to my guys and wink. There was no way they were going to let me walk around with Breaker unattended.

Verkor and Stolas walk back into the kitchen. Obsidian moves to the side and lightly runs his fingers down my arm as Breaker and I walk past. I relax a little at his touch. He follows us in. Sitting at the kitchen table is Cain and Jett. The cooks are placing plates of food in the center. Once the last plate is on the table, they make a hasty retreat.

Breaker guides me over to the empty seat on the left side of the chair that's at the head of the table. Cain is sitting in the chair on the right and Jett is right beside him. The second I'm in my seat, Obsidian takes the one next to me, with Stolas sitting beside him. Verkor takes the last seat at the opposite of Breaker.

"So, Finley, tell me about yourself," Breaker says as he picks a dish filled with mashed potatoes. He serves me before serving himself then passes the dish to Cain. Obsidian growls low from beside me. I reach under the table, grab his leg right above his knee and give it a gentle squeeze. He quiets down.

"What do you want to know?" I ask.

"Everything," he replies. Yeah, that's not happening. I chuckle, playing along.

"Well, besides being mated, I guess the most important thing to know about me is that I love playing the violin."

"Is that so? You'll have to play for me sometime." I nod and give him a little smile. It's the last thing I want to do, but I will if it helps us.

OBSIDIAN

If it wasn't for Finley gripping my thigh, I would have reached across the table and punched Breaker in the face. Actually, I really want to rip his throat out. I don't know how much longer I can last with him touching her and looking at her like he wants to eat her, in a sexual way. I want to throw her over my shoulder and hall ass out of here. But I'm forcing myself to sit here and listen to all the dribble coming out of his mouth. The sound of his voice is grating on my nerves. The worst part is watching him feed my mate, serving her food. I know everything that he has done tonight is to just get under my skin, and it's working.

I'm so pissed and irritated that I'm stabbing the steak on my plate harder than I need to, and I don't taste what I'm sure is a delicious meal. My thoughts keep circling back to how fast I can get Finley out of here and away from Breaker. I have to give her credit; she's hiding her true feelings extremely well. If it wasn't for the slight squeezing she does every so often to my knee, I wouldn't suspect anything.

I quickly glance at Verkor and Stolas. Verkor has his eyes narrowed at Breaker, and Stolas' knuckles are white from the grip he has on his fork. I move my gaze to Cain and Jett, who have been quiet this whole time. I see the corner of Cain's eye twitch. He doesn't like something. Wonder what it is? Jett has a mask of indifference on his face.

If I had to guess, Cain doesn't like something that his Pack-master is doing. I wonder if he wants Breaker's position. Jett, on the other hand, is just a follower; he'd never be able to lead anyone. I flit my gaze back to Breaker. There's a gleam in his eyes as he looks at Finley, and I don't like it. He's ignored everyone tonight except for her, and I think it's time I take his attention away from her.

"Breaker, how did you become Packmaster? Axel was one tough son of a bitch," I say, voicing my earlier thoughts. It accomplishes what I want, Breaker's attention on me instead of Finley. Breaker looks at me, narrowing his eyes. Out of the corner of my eye, I see Cain and Jett sit up straighter in their chairs.

"I don't see how that is any of your business," Breaker sneers. "You are no longer pack and aren't privy to such information." I sit back in my chair, crossing my arms over my chest.

"As far as I know, as long as my parents are still pack, so am I by association. Also, I was never handed a formal letter excusing me from the pack." A smirk crosses my face when his lips pull back. He's not happy about the loopholes in the pack law. Just when I think I have the upper hand on him, I see the change in his demeanor, and I know I'm not going to like what he says next.

"Well, I can issue a formal letter tonight before you leave, or..." he leans forward in direction, placing his forearms on the table. "Or, I can wait until the day you leave here again, because we all know you're not going to stay. You like to run from your problems instead of handling them like a man."

I growl low, my chest vibrates from the sound. He smiles because like a fool I played right into his hands again by reacting to what he said. Breaker shifts in his seat, angling toward me. He leans back, leaving one hand on the table, and thrums his fingers against it.

"Yes, I think I'll wait until you leave here again. It'll be a satisfying end to our game. And speaking of your parents, I can't wait until you find out about them." A sick grin twists his face. *You can't react. You can't let him see anymore. You have to be stronger.*

"We are stronger," my shifter essence answers. *"We could take over the pack."*

"No, that's not what I want."

"It's what we deserve. We need to kill them."

"We will, one day. But not now. We must protect our mate." The essence hums its agreement and quiets down.

I need to play this off then I need to get us out of here. I look Breaker directly in the eye and shrug my shoulders.

"Do you honestly think I care about what happened to them? If you think I do, then I'm sorry to disappoint you. I don't give a fuck." I push back my chair and stand. Everyone at the table, except Finley and Breaker, do the same. "As fun as this has been, it's time we take off for the night."

I hold my hand out to Finley. She places her hand in mine, and I lace our fingers together. I help her stand and tug her close to my body. She loops an arm around my waist, hugging me. I make sure to keep eye contact with Breaker the whole time.

"Let's get you back to the bed and breakfast, Finley. You have to be tired from all the running around we did today."

It's a blatant lie, but Breaker doesn't need to know that.

This is more of me marking my territory and showing my claim on her. The hand that Breaker has on the table clenches into a fist, and I smirk. That's right; she's mine and is going home with me, warming my bed tonight.

Finley yawns and nuzzles her head against my chest. "You know, I am feeling pretty tired. It's been a busy day," she says playing along. God, she's perfect.

"I hate to cut this dinner and evening short, but as my mate just said she's tired. I'm going to take her home and put her to bed. My mate's needs will always come first." Breaker's lip curls and he understands the meaning behind my words, and if the pinch Finley gives me on my side is any indication, she understood the meaning too. Breaker stands and forces a smile at us.

"Of course." He turns his attention back to Finley. "It was an honor having you tonight, and I hope we can do it again soon. Maybe you'll even get to stay for dessert."

"Maybe," Finely replies.

I turn us in the direction of the living room, hoping to make a quick escape, but we don't get far before Breaker is calling out to us.

"Oh, Finley." We stop and Finley looks over her shoulder to Breaker. "On Saturday night there's going to be a party down at the beach. We're celebrating a rare occurrence, the Super Blood Moon. It's something that only happens once every five or more years. It's a sight to behold. You're invited to attend, as well as your mates."

"Thank you for the invitation. We wouldn't miss it."

"Excellent," Breaker says and claps his hands together once. "I'll be sure to send you a formal invitation."

"I look forward to it." No, she's not. I hear the strain in her voice at having to expect the invite. She's not the only one who doesn't like this.

Finley turns back around and follows Stolas and Verkor through the living room and out the door.

CHAPTER 9

VERKOR

We make it back to the bed and breakfast in record time. Everyone is on edge. Obsidian is pacing the small confines of the room, Stolas is bouncing his leg up and down, Finley is fidgeting with the hem of her shirt, and I keep running my hands up and down my thighs. That whole dinner was a sham. The only purpose it served was to just irritate us, and it worked.

"That was fun," Stolas says. I look over at him, sitting on the edge of one of the beds. For once there's no hint of joking in his voice or on his face. There's a scowl present that could rival Obsidian's. There are very few things that anger Stolas to this point, and Breaker just made it on that list.

"I, for one, am glad we got out of there when we did. He gives me the creeps," Finley says with a shiver. She turns her attention to Obsidian, who stopped pacing when she started talking. A playful smirk crosses her face. "Like the pissing contest you were having there at the end. Claiming me in front of him. Any other time I would have been pissed, but in this case, it's warranted. He doesn't seem to be taking the hint." Her eyes narrow and she crosses her arms under her chest. "I mean, who tries to continue to go after someone else's mate. Breaker is skeezy."

I chuckle. "That's putting it mildly." Finley looks over at me and smiles.

"What's with this Super Blood Moon he was talking about?" She directs her question to Obsidian. "Could that be the party in the moonlight the poem mentions?"

"I don't know," he replies while running his fingers through his hair. "It's something new that they're doing, because we never celebrated it before. I'm going to wager that this is exactly the party the poem is talking about. That's not the only thing that I'm questioning. I want to know how the hell Breaker became Packmaster. He avoided my question about Axel. Any other person would have reveled in the story of how he took down the Packmaster. Something else is going on," he growls. Obsidian is completely frustrated. There's only one way to get the answers that we seek.

"Then I say we start nosing around town and asking questions, subtlety," I state.

"No, we don't. We're only here for the map. We need to stick with that. This realm, this region is none of our concern. We need to stay focused on why we're here in the first place. Why bother with anything else?" Obsidian questions. As much as he says he doesn't want answers, there has to be a small part of him that does.

"Because you know you'll want answers," Finley and I say at the same time.

"I think I know where the map is." All of us turn our attention to Finley.

"What do you mean you know where the map is?" I ask.

"First, I said I *think* I know where the map is, not that I *do* know where. Second, when Breaker was so graciously," she rolls her eyes, "giving us a tour, he showed us his office." We all nod. "I didn't get a chance to see what the holographic image was that Cain and Jett were looking at when Breaker first opened the door, but I did see the painting on the wall behind the desk. At first, I was only looking at it because it caught my eye. There's a hyena in the front followed by all types of different animals. I assume it's meant to represent the shifters in this region." Finley turns her gaze to Obsidian, seeing if her assumption was right.

"Do you know what animals were behind the hyena?" Obsidian asks.

"Yeah, there were two wolves, each a different color, followed by bears. All of those animals were the biggest. There were others in the picture, but they were small in more in the background," Finley replies.

"That's because the biggest animals in the painting are your Packmaster, Beta, Omega, and Enforcers. Breaker is a hyena, so that animal was probably the biggest and front and center. The wolves are Cain and Jett, and the bears are his Enforcers. The other animals would be the different types of shifters that live in this region," Obsidian explains.

"Huh, Breakers laugh makes so much more since now," Finley states. "Anyway, as I was looking at the painting, I noticed that it didn't lay flat against the wall." I get where she's going with this. "Which means, there's a chance that there is something behind it, say a safe that might hold a piece of the map."

"That's likely. I didn't see anywhere else that he would stash something that important," I say.

"Did the house seem eerily empty to anyone?" Stolas questions.

"What does that have to do with anything?" I ask.

"I don't know," Stolas shrugs. "It's the pack house. I thought there would be more shifters running around the place." We all turn toward Obsidian for confirmation.

"I can't tell you. I did everything I could not to be around the pack house. The times that I was there, I never made it past the door on the left," he responds.

"Well, we'll have to add that to the list of questions we have," I state.

"Is that what we're doing tomorrow, going around and asking questions?" Finley asks.

"I guess. We didn't have anything else planned, did we?" Stolas inquiries.

"No," Obsidian says.

"Then that's what we'll do."

"On a side note, are we going to wait until the Super Blood Moon party before trying to take the map?" Finley asks.

"That would be the best time. We can use that as a distraction," Stolas says with a smile.

"What was the last part of the poem?" I ask.

"The last piece of the puzzle you will find, in a place where only the moon shines. A party in the moonlight will be quite the sight but be prepared to fight. Assemble the pieces and follow the trail, you'll end up in a distant land. A throne is what they sought, now go and take back what they took," Finley rattles off.

"Okay, so we completed the first line. We're here in the Shifter Realm," I state.

"The Super Blood Moon party we assume will be the party in the moonlight. That will be our best chance at retrieving the last piece of the map. Like I said, we use the party as our distraction. I'm sure no one will notice if we're gone for a few minutes," Stolas says.

"That's fine, but the poem says be prepared to fight. Something is going to go down that night," Finley states. "The rest of the poem deals with after we have the piece. So, for now I say we focus on how we're going to get back inside the pack house."

"What, why?" Obsidian bellows, cutting Finley off. She turns her attention to him.

"We need to be sure there is a safe behind that picture. There's no point in making plans for it to be there and it turns out that we're wrong. We need to make sure. We already have to worry about when and where this fight will happen, let's try to make this a little easier on us."

"Easier on us," Obsidian scoffs. "Nothing about this has been easy for me." He runs his fingers through his hair, tugging on the ends. "I don't want to go back to that house. Hell, I don't even want to be here."

"Then leave and go back home," Finley growls. A little smoke escapes her nose. She's getting angry.

"Like hell I will," Obsidian says, getting up into Finley's face. She plants her hands on her hips and narrows her eyes at him.

"Then man up, shut the fuck up, and help us with this. You know this place and the people better than anyone. You're our best chance at getting out of here alive and relatively unharmed."

"Fine, but just it be known I hate this, and I'm not happy about it," Obsidian says before sitting down on the edge of the bed. I watch indecision cross Finley's eyes. Obsidian caved on this argument quickly. Finley bites her lower lip then narrows her eyes. She's working something out in her head. After a few minutes, she sighs and her shoulder slump.

"I'm sorry," she says softly. Obsidian whips his gaze to her. "I know I shouldn't be pushing you. I'm sorry for not taking into account how hard this must be for you. I should have considered that before jumping down your throat." Finley quickly looks over to Stolas, narrowing her eyes. "Not a word," she tells him. Stolas has his mouth open like he was going to say something, but Finley stopped him before he could. Stolas smirks at her and winks. He was definitely going to say something inappropriate. Finley turns her attention back to Obsidian.

He opens his arms and she walks right into them. "It's fine, doll, and thank you." He kisses the top of her head, before she pulls back.

"I promise to be more considerate of your feelings going forward." Obsidian nods at her. "What do you think we should do?"

"Getting back into the pack house will be difficult, unless we're invited back in, but I don't see that happening," Obsidian states. "We're going to have to sneak in, and that won't be easy," he says.

"Well, while we're out subtly asking around about the Pack-master and the Super Blood Moon party, what if we noncha-lantly case the pack house?" Finley says. All of us look at her, then Stolas and I look to Obsidian.

"That works for me. We can see how many shifters guard the grounds outside and watch the coming and going of who enters and leaves the house, and how often," Obsidian says, nodding his head. He runs a hand over his beard. "Let's start with that then go from there. We have until Friday night to finalize plans. We'll need to make sure all of our bases are covered, with the crazies that live here."

I go to open my mouth to voice a thought when a muffled commotion outside of the window catches all of our attention. We all stand from the bed and walk over to the window. Finley gets there first, unlatches the locks on the window, and shoves it up. The muffled voices are now clear as day through the open window.

"I'm tired of the way you run things. You're worse than Axel was. I challenge you for the position of Packmaster." From the angle of the confrontation, I can't see the face of the person issuing the challenge, but the other person is visible. Breaker.

I look closely, but I don't see Cain, Jett, or any Enforcer nearby. That doesn't mean that they aren't there, it's just that I can't see them. Breaker's high-pitched laugh echoes through the street. Not one sound can be heard.

"Challenge accepted. Be at the pack house this time tomorrow," Breaker answers.

Without another word, Breaker turns and walks away. The other shifter stares after him for a moment before turning and walking in the other direction. The shifter briefly steps beneath a streetlight, and I get a glimpse at his features. Short blonde hair, sharp jaw, long pointed nose. I can't see his eyes color, but they glow green.

"Who was that? What's going to happen? Are we going to watch the challenge?" Finley rapid fires her questions. I turn to look at her, but her eyes are glued to the spot where Breaker and the unknown shifter were standing. I look back toward the streetlight, but the shifter is gone.

"Do you know who that was?" I direct my question to Obsidian. He shakes his head.

"No, but that doesn't mean much. This region is pretty big, and shifters can move freely within it. The only time permission is needed is when a shifter from a different region wants to move to this one. There has to be an agreement between the two Packmasters. He could have petitioned to move here. I don't know. It's been so long since I've been here. Maybe some of the rules have changed."

"What's going to happen, and are we going to watch the challenge?" Finley revoices her questions.

"Unfortunately, we do have to go. Challenges are mandatory." We all move away from the window and resume sitting on the beds. "What's going to happen is that Breaker and the challenger will decide if they will fight human or shifted. Most shifters prefer to fight shifted. You're stronger in your animal form and can handle the pain better." A weird look crosses Obsidian's face, and her furrows his brows. "Though, I don't know why Breaker is waiting until tomorrow. Usually, once the challenge is issued, the participants only have a few hours to prepare."

"What do you think it means? That he's waiting?" I ask. Obsidian looks up meeting my eyes.

"I don't know, but Maxwell clammed up pretty quickly when I asked how Breaker was still Packmaster. Plus, he said the challenge with Axel was weird. I bet any money something is happening before the challenge, and I don't think it was the only time," Obsidian replies. Everyone is quiet after that.

CHAPTER 10

FINLEY

Someone pounding on the door wakes me up. Sleepily, I roll over and start to push back the covers to get out of bed and answer it. Mostly, I just want to yell at the person for daring to interrupt my sleep. I'm not a morning person. An arm falls across me, pulling me back against the warm body I'm sharing the bed with. Verkor snuggles up against my side, buries his face in the crook of my neck, and inhales deeply.

"Don't worry about the door, one of the others will get it," he mumbles against my skin. "Just go back to sleep." Good, because I wasn't ready to get up yet. I fix my covers and sink into Verkor's arms. Just as I'm getting comfortable, a loud, deep growl permeates the room. My eyes open like a flash, and both Verkor and I sit up in the bed.

"What the hell?" I voice. I look over to the other bed and see that it's empty. Obsidian and Stolas are already awake.

I look over to the door and see Obsidian's back heaving. His fists clenched at his sides, and I don't have to see his face to know that he's pissed. Stolas is standing in front of him with an open box in one hand and an envelope in the other. Whatever is in the box and whatever the note in the envelope says can't be good, especially to rile up Obsidian first thing in the morning. I scramble from the bed and plant myself between the Obsidian and Stolas.

"What's going on?" I ask, putting my full attention on Stolas.

I feel hands on my waist and a gentle urging of me to move backward. I do what Obsidian wants, and lean back into him, resting my back on his front. His nose goes to my hair and he takes a deep breath. I let Obsidian do his thing. If me being near him, touching him, will help calm him down so he can explain what's going on, then I'm down. Who am I kidding, I love when all of my mates touch me. Their touch has the same effect on me. I reach down and put one of Obsidian's hands on my belly and start rubbing up and down on his forearm. I feel him relax against me. I keep up the motion as I wait for Stolas to answer me.

"These came this morning." Stolas raises both hands, which are filled.

"I gather that, but why is Obsidian already in a bad mood this morning?" I question.

"Because of what's in the box and the letter," Stolas replies.

I use my free hand to motion for him to continue. Stolas sighs. He moves around Obsidian and me. I turn to watch him, with Obsidian moving with me, never letting me go. Stolas places the box on the end of the bed Verkor and I were just sleeping in. He takes the letter out of the envelope and unfolds it.

"My Dearest Finley," Stolas starts.

I cringe. That alone would piss Obsidian off, and if I'm not mistaken, there's a bit of a bite in Stolas' voice when he read the line. Stolas isn't happy about this either it would seem.

"It was truly an honor to have you at dinner last night. I'm sorry our time was cut short. We didn't even get to the dessert portion of the meal, which I'm sure you would have loved. But there will be time for that at a later date.

In the box, I have sent a dress I would like for you to wear tonight to the challenge. You would do me a great honor by being my special guest. Also, I have included a formal invitation for you and your crew to attend the Super Blood Moon party this Saturday.

I can't wait to see you this evening. Please, enjoy the rest of your morning.

Yours,

Breaker," Stolas finishes.

I'm too shocked to move or form words, but Verkor has no such problems. I watch as he walks over to the box and pulls a beautiful red dress from it. As much as I don't like Breaker, and the fact that I find him creepy, whomever he sent to buy the dress has great taste.

There are sheer sections to the dress that are noticeable through the sunlight streaming in from the window. That reminds me, I want to see as much of the region in daylight as I can before the sun goes down. You might think that four hours is a long time, but it's not, and it goes by fast. But I digress.

I move from Obsidian's hold and walk over to Verkor. I finger the dress and see that the majority of the dress is made of tulle, and that the only parts that aren't sheer are the cups of the breasts, and a piece under the tulle that goes from the hips down to mid-thigh. The floral embellishments that cover the skirt, sides, and breast cups are gorgeous.

I look over to the box and see that there is a pair of red strappy heels that match. My gaze settles on Obsidian.

"Is it normal to dress so fancy for a challenge?" I don't know what the protocol is for this. Obsidian's lip curls, but I know it's not directed at me.

"No," he growls. "I don't know what Breaker thinks he's

doing, but he needs to stop. I can't take him hitting on you for much longer."

"Same," Stolas growls from my side. I look up at Verkor and he nods, agreeing with them.

"You know that I don't want him to. I don't even like the guy," I state.

"We know that, baby, but Breaker is really pushing the limits."

"Verkor's right," Stolas says. "No *good* mate would let this continue." I turn my gaze to Obsidian who hasn't moved an inch.

"He's already crossed the line and it would be within my right to kill him." I open and close my mouth, not really knowing what to say. "The only reason I'm not hunting him down as we speak is because I won't put you in danger. I also don't want to be Packmaster here."

"I think you would be good at it," I say. Obsidian scoffs, and the corner of my mouth turns up into a smile.

"I hate people, and there's no way I want to help people deal with their problems when I have enough of my own." I fully smile at that. I move over to him and wrap my arms around his waist, looking up into his amber eyes.

"I know that. I was just pulling your chain." Obsidian wraps his arms around me and kisses my lips.

"This is going to be the longest week of my life," he groans. I giggle.

"It won't be too bad." Obsidian pulls back and quirks an eyebrow at me. "You'll have me and your best friends here." He rolls his eyes and does his best to try to hide the smirk on his face.

"Yeah, there's that," he replies.

I step back from Obsidian and position myself so I can see all of my guys.

"Look on the bright side guys." They look at me confused.

"This will give us an opportunity to sneak back into the pack house. Everyone will be focused on the challenge and won't notice if Verkor uses his shadow magic to hide and snoop around." Stolas smiles, Verkor has a shocked look on his face, and Obsidian has his ever-present scowl.

"Have I ever told you, you are the best, love?" Stolas says.

"No but continue." I pretend to preen under his comments. He laughs and swats at my ass.

"Go and get changed. We have a lot of ground to cover. Plus, we'll get food."

"Well, in that case," I walk over to the closet, open the door, and drag my bag closer to me. I grab the first thing that my hand lands on and pull it out of the bag. I stand and walk over to the bedroom. "Give me just a minute, and I'll be ready to go."

I shut the door behind me and hear Stolas chuckle before saying, "I told you food was the fastest way to get her moving." I grin at that. Food is always a good motivator for me, whether I'm pregnant or not.

It doesn't take me long to get ready. I pick up the clothes I brought in and see that I have a pair of black yoga pants and a plain blue t-shirt. Nice, I get dressed as fast as I can. I brush my teeth and put deodorant on. I don't bother with any kind of spray or perfume. The guys seem to like my natural scent the best. Quickly, I brush through my hair and slap it up into a ponytail.

I take a step back, assessing myself. I turn to the side and I smile. I swear my belly is getting bigger by the day. I run my hand over the slight swelling. I never knew instant love was a thing, but that's what this was. I'm nervous and excited about becoming a mother. I don't have anything good to go off of and I'm terrified I'll screw this kid up. I also know what I missed and wished I would have had in my life, and I'll have the guys to help me. I know they won't let anything happen to me or this baby. I stare at my belly a little longer in the mirror. I look up and see my gray eyes and pink hair, and shrug my shoulders, good enough. I don't want to get all dressed up now, when I have to do that later.

I shiver at the thought of Breaker, and not in a good way. There's just something off about someone who knows the rules for when it comes to mates yet still tries to go after one that is already taken. He's slimy, gross, and overzealous, and if I didn't fear that I would be punished, or worse, Obsidian would be in some way, I would decline. But this is a means to an end, and I will do what I have to get what we came for. Besides, Obsidian is here when he doesn't want to be, and I can't let him down. I can't let him fight through his demons and his memories of his traumatic past and have it be for nothing. No, I will do what I need, to a point, to get this done. Thankfully, I don't have to worry about seeing Breaker until later tonight. *For now, just go out and see if you can figure out what the hell is going on around here.*

I open the bathroom door and see Stolas lounging back on the bed closest to the bathroom. He's wearing blue jeans, a dark green t-shirt, and a pair of black boots. His black hair is getting messy from laying on it, but it doesn't distract you from how good looking this man is. His arms are under his head as he uses them for a pillow. There is a sliver of tan skin on display where his shirt has ridden up. I'm dying to run my fingers across it.

I move my gaze to Verkor who is sitting on the edge of the other bed with my boots in his hand. His blonde hair is longer than he normally keeps it, just past his shoulders but I'm not complaining. That man is sex on legs. He's also wearing blue jeans and a plain blue t-shirt, paired with his ostrich skin cowboy boots. What I wouldn't give to ride him. The only thing missing is his black wings. Man, do I love those things. Verkor loves when I pull and tug at the onyx feathers while we have sex. I run my tongue over my lips just thinking about it.

I shift my eyes to Obsidian who is standing by the window.

My ginger haired mate. The man is a walking piece of art, quite literally. He's covered in tattoos, which I just learned he has to hide the scars from years of abuse at the hands of his father, his tormentors, and the Packmaster. Obsidian stands there in black jeans and a black t-shirt with shit kicker boots on his feet. He's the biggest of all of my mates, and it's hard to imagine a time when he wasn't this hard muscled wall. I look at him and feel nothing but love, even when we argue with each other.

I don't understand how anyone would hurt a child. He's so strong that it's tough to see him struggling and trying to hold all his emotions in, because even if he doesn't see that he's doing that, I do. I will help him as much as I can. I will help carry the burden, even if he doesn't want me to.

The second I step out of the bathroom, all of them turn their attention to me. Stolas and Obsidian inhale deeply and let loose a couple of growls.

"What?" I ask.

"What were you doing in there, love?" Stolas asks as he sits up in the bed, swinging his feet over the side.

"Getting ready, why?" I question, confused by what else he thinks I was doing.

"I can smell your arousal," Stolas says with a huskiness in his voice. I see Obsidian nodding his head in agreement from the corner of my eye. It dawns on me then what they think I was doing.

"Well, you can blame yourselves. All of you." I gesture around the room. "Maybe if you guys didn't look so good all the damn time. Why, did you think I was pleasuring myself without you?" I say, waving my fingers at them. There's a round of growls and I'm pretty sure that included Verkor. "Don't worry guys; I have you to fill my *every* need." I smile at them. They all growl again.

"Damn right we will," Stolas says.

. . .

STOLAS

"As much as I would like to continue this, daylight is a wasting, literally. We have things we need to do before this challenge tonight," Finley says and heads toward the bedroom door.

As she walks past me, I get a stronger smell of her arousal and I groan. She smells so good. I want to bury my face between her thighs. I stand, adjusting my hard cock in my pants. I swear I've been a walking hard-on since we learned she was pregnant, and it's getting worse as I watch her belly grow with my child. Don't get me wrong, just being around Finley makes me hard, but it was easier to control, and I didn't want to pounce on her every chance I had, but now... I shake my head. I can't seem to get enough.

"Stolas, are you coming or are you going to stand there daydreaming all day?" Finley calls out from the bedroom doorway. I look over and see Obsidian and Verkor are waiting just outside the door. I'm the one holding everyone up.

"I'm coming." I hope in more ways than one. I walk over to the others, close, and lock our bedroom door behind me.

"What are we doing first?" Finley asks.

I throw my arm over her shoulder, pulling her close to my body. Her hand comes up and rests on my lower stomach, right about the waistband of my jeans. My stomach clenches from the touch. I want her hands on me a little bit lower and preferably without any clothes on.

"We're going to get something to eat," Verkor answers. I'm glad he does because my mind is fully in the gutter right now. "Then we're going to try to get some answers from the shifters around town."

"Do you think they'll talk to us?" she questions.

"Probably not," Obsidian voices.

"Why do you say that?" Finley inquires. Obsidian pushes open the bed and breakfast door; Verkor walks out first, followed by Finley and myself, and Obsidian last. We start walking down the street before Obsidian responds.

"If Breaker is anything like Axel, and I think he is, then they'll be too scared to talk. They'll be afraid of repercussions. It's easier to pretend things aren't happening and mind your own business, than getting mixed up in something. If you have an opinion, your best and safest bet is to keep it to yourself."

"I don't understand why the town hasn't banded together to try to overthrow, or whatever it's called, the Packmaster. Safety in numbers."

Obsidian shakes his head at Finley. "You would think, but fear is a powerful thing. Most shifters want to protect their families. They might see what's going on and want to help, and wish things were different, but the consequences for stepping in are too high."

Finley sighs. "That's a shame," she whispers. "Why do people have to be so cruel? There's enough nastiness going on in all the realms, why add to it?"

I pull her a little tighter against me and kiss the top of her head. "You have a good heart, love. The sad thing is we can't fix everything, but we can try to change the things we have the power to."

Verkor stands a little closer to Finley and interlaces his fingers with hers. "That's what we're doing today. We're gathering information and hopefully we can find the right person to pass it to and hope that something good will come out of it," he states. Finley sighs and nods her head.

"Okay," she says. The rest of the walk to the diner is silent.

FINLEY GROANS FROM BESIDE ME. WE'RE TAKING A QUICK break from walking around town, to sit on a bench by the section of woods. "I knew Obsidian said it would be hard trying to get people to talk, but shit, this is like pulling teeth," she says leaning into my side. I chuckle. She's really impatient.

"Shifters aren't going to open to people that don't live here. The only one they know is Obsidian, and they seem scared of him," Verkor responds.

He puts his hands-on Finley's shoulders and starts to massage them. Her head falls forward and she moans. The sound goes right to my dick. Now is not the time.

"Then what are we supposed to do if no one will talk to us?" she questions.

"We can't help someone if they don't want it," Verkor says.

"I don't understand why though. Is it really better to continue on living like this, in fear, than to reach out for help?" she inquires.

"They don't know any other way," Obsidian interjects. "Take it from someone who knows. I tried to stand up for myself and for others and it didn't bring me anything but more pain and suffering. You get to a point where protecting yourself from harm overrides everything."

I glance at Obsidian who is sitting next to Finley on the bench. He absentmindedly rubs his arm. I think he's remembering how he got a few of those scars. Finley must sense a change in him because she looks up and places her hand on his forearm. Obsidian doesn't say anything. He places his hand over hers.

We all sit here quietly taking in our surroundings. The shops are open but there are very few people milling about. You would think with it being so close to the Super Blood Moon party that people would be rushing around gathering things, but it's like a ghost town.

There is a ruffling sound behind me. I turn my head slightly toward it. Someone is walking through the woods behind us.

"Has anyone seen Ryan?" a soft voice asks.

"No," a deeper one answers.

"You don't think..." the soft voice trails off.

"I think we have to assume the worst has happened," the male voice responds. There's a feminine sigh.

"He was our best chance. I would petition to move regions, but we know Breaker would never allow it," she says.

Finley reaches over and grabs my thigh. I look down at her and her eyes are wide. I mouth, "Can you hear them?" and she nods. Seems like she's gaining some of the shifter hearing.

"Did you hear that Obsidian, his mate, and friends are going around trying to find out information on Breaker and what he's like," the male voice says. Their voices are starting to get softer as they move away from us.

"I did, but Obsidian should know better than anyone what Breaker is capable of," the female voice responds.

"Super Blood Moon is nearing, has there been any word on who it will be this year?" the male voice asks. By the time the female voice responds they are too far out of my hearing range to hear an answer. None of us say anything for a few moments.

"Do you hear an answer?" I ask Obsidian.

"No, her voice was too soft," he replies.

"What do you think that was about?" Finley questions, turning to face Obsidian.

"I don't know, doll, but I don't think that it's anything good."

For once, I agree with Obsidian. It seems like there is more to this Super Blood Moon party than what Breaker is letting on. Word is spreading that we're asking questions, and I think we need to be more careful and be aware of our surroundings.

Verkor takes the words right out of my head. "They're talking about us; you know it'll only be a matter of time before Breaker finds out." Obsidian shrugs.

"What's he going to do? We're only asking questions. We haven't actively sought him out for anything," I state.

"No, but he might take it as we are trying to take his place.

We just have to be careful around him. Everyone needs to be very aware this evening." Obsidian focuses his attention on Finley. "I wouldn't wear the heels Breaker sent with the dress. Wear your boots instead. You still have the throwing stars hidden in them?"

"Of course," Finley replies.

"Good. We'll place a dagger high on your thigh because of how sheer the bottom of the dress is and we'll place some inside your boots as well," Obsidian states.

"Don't forget her pointed hair chopstick things you got her," I say. Obsidian nods.

"We still have a few hours before the challenge tonight, and I doubt anyone will talk to us. Word seems to be spreading like wildfire around here," Verkor says. "What do you want to do in the meantime?"

"I have something I want to do, but I don't know how I will handle it," Obsidian says, staring off in front of him.

"What's that?" Finley probes lightly. Obsidian turns his gaze to her.

"I want to see my mother."

Well, shit. Out of everything he could have said that wasn't something I would have ever expected.

CHAPTER 11

OBSIDIAN

This was the one thing that I didn't want to do, but ever since Breaker had mentioned that something happened to my parents, it's been nagging at me. I need to see for myself if what he said is true. The trip should be easier with Finley and the others going with me. I don't know if I would have gone by myself.

My pace starts to slow the closer we get to my childhood home. The street is quiet and everyone looks holed up in their houses. It's very different than when I lived here. There used to be kids playing in the yard and families getting together, except for mine. My father wouldn't allow it. He was too afraid that my mother or me would let something slip. I wasn't dumb enough to do that. I didn't want to see what the punishment would be for something like that.

A small hand slips into mine. I look down and see a worried expression on Finley's face. I give her hand a gentle squeeze, letting her know I will be okay. I hope. We continue walking down the street, hand-in-hand, until we get to a white, two-story home with a white picket fence. The memories of living here start to flood my mind. Very few of them good. Nothing traumatic happened outside. Realms forbid the neighbors find out that we weren't the happy, perfect family we pretended to be.

We stop just outside the gate of the fence. Finley is still holding my hand, and Stolas and Verkor are standing behind us.

"Are you sure you want to do this?" Finley questions.

"No, but if I don't, I know I will regret it. It'll be easier with you here with me," I reply.

I watch as my hand trembles as I reach for the gate. I pause halfway there, clench and unclench my fist a few times, trying to get rid of the nerves. *You're not that little kid anymore. You're stronger now. He can't hurt you anymore.* I take a deep breath, letting it out slowly. I reach for the gate again with a much steadier hand. It squeaks as I push it open and let Finley walk ahead of me. Stolas and Verkor follow.

There's a stone pathway that leads up to the red wooden front door. The grass is overgrown like no one has cut in a while; the flower beds have seen better days. I'm surprised that my father let it get this bad. Everything had to be perfect and in place to keep up the perfect family appearance.

We walk up to the front door and I ring the doorbell. I can hear the sound of it echo through the house. I wait a few minutes before ringing it again. When no one answers, I ring the doorbell for a third time. This time when no one answers, my brows furrow. I can't remember a time when my mother or father didn't answer the doorbell after the first ring.

I try the doorknob, turning it. I'm surprised when the door opens. Pushing it the rest of the way open, I peek my head inside, looking to see if there is an immediate threat. When I don't spot anything, I gesture for Finley to enter. She takes a few steps inside, leaving room for all of us to enter.

There's a stale smell to the air, like no one has been here for a while. I walk down the foyer and into the living room and I'm shocked at the sight. There are papers thrown everywhere, chairs flipped over, cushions on the floor.

"What the hell happened here?" Finley says from beside me. I shrug my shoulders because I don't have an answer for that, but it's clear that something did.

I walk further into the room, and I can feel my chest getting tight. The horrible memories I have are trying to crash through, but I can't let them. I can't let what happened to me in that alley happen here. It seems like the harder that I try to push them away the harder they try to break through. I take a couple of deep breaths and close my eyes, trying to ward off the negative thoughts and feelings. It's not working and the memories flood through.

"What did I tell you?" my father screams at me. CRACK! I wince as the belt makes contact with my flesh. "How many times have I told you not to embarrass me!" CRACK! This one lands on my back.

I learned a long time ago not to make any noises. The beatings lasted longer when I cried. CRACK! My arm feels like it's on fire from the hit. CRACK! I hate when he hits the same place more than once. CRACK! My back has gone numb from the pain. At least when he hits me again it won't hurt so much. CRACK! I barely flinch at this blow. I hear the belt fall to the floor, but I know not to move until he tells me too.

My memory fades into the next.

My head whips to the side as my father backhands me across the face. "You stupid mutt." He shoves me, the back of my legs hit the coffee table, and I fall. "Stand up!" he yells. I scramble to my feet. He grabs my hair and yanks me forward. The smell of alcohol is heavy on his breath. "Why can't you do anything right? Is that too much to ask for?" he shouts as he punches me in the stomach.

The memory fades into another.

I hit the floor hard so hard my head bounces, black spots dot my vision, and I lose my breath. I try so hard to suck in air, but I can't. I blink my eyes a few times, and when my vision is clear, I see that the reason I can't breathe is because my father has his foot on my chest. I grip and scratch at his ankle, trying to remove it. I know that trying to fight back will only worsen or prolong this abuse, but I need to do something before I die. I know he won't care if I do. There's no one who would miss me.

Just when I think he's not going to let up, he does. I suck in much needed oxygen, only to have to have it ripped from me again by him kicking me in the ribs. The pain is sharp. I think he broke a rib. I'm positive he did. It wouldn't be the first time, and I'm sure it won't be the last. I just need to live long enough to escape. It's almost here.

I don't even know what I did this time. It may not even be my fault. It doesn't take much to anger him anymore. It started when I got a bad grade or talked back. It slowly escalated from there. Now, whenever he gets angry, he just takes it out on me. My mother hides from him when he's like this, and I can't say I blame her, but it would be nice if she stepped in to stop it. It would be nice if anyone would step in to stop it.

There's another swift kick. It lands on my back. I huddle into a ball, throwing my hands over my head to protect it. The motion of curling up puts a strain on my ribs and it hurts worse now. I can handle this; he'll stop soon, I think as I get another kick lands on my back.

Another memory assaults me.

"Are you really so pathetic that you let three weak ass shifter kids beat the hell out of you?" my father yells.

"It's not like I wanted to let them. They held me down," I yelled back.

"You're just as weak and helpless as they are." He stalks closer to me. He unloops his belt and folds it in half. "Maybe I should teach you how to toughen up. No son of mine is going to be a pansy." CRACK! The belt hits my shoulder blade. It's followed by another and another. The sound of the belt hitting my flesh echoes in the silent room.

"Obsidian, I need you to come back to me. Whatever you're seeing isn't happening. You're fine and standing in front of me. Let your past go. Please, Obsidian," Finley's voice begs.

It's then that I feel her small hands on my chest, rubbing them up and down. I take another breath, inhaling her scent of strawberries, vanilla, and sulfur. I listen to the sound of her voice. All of it is grounding me. It takes me a few minutes to fully come back, and when I do, I quickly wrap Finley up in a hug.

"Thank you, doll," I whisper. I just hold on to her until I know that I can look at the room again.

I take a step back from her and square my shoulders. The first thing I see are all the family photos on the fireplace. My mother, father, and I are all smiling, but it's fake. None of us were happy, but we had to keep up appearances. I can't stand to look at them any longer. I stalk over to the fireplace and run my arm along the top of the mantle, knocking all the pictures to the floor. The sound of glass breaking is deafening in the silent room. I thought I would feel better, but I don't. If anything, I'm angrier and I want to rip this house to shreds, but I don't. I'm better than this, than what I was.

"Obsidian, we can go. We don't have to do this," Finley says. I know I don't have to be here, but I need to do this. I can't let this house and these people get to me any longer.

"Just give me a minute," I say through gritted teeth as I grip the edge of the fireplace. All of them give that to me. I can hear them talking to each other, and their voices ground me a little more. My anger starts to fade away. As I look at the shattered pieces of glass and the old pictures laying at my feet, I realize that I wouldn't be where I am today if all this ugliness hadn't happen to me. I'm not perfect. I have a long way to go, but right now, I'm happy. Finley makes me happy. She is helping to heal me piece by broken piece. I couldn't ask for more.

"This place is awfully dusty. I don't think anyone has been here for a while," Finley's voice drifts to me.

I look at the mantle and see bare spots from where the pictures were standing. She's right, there's a thick layer of dust. I know there's no way my father would have let this go. They're not here anymore and they haven't been for a while. Breaker said to wait until I knew what had happened to my parents, but if they're not here, then where the hell are they? What did he do to them, and more importantly, do I care?

FINLEY

"What do you want to do, Obsidian?" I ask. It's his home and his parents and gauging from his reaction to just being here maybe it's better that he doesn't look for them. I'm sure that whatever happened to them they deserved.

"Breaker knows something. He said as much at the dinner." He rakes his fingers through his hair. "I know what I'll be doing after the challenge tonight. He's going to be answering a few questions," Obsidian growls. I nod.

"Maybe his answers can give you some peace about them. Is there anything you want from here? Do you even want to continue looking around?" I ask softly.

"Not really. You can if you want," he responds.

I don't want to go through the house without him. I also don't want to trigger any more memories, but I'm curious about what his bedroom looks like. Well, how he left it.

"The only place I want to see is your bedroom, but we don't have to go and look if it's too much."

Obsidian shakes his head. "I should be fine, but if not, I'll deal with it."

This time it's me that shakes my head. "No, Siddy, that's not right." Now I feel like an ass. I shouldn't be pushing him to do this. I should be dragging him the hell out of here. Why would I put him through more heartache? I'm the worst mate.

"It's fine, doll. If I truly didn't want to do it, I wouldn't."

Obsidian walks over to me and grips my hand. He starts tugging me to a set of stairs on the other side of the living room. The steps creak as we walk up them. At the top of the landing, we turn right and walk all the way down the short hallway. Obsidian opens the door on the right and pulls me inside.

I look around the room and whip my gaze to Obsidian. He shrugs then looks around the room himself. My eyes don't know where to land. There's barely anything in the room. It feels like a prison cell.

There's a small twin bed on the floor, pushed up against the far wall. A dark blue blanket is balled up in the center and there's no pillow in sight. Bars cover the only window in the room, and holes litter the walls. The closet door is wide open, and only half of it is filled. Off to the side is a small desk, but the chair behind it sits at an odd angle. There's no posters, books, or pictures. Nothing to suggest that a young boy or even teenage boy stayed here.

"Geez, Siddy." My gaze settles back on him. My eyes are starting to burn because I haven't blinked since stepping in here. "This was your room?" I finally blink, and when I do, I feel the tears welling up in my eyes. I may not have had a great childhood either, but this... this is something else. There has to be a reason why his father treated him so horribly.

Obsidian pulls me into his arms and kisses the top of my head. "Oh, doll. Don't waste your tears on me. This is my past. Yes, there isn't much here, and yes, it sucked, but what I have now makes going through all of this worth it."

"I-I-I just don't understand," I hiccup.

"I know, doll, but there is one thing I can promise you." Obsidian pulls back and cups my face. He uses his thumbs to wipe away my tears. Stupid hormones.

"What's that?"

"You will never have to worry about me treating any child we have like my father treated me." His eyes bounce back and forth between mine.

"It never crossed my mind that you would." I frown because I'm confused on why he would think that I would. I reach up and wrap my hands around his wrist. "You have never laid a hand on me in any way that I didn't want. Your touch is always gentle and caring. Hell, you barely raise your voice to me when we argue. You have never raised a hand at me in anger. You're a great mate, and I know you'll be a wonderful father. Remember what you told me. We already know what we don't want to be like as parents.

"Yeah, we'll make mistakes, but we'll have each other, plus Verkor and Stolas to lean on. I don't think you'll have anything to worry about." I nuzzle the side of my face into his palm before placing a kiss on it. I smirk at him. "Besides, you know I'll beat you down if you tried anything stupid. I'll have Verkor and Stolas help me."

"Damn straight we will," Stolas says from the doorway. Obsidian drops his hands, and I let go of his wrist. When I turn toward the doorway, I see it's not just Stolas, but Verkor as well. I didn't know that they followed us upstairs.

"It's getting late and we still have to go and change for the challenge," Verkor says. We all groan.

"Fine, but there better be food. I'm starving again." The guys chuckle. "You guys won't be laughing when I start gnawing on you from hunger."

"You can gnaw on me anytime, love." Stolas winks at me then turns and leaves. Verkor is shaking his head, but there's a soft smile on his face as he follows him. I turn my attention back to Obsidian.

"I'm with Stolas on this one," he says with a grin.

"Yes," Stolas' voice echoes down the hall. I roll my eyes, but giggle.

"Come on," I say, lacing my fingers through Obsidian's. "We have a recon mission to go on."

CHAPTER 12

FINLEY

"Are you sure we can't skip this?" I call out from the bathroom.

"You know we can't, love," Stolas replies. "Come on out. It can't be that bad."

I huff, as I look at myself in the mirror. The red dress Breaker sent is beautiful and only clashes with my pink hair a little. No, the problem with the dress comes in where the sheer pieces are placed. I'm practically naked. The only places covered are my breasts, which let's be honest for a minute, it isn't covering much because my boobs are slightly larger since becoming pregnant, which my belly is on fully display. There is no missing that I'm pregnant. The other place covered is my va-jay, but barely. The little slip under the dress, when I saw it, looked like it would hit me mid-thigh, but I was wrong. There's no way I can sit down tonight and not flash my goods.

There's a knock on the bathroom door before Verkor's voice filters through. "Finley, baby, come out. We want to see you."

"You're not going to be happy." I take one last look at myself in the mirror and sigh.

I open the door and step out to the bedroom. I cross my arms under my chest. My guys eyes shift up and down my body. Stolas winks at me but his silver eyes are filled with desire and lust. Verkor is standing there with his mouth open, wide-eyed in complete shock. Obsidian looks angry.

"No," Obsidian growls. "No way in hell is she going to be paraded around Breaker looking like that. What the fuck was he thinking sending that over here?" Obsidian's voice rose with every word he said. "What is Breaker going to do when he sees her belly? I don't think he's noticed yet, and I would like to keep it that way because I don't know how he will react."

"Thank you," I say. "I said you guys wouldn't be happy. Hell, I'm not happy. Can I go and take this off now?"

"You can't," Obsidian says through gritted teeth. "He did this on purpose." I'm pretty sure he's going to break his teeth with how hard he's grinding them.

"Out of curiosity, what was the last animal meat you ate?" I ask.

"I haven't eaten a piece since we were in the Hell Realm."

"Wait, so you can still turn into Abaddon, or is there a time limit?" I question.

"The ability to shift into whatever animal I have eaten stays until I eat a new piece of meat of a new animal. There's no time limit."

I tap my chin with the tip of my index finger then grin. "How bad do you think we could scare Breaker and his posse if you changed into the King of the Abyss?"

"I like the way you think, love," Stolas says. He walks over to me throwing his arm around my shoulders.

"I'm not turning into Abaddon just to scare Breaker. I would rather rip him apart limb from limb," Obsidian states.

"Someone's been bloodthirsty since being here. I kind of like it," I say, giving Obsidian a wink. He shakes his head but relaxes a little.

"How about we find you a coat to go with the dress and say you were cold? It can function to cover you and hide your belly," Verkor says, finally joining the conversation.

"Fine, if you want to take all the fun out of it." I say, pretending to be mad, but I'm not. "Who's going to go and get it?" There's no way I'm walking outside like this.

"We will," Verkor gestures to himself and Stolas. Verkor thinks he's sly, but he's doing this to give me some time to talk to Obsidian.

"Thank you." Verkor and Stolas each place a kiss to my lips before leaving.

I walk over to one of the beds and sit, patting the seat next to me. Obsidian listens and makes his way over to me.

"What started this whole thing between you and Breaker?" I ask.

"Your guess would be as good as mine. It's been so long that I don't even remember the real reason. I can tell you why I'm still angry with him after all these years though." I nod. "The majority of the reason is because of all the marks he left on my body. I have scars because of him. I try to hide them with tattoos, but that only works on the outside. I would rather someone asks me about my ink than ask why I have so many scars. Scars bring pity and that's something I don't need. I survived, and that's all that should matter."

"What are the other reasons?" I ask softly.

"I always had a feeling everything they did to me was because I was different. There were no other hamrammrs in this region. There were a few in the others." I frown at him.

"Um, isn't one of your parents a hamrammr?"

"No, my mother is a rabbit shifter and my father a wolf. I guess they tried for years to have children but couldn't. They adopted me. The agency didn't know what kind of shifter I was because I was left on their doorstep with nothing but the clothes on my back and a blanket." Oh shit. "I think the reason my father hated me was because I wasn't his, but also because of the type of shifter I am. It was a shock when they found out. It was by accident too. He was teaching how to hunt; I was trying different kinds of animal meats. At this point, I still haven't shifted and we didn't know why, but I was still pretty young; I could have been a late bloomer.

"I had just eaten a piece of bear meat when I was scared by the noises I heard in the woods. It triggered my shift and I turned into a bear. My father was proud, thinking that was the shifter I was." I reach over and grip his hand. "When I shifted back, he continued on in his lesson, he had me try rabbit meat next, when an animal charged into our clearing, scaring me. I shifted right then, but it wasn't into a bear, it was into a rabbit. I didn't know what was happening. It didn't take long after we returned home that my father found out what I was. He tried to keep it a secret, but we all know those eventually come out.

"I think it's why he tried so hard to make us look perfect. He was fine until people started finding out what I was. Remember when I said people fear things they don't understand?" I nod in agreement. "I'm living proof of that. My life got significantly worse once people knew. I don't think I need to elaborate how."

"I'm sorry." It seems inadequate, but I don't know what else to say.

"Can't change it now."

"Do you know who your birth parents are?"

"No, and I never looked for them. Clearly, they didn't want anything to do with me."

"If you ever want to look, I'll help you. Maybe we can look for our birth families together," I say with a shrug, trying not to make a big deal about it.

"Maybe," he replies.

I lean against him. "So, what other reasons do you hate Breaker and his gang?" I ask, changing the topic.

"They got away with everything. You know those kids in the alley our first day here, when I walked down that alley all I saw was myself in the same position. When we figured out that the kids doing the bullying were related to Breaker, Cain, and Jett, I knew nothing would happen to them. It was the same when I was a kid. Breaker was Axel's nephew. Cain and Jett just tagged along and did whatever Breaker wanted. I tried to make friends thinking that they would help me, but all the kids were afraid of what I would do to them. I grew up alone, constantly looking over my shoulder. If I wasn't getting harassed at school, then it was happening at home.

"As I got older, the more it happened. No matter how many times I tried to fight back, nothing worked. I wanted to escape, but as a kid, I had no idea where to go or what to do. I toughed it out until I turned eighteen, and the moment I did, I left. I took very little with me. I ended up in the Magic Realm. I took odd-and-end jobs to cover what I needed. It wasn't until I was getting jumped one night that someone finally took notice of me. The guy said I had potential. He offered to give me free lessons on how to fight and take care of myself.

"I continued with them even after I didn't need them anymore and I'm glad I did. The guy that I worked for saw me and offered me a job. At first it was just bodyguard work, but it paid better than anything I had, so I took it."

My fingers caress the inside of Obsidian's arm as he tells me his story.

"One day, his client got out of control and I used the knowledge that I gained and quickly took control of the situation. After that, my employer trained me in what I do now, and I eventually got hooked up with Verkor and Stolas. We stayed until we could afford to strike it out on our own."

"I'm glad you met them," I say.

"Me too. The one thing I didn't mention was my anger problems. I would get angry over everything."

I snicker. "You still do." He chuckles.

"I do, but it's not all consuming as it used to be. You help me."

I look up at Obsidian and smile. "You help me as well." I look down at his forearm and start tracing over the lines of a wolf and star tattoo. "Will you tell me about one of your tattoos?"

"The one that you're touching, the wolf was to remind me to always stay hungry and to never follow anyone. I lead my life and where it goes. The stars represent my escape and freedom. There's a yin and yang symbol." He rotates his arm and points to a spot near his elbow. "I'm quick to anger, yet quick to calm down if I'm left alone. That symbol represents balance, and that's something that I always have to work on. I have an idea for a couple of new tattoos. Though one will have to wait for a few years I think, but the other one I'll get when we have time."

"Oh, and what are these new tattoo ideas, and where the hell are you going to put them?" I question.

"One tattoo is for you. I'm still working out the exact idea, but there is a spot on my chest that needs filled."

"You'd get a tattoo for me? You know that shit is permanent, right?"

"So are you." Well, damn what is a girl supposed to say to that? I clear my throat and decide not to comment on it.

"What's the other idea?"

"I have to wait until we're done having kids. I'd get a piece for them. There's space on the side of my ribs." I feel tears gathering in my eyes. Stupid hormones.

"I don't care what you say; you're one of the sweetest men I know." I lean up and place a kiss to Obsidian's lips. In what was supposed to be a quick peck, turns into something more.

I lean into Obsidian, and he wraps an arm around my waist pulling me close to him. His other hand goes to the back of my bare neck, since my hair is up in a bun and held in place by my knife chopsticks. I place my hands on his chest, trying to keep my balance. Obsidian nips at my bottom lip and moan. I part my lips and he dives in. I could kiss this man forever. I love the way his beard feels against my smooth skin. I'll proudly wear beard burn. He changes the angle of the kiss, and I start to move my hands up and down his chest, causing him to growl, but in a sexy way. The sound runs through my body and straight to my clit. I clench my thighs together trying to alleviate some of the ache that is forming. A throat clears from somewhere inside the room, but I don't focus too much attention on it. My sole focus is on the man expertly kissing my mouth in ways that I wish he was doing to my pussy.

"They'll come up for air eventually," I hear Verkor say.

"If not, I call dibs on giving mouth-to-mouth to Finley, you can have Obsidian," Stolas states. I smile against Obsidian's lips and the mood is effectively broken. Obsidian pulls back and glares at Stolas. "What?" Stolas says with a shrug and a smile. "She's prettier than you." I giggle.

Verkor holds up a bag. "We got up something."

I place a quick kiss on Obsidian's cheek before extracting myself from his arms. Let me tell you, it was a hard feat. The man is too good looking. I walk over to Verkor and take the bag from his hand. I open it and pull out a gorgeous, long red trench coat. The fabric is soft to the touch. I put it on and tie the belt around the waist. This feels like heaven against my skin. I do a little twirl, and smile.

"I love it. Thank you." I go over to him and give him a hug and a kiss.

"Hey," Stolas whines. "I helped too." I look over at him and see that he is pouting. I roll my eyes but walk over giving him a hug and a kiss too.

"Thank you."

"You're welcome, love. Now, we won't have to rip out the eyes of any man trying to look at you tonight."

Normally, I would have been mad at what Stolas said, but honestly, I'm not. I don't want anyone looking at me but them. We don't need to stir up any more trouble while we're here. Besides, this will serve Breaker right, thinking he can try to swoop in and take another man's mate.

"Let's get going, we're already running late," Verkor says.

VERKOR

I hold onto Finley's hand tightly as we walk through the woods to a clearing behind the Packmaster's house. The second Breaker sees us a frown mars his face. I follow his gaze and see that he's looking directly at Finley. I internally smile, because he was hoping she was going to waltz right in here in nothing but the dress and shoes he sent over. I get a sick sort of satisfaction in his disappointment.

Don't get me wrong, when Finley stepped out of the bathroom earlier, I was shocked. She looked absolutely gorgeous. The only problem was there was practically nothing to her dress, fabric wise. Too much of her skin was on display, and her naughty bits were barely covered. No one gets to see that much of her body except her mates.

See, there was a problem though, because she had to either wear the dress or enrage Breaker by disobeying and there's no way in any realm that we would put Finley at risk. So, I came up with another solution. A coat. Finley could wear the dress and prove that she has it on by pulling open the bottom of the coat, but she's covered, and like Stolas said we won't have to attack anyone for staring at her for too long.

"There she is," Breaker says. He walk over to us and stops in front of Finley. "Did you not like the items I sent?"

I watch as Finley paste a fake smile on her face. "Oh, no I did, see." She opens the coat just enough to reveal the dress. "I just got cold. The shoes are beautiful, but I thought it would be safer walking in the woods in boots than heels."

Breaker licks his lips as he takes in Finley from head to toe. I hate the leering look he has on his face and I would like nothing more than to remove it for him.

"You look as lovely as I imagined you would," Breaker says. Finley doesn't let him look any longer and closes the coat. That snaps him back to attention. "Please, come with me."

He holds out his elbow for her. Reluctantly, she accepts and loops her arm through his. Obsidian and Stolas growl behind me. That only pleases Breaker and he flashes them both a grin.

"Is that water I hear?" Finley asks. I see her sneak a look at us from the corner of her eye. She's trying to take the attention off Obsidian. Breaker smiles and nods his head.

"Yup. The ocean isn't far from here," he replies.

Breaker places his hand over the one she has resting in the crook of his elbow. I see her body tense up at the touch, but otherwise doesn't give away that she doesn't like him. He guides her over to the open spot in the middle of the clearing, which gives me a chance to talk to Obsidian and Stolas.

"You two need to tone it down. He's only doing this because he knows it's getting to you," I whisper.

"I can't help it," Obsidian says. "I hate him, and I hate that he's touching our mate."

"I'm with Obsidian on this. The more he's around and doing things for her the more it's agitating me and my hellhound. He's pacing in my mind right now, trying to convince me to rip him to shreds. He thinks he's taking our mate and pup and he's not happy," Stolas says with an angry glare on his face.

"By pack law, we are well within our rights to kill him. He's extremely pushing his limits, and the only reason I'm not attacking him right now is because of Finley. The second I attack Breaker, his Beta, Omega, and Enforcers will come running and that will put her in danger," Obsidian says, never taking his eyes off Finley and Breaker. He's watching every move they make like a hawk. Our conversation stops because Breaker raises his hand and all the shifters that have gathered in the clearing quiet.

"As you all know, Ryan had issued a challenge to me yesterday," Breaker's voice booms.

He snaps his fingers and one of his Enforcers appears with a body over his shoulder. Once the Enforcer steps into the clearing with Breaker, he drops the body on the ground. It lands with a loud thud, and dust from the dirt rises in a cloud, causing Finley to cough. Stolas and Obsidian take a step toward her but stop when Breaker starts to speak again.

"Unfortunately, there will no longer be a challenge fight tonight. As you can see, Ryan was killed at some point last night or early this morning." Hushed whispers fill the quiet air.

I take a look at the body on the ground in front of Breaker and Finley and see that it's the same guy we saw last night outside of the bed and breakfast, at least I'm pretty sure it's the same guy. He's practically unrecognizable. It's hard to tell from how mangled, cut, torn, and bruised the body is. There's not an article of clothing that isn't saturated with blood. Whatever happened to him, it was not pretty. I'm not surprised he didn't live; no one could survive a beating like that. Breaker raises his hand again, and all sound dies down.

"Rest assured that we are doing everything we can to find his killer. Since you are all here, please enjoy the after-challenge festivities."

Breaker and Finley walk in our direction, stopping before us. "I have some pack business to attend to, but I'll be back for you shortly," Breaker says to Finley, then leans forward, placing a kiss on her cheek.

Obsidian and Stolas both growl and snarl at him. If Breaker keeps this up, I'm not going to be able to stop them from attacking, and honestly at this point, I wouldn't. I'm tired of seeing him with his hands all over her. She's not his; she's ours.

"Until then, relax," Breaker says before strolling away.

"Ugh, I really need to start carrying wipes with me so I can remove his germs from my body," Finley says, wiping at the cheek Breaker kissed with a disgusted look on her face.

"Or, he can stop fucking touching you," Obsidian says through gritted teeth.

Finley reaches over and pats him on the chest. "Only a few more days, and we can all get the hell out of this nightmare."

"He's not going to make it that long," Obsidian replies. Finley steps closer to Obsidian and wraps her arms around his waist, placing her cheek against his chest and nuzzling him. He hugs her back, burying his nose in her hair and inhaling deeply.

"As much as I would like to see you give Breaker what he has coming to him, now's not the time," Finley states. She steps back out of his embrace and turns to face me. "However, now would be the perfect time for you to go all shadowy and eavesdrop on him." She's right.

"What are you guys going to do?" I ask.

"I figure we can ask around about this," she waves her hand over in Ryan, the dead shifters, direction. No one has removed the body.

"Do you think anyone will talk?"

She shrugs her shoulders. "It can't hurt to try. Someone here has to be tired of the way things are."

I hope she's right. I open my arms and she walks into them. I pull her close, loving how her body feels against mine. I love the sparkle in her stormy gray eyes.

"Just be careful and keep Stolas and Obsidian close."

"I will."

I lean down and give her a kiss. I step back and call the shadows to me, concealing my body. Time to go and spy on the Packmaster.

CHAPTER 13

STOLAS

We watch as Verkor slowly disappears from sight. It doesn't take him long to hide in the shadows. I hope he finds something useful, because I don't think either Obsidian or I will last until the Super Blood Moon party. Breaker is pushing every button I didn't know I had. My hellhound has never been more agitated. He wants to kill Breaker and send him to hell, find him, and torture him. Having Finley closer to us has eased him some. Not enough to stop his singular thoughts, but enough that I can block them and focus on the task at hand.

"Okay, if you had to pick someone out of this crowd to be a narc, who would you pick?" Finley asks, while scanning the crowd of shifters.

"Your best bet is to find someone that is off by themselves," I say.

"Or, how about someone who keeps glancing our way," she says.

I keep scanning the crowd trying to find who she's talking about, but no one is standing out.

"The tree line over to your right. The skinny girl with the blonde hair."

As subtly as I can, I turn my attention that way and see about the girl. Every few seconds her eyes land on us, but she quickly looks away. She keeps fidgeting with the hem of her shirt then switches to tucking her hands into her long-sleeved shirt.

"Maybe, but it looks like she would run away if Obsidian or I walked over to her."

"So, don't." I look over at Finley and raise a single eyebrow. "I'll go over and talk to her."

"I don't want you going over there alone," Obsidian growls.

"Who said I was?" She smirks at him. "I just need to talk to her alone, but you guys can be hovering nearby."

"Fine, but let's make this quick," Obsidian says.

As one unit, we circle around the other shifters. The closer we get to the female shifter, the more leeway we give Finley. She's always a few feet from one of us. Eventually, Finley makes her way over to the shifter. I'm over to Finley's left and Obsidian is hiding behind a nearby tree. We're both close enough to be able to hear the conversation.

"Hi, I'm Finley," she holds out her hand to the shifter. Tentatively, the female extends her hand and shakes Finley's.

"Hi, I'm Nova." Finley smiles wide at her; Nova doesn't return it, but that doesn't stop Finley.

"I'm new to this sort of thing," Finley says, waving her hand around in the air. Nova's eyes rapidly look around.

"Are you going to be Breaker's mate?" Nova asks.

I hear a small growl come from nearby, and I know it's Obsidian, but I return his sentiment. No way in hell is Breaker taking our mate and pup from us. My hellhound growls in my mind, and I have to try hard to keep my skin. I haven't had trouble controlling my hound since I was a pup learning how to shift, but this place, more specifically Breaker, is testing my very control. I'm starting to act more like Obsidian, which in this case isn't that bad of a thing. I can't wait until we get the hell out of here. The sound of Finley snorting breaks through my thoughts.

"Yeah, no. I have a mate, well three, and Breaker is not one of them," Finley replies. At her answer, Nova relaxes.

"Sorry, I had to ask because I saw you on his arm a little bit ago." Nova's eyes look everywhere but at Finley.

"Trust me, that is not where I wanted to be. I haven't been here long, but I can tell it's just better to go along with him than try to fight." Nova nods.

"I tried to tell Ryan that, but he wouldn't listen." Nova voice hitches at the end, and I can tell she's about to break down. "Nothing good ever comes out of dealing with the Packmaster." Tears stream down Nova's face. Ryan was important to her.

"Does this kind of thing happen often?" Finley questions. Nova shakes her head. She wipes the tears from her face with the sleeve of her shirt.

"Breaker rarely gets challenged anymore," Nova says softly. "But when he does, this is what happens." She points to Ryan's lifeless body.

"He was special to you, wasn't he?" Finley questions, noticing what I did.

Nova nods then meets Finley's eyes. "He was my mate."

There's a small change in Finley at her words. She doesn't hesitate and pulls Nova into her arms, hugging the female. She just holds her while Nova cries. Finley glances around until she meets my eyes, and there, I see the steel resolve in them. My mate is determined, and I know she won't stop until she gets what she wants.

It takes some time, but eventually Nova stops crying and takes a step back from Finley.

"I'm sorry," Nova says.

"Don't worry about it. I know I would be the same way if something were to happen to one of my guys," Finley states.

I snort. I know she would be upset, but I don't think she would cry at first. No, my mate would hunt down whoever killed us and then kill them. My mate would avenge us first. Only after that was done, do I think she would cry.

"Can you tell me what you meant by this is what happens when the Packmaster is challenged?"

"I can't tell you much because no one knows what's really happening," Nova responds.

"Tell me what you can."

Nova fidgets with the hem of her shirt for a moment before replying. "Whenever someone challenges the Packmaster, he always makes it for the following day."

"No one sees what's actually happening to these shifters?" Nova shakes her head.

"I knew something was wrong when he didn't come home last night, but I know better than to ask around," she whispers, wiping away the tears streaming down her face.

"What happened yesterday? Did anything seem out of the ordinary?" Finley questions. Nova sighs.

"Ryan would occasionally bring up how unfit Breaker is as Packmaster." She quickly glances around the clearing to see if anyone is watching or listening in. "He's not the only one. There are a lot of us that feel this way," she whispers. "Him and a couple of the other guys would talk about the changes they would make if one of them could take out Breaker. At first, I thought it was just them talking and wishing of a different life for all of us. Then it turned into them making plans to go through with it. I begged him not to. I thought I had talked some sense into him, because he dropped the subject. He never talked about it again in front of me. Everything went back to normal, or so I thought. It turns out they all were training and still making plans," her eyes well with fresh tears.

"I didn't think Ryan was going to outright challenge him. I thought it was going to be a group effort, especially with the rumors spreading of how none of the challengers live to actually fight in the challenge. I thought they'd band together to take him down, but that's not what happened.

"Ryan came home a little later than normal last night. He told me he issued the challenge. We got into a huge argument and he stomped out. He didn't come back home." The tears are flowing freely down Nova's face. She turns her gaze back to her mate's dead body. "Our last words were said in anger. I didn't get to tell him how much I love him and how proud I am of him, even if I didn't agree with his idea." She lets out this sorrow-filled wail, and it guts me. I would burn all the realms to the ground with hellfire if something were to happen to Finley.

"Oh, sweetie," Finley whispers, before gathering her up in her arms. "It's never too late to tell him how you feel. I know he knew how much you loved him. You didn't have to tell him; I bet he felt it." Finley lets Nova cry in her arms for a while, before she pulls back.

"Can I ask you a question?" Finley asks. Nova nods, shoving the sleeves of her shirt over her hands. "Why are you telling me this?"

For the first time since seeing Nova and hearing her talk, I see a rage simmering behind her blue eyes. "Because someone needs to stop him. Someone needs to put an end to all the killing, bullying, and punishments. No one here is willing to step up anymore, and I thought..." she trails off.

"You thought what?" There's a slight edge in Finley's voice. I take a step forward ready to cut in if I have to. I see Obsidian move from behind a tree.

"I thought..." Nova runs her fingers through her hair. "I thought you were here to be Breaker's mate. I was hoping that with you being here that maybe you could have changed things. Then when you just said you already had a mate, I thought maybe that was why you were here, that you guys were sent here to help."

Finley shakes her head. "Sorry, but that's not why we're here. One of my mates is from here and he only came back to show me where he comes from. We would already be on our way home if Breaker hadn't shown an interest in me. The interest is not returned." Finley sighs. "I recently found out that Breaker and my mate had some rivalry when they were younger, and when Breaker found out I was his enemies' mate, he's been going out of his way to irritate him." Nova sucks in a sharp breath then leans in closer to Finley.

"Your mate has every right to attack and kill Breaker for that." I can hear the hope in Nova's voice, but like Finley said we're not here to take over.

"I know, my mate said as much, but he doesn't want to be Packmaster. The only thing I can offer is to help figure out what's going on here, but we're only here until Saturday. Once the Super Blood Moon party is over, we're going home."

Nova flinches when Finley mentions Super Blood Moon. I tilt my head to the side. I think we just got additional confirmation that something more is going on where that party is concerned, and I hope Finley pushes for more information.

"Why did you just flinch?" Finley asks. I smile, that's my girl.

"It's nothing." Nova waves her hand dismissively. She clears her throat. "The party is going to be hard this year without Ryan." At the mention of his name, tears start to well up in Nova's eyes, and her gaze drifts to his body, which is still laying in the clearing.

"I'm sorry about your mate," Finley says softly.

Nova nods and whispers, "Thank you."

"Look, we're not here to take over, but like I said, we can try to help find out some information for you while we're here. It might not be much, because we're only going to be here a handful more days, but something is better than nothing, right? And if we do find something maybe that can help the next challenger."

Nova meets Finley's eyes and offers a sad smile. "That would be great."

"Okay, is there anything more you can tell me?" Finley questions.

"Not really. All I know is that Breaker almost lost the first challenge he was issued. He followed pack law and had the challenge that night. Ever since then, Breaker accepts the challenge because he can't say no, but the challenge is always set for the following night and the challenger always winds up dead."

"There are no witnesses to this? No one sees anything?"

"No. If there are, they're smart enough to keep their mouth shut so they don't end up the same way. I knew what would happen to Ryan if he did this, and he knew too, but he challenged Breaker anyway, and now...now, I'm mateless."

Finley pulls Nova in for another hug. "We'll try to find something before we leave." Nova pulls back, wiping her eyes.

"It's okay if you don't. We've been living this way for so long; I don't know if any of us would know how to function without the fear." Nova shrugs her shoulders. "Thank you all the same." Without another word, Nova turns and disappears into the crowd.

Both Obsidian and I walk over to Finley. She wastes no time voicing her opinion.

"We all know Breaker and his goons are behind what's happening to those shifters. He knows he's not strong enough to win these challenges. So, he's either kidnapping them, or making them come to him." She points over Ryan's lifeless body. "Clearly we know he's torturing them. The evidence is staring us right in the face. The coward can't even fight fair."

"I know, love, but there's nothing we can do right now, not if we want to get the last piece of the map. Before we leave, if we can, we'll try to help these shifters." I place an arm around her shoulders, pulling her close to me. I see Obsidian reach out and rub small circles on her back. "For now, let's go back toward the house and wait for Verkor." She nods, and we guide her back to where Verkor had left us standing.

As we pass by Ryan's body, Finley pauses. "I would lose my mind if anything would happen to any of you. I would tear all the realms apart to hunt down and kill whoever harmed you." There's a growl to her voice and a puff of smoke escapes her nose.

She's becoming a very fierce protector. If she's this way with us, she'll be more so with our pup. Seeing her like this is getting me all hot and bothered, and if we weren't waiting for Verkor, I would scoop her up in my arms and head back to the bed and breakfast and show her exactly how much I like seeing her this way.

"You're not the only one who feels that way," Obsidian says.

"We would do the same," I interject.

We stand there for a while with Finley cuddled up next to me when I start to get worried about Verkor. He's been gone for a while. I feel like he should have been back by now.

"Anyone else think Verkor is taking too long?" I voice. Both Finley and Obsidian look at me with frowns on their faces.

"Now that you mention it, it does seem like he's been gone too long," Finley states. "Should we worry? Should we go looking for him?"

"Not quite yet," Obsidian says. "Let's give him a few more minutes. He could be in a spot where he can't leave just yet. If we see Breaker before we see Verkor, then I think we should worry."

I nod in agreement even though I feel like we should go searching for him. I don't like this. He should be back by now.

. . .

VERKOR

I never get tired of seeing Finley's eyes light up when I use my magic. It's why I let the shadows slowly take over my body. I can call them instantly, but her eyes sparkle, and I can't deny her anything. So, I take my time and let the shadows creep up my body until I'm hidden. The second I am, I head off toward the pack house.

Instead of going inside the house, I detour and walk around it, clinging to the shadows. I take in every guard. Two on each side of the house, plus one in the woods on each side. I don't remember there being this many guards when we came for dinner, but I wasn't really paying attention. There could be this many tonight because of the amount of people here, and because of the challenge.

I make my way back to the backdoor. I glance around me quickly, making sure no one is close enough to see the door open and close by itself. No one is paying any attention. I reach for the doorknob and slip inside. The house is silent, but I still don't drop the shadows. Last thing I need is to get caught. Wasting no time, I head to Breaker's office.

The closer I get, I can hear murmured voices, but can't make out what they're saying. What I wouldn't give to have Obsidian's or Stolas' hearing. I creep closer to the door and place my ear to it. The voices aren't completely clear, but I can hear some of what they're saying. I recognize the voices, Cain and Jett.

"Has Breaker picked yet?" Jett asks.

"No, but I have a feeling I know who he's going too," Cain responds.

"Do you ever regret helping him become Packmaster?" Jett questions.

"All the fucking time," Cain growls. "I don't know why I did it. It should be me. I'm stronger than him, yet I let him take the job," he bites out.

"I never understood why you did that," Jett states.

"Because I thought that being his right-hand man would give me more power. I could whisper things to him, plant ideas in his head. I could run the region and not have to worry about the challenges, but I was wrong. You see how he is; he doesn't listen to a goddamn thing I say." You can hear the frustration in his voice.

I don't think the shifters would be better off in his hands. From what Obsidian has said, Cain played a big part in his bullying and torment. In a weird way, I hope everything he has done is coming back to bite him in the ass. If not now, it will one day.

The sound of floorboards creaking comes from above me. Cain and Jett stop talking. That must be where Breaker is because he entered the house before I did. I don't move from my spot. I wait until I hear footsteps pounding down the hall. There's a quick succession of steps as someone comes down the stairs. I look over and see it's Breaker. I move back away from the door as he steps off the bottom stair, putting just enough distance between us.

A second later Breaker opens the door to his office, walks in, and shuts it behind him. I almost groan. Why couldn't you leave it open, or crack the door a little? I move back to the door and place my ear back on it.

"I told you guys she would wear the dress." There's a smugness in his voice. "I'll win her over. I mean, who in their right mind wouldn't pick a Packmaster over some Berserker mutt. I can offer her more than he ever could." One of the others clears their throat.

"Obsidian isn't a little kid anymore. I don't know if you've noticed but he's fucking huge. He's harder than he was when he was last here. Plus, you don't know what he'll do to protect his mate," Jett says.

Interesting. He sounds scared. He should be.

"What exactly are you trying to say?" Breaker sneers.

"No-Nothing, I-I was just pointing out that he's different," Jett stammers.

"No matter. I will have her, and there's nothing Obsidian can do about it." Breaker lets out a high-pitched, crazy laugh. "Now, is everything else taken care of and ready to go?"

"Yeah," Cain clips out.

"Good. Let's go out and enjoy the festivities. I have a certain pink haired female to woo."

I almost don't step back in time before the door opens. I plaster myself against the wall and hold my breath. I stay that way until all three have left. I finally release the breath when I hear them slam the backdoor shut. Shit, that was close. I can't stand around here. I need to confirm what Finley saw.

I move to the office door, grab the handle, and push open the door. It's pitch black in here, and I wish I had Stolas' or Obsidian's ability to see in the dark. I close the door behind me and run my hands over the wall, hoping to hit a light switch. I come up empty on the right side but find it on the left. I blink my eyes a few times, trying to adjust to the lighting.

I sweep my gaze over the room. It's an office, you've seen one, you've seen them all. Except, I stop at the painting on the wall behind the desk. It's like Finley said. I drop the shadows and walk over to it. The bottom left corner isn't lying flat. I grab the sides of the painting and try to lift it off the wall, but it doesn't budge. I move my hands along the sides and feel metal on the right side but none on the left. The painting must have hinges. I curl my fingers around the left side of the canvas and swing it open.

Finley was right. There's a safe in the wall that looks pretty standard. It has a simple turn dial lock. It should be easy enough to break into, but the process would go faster and be simpler if I had the combination. I close the painting and start searching the desk. Hopefully, Breaker has the safe numbers written down somewhere.

I pull the chair out from behind the desk and sit in it. The only thing on the top of the desk are some pens, a small note-book, and a couple of file folders. I pick up the notebook and leaf through it, finding nothing useful. I grab the file and open it to see a picture of Obsidian. It's a recent one, from the first day we were here. There's basic information on him, but nothing too damning. I look through the rest of the files and see there is one on Stolas, Finley, and myself. The pictures of us are also from the first day we arrived. Stolas and I have the same basic info as Obsidian. Finley's file has very little to almost no information.

Could this be part of the reason he's obsessing over her? The first reason is definitely Obsidian. Breaker has an unhealthy fixation on trying to torment him and it's spilling over to Finley. I close all the files and place them back where they were. I start opening the drawers not finding anything. Mostly, it's just office supplies. I did find the pack ledger. I open it and find that the pack is financially stable.

There's one drawer that won't open. I re-search the drawers and there's no key. If I had time, I would try to break into it, but I'm already taking too long. I hear a door slam and I jump. I quickly stand, push in the chair, and flip the lights off. I barely call the shadows to me, making me invisible, when the office door swings open and the lights flicker back on. Jett steps in and pauses just inside the doorway. He inhales deeply and a frown falls over his face. *Come on and move out the way.* After another moment he does, walking over to the desk.

I scoot along the wall and slip out the door he left open. I stay in the shadows and make it back to the backdoor. I don't hesitate to open it. I glide out the door, closing it behind me. A quick glance around the yard and I spot Finley and the others standing off to the side. Finley and Obsidian are going at it, while Stolas is trying to calm them down. I walk over to them but move to the trees nearby. I release the shadows and step from behind it.

"You said we would go look for him if Breaker came back before he did. Well, Breaker is over there, and there's still no Verkor," Finley seethes. "If something happens to him, I'm blaming you and I will find a way to make you pay." My lips turn up into a smile.

"I'm fine, baby," I say. As much as I love seeing her getting protective of me, I need to stop this before they make a scene. Finley whips around.

"Verkor," she says, then launches herself at me. I chuckle but catch her. She places a quick kiss to my lips before pulling back. Her eyes run over my face. "You're okay?"

"Yeah, baby. I'm good, I promise." She places another kiss on my lips. I place her back on her feet, making sure she's steady before I let go. The second I do; she smacks me across my chest. "Ow. What was that for?" I rub at the spot she just hit. Finley narrows her eyes at me and places her hands on her hips.

"For scaring the shit out of me." She turns and smacks Obsidian across the chest.

"What the hell? Why did you hit me?" he growls.

"Because you weren't going to go look for him and help him." There's a hitch in Finley's voice. I know she's about to breakdown and cry.

"I've worked with Verkor for years. If I truly thought he was in any danger, I would have gone looking for him," Obsidian says.

I walk up behind Finley and wrap my arms around her, pulling her close to my body. I dip my head, placing my face in the crook of her neck.

"He's right, baby. I promise you I was in no danger." Her body shivers against me. She takes a couple deep breaths. She removes my arms around her and spins to face me. There is anger shining in her gray eyes. In this moment, they truly do look like storm clouds.

"I don't care." She jabs her finger in my chest. "You guys refuse to let me do anything dangerous by myself, so why would I be okay with letting one of you. I don't care how long you guys have known each other, or how long you've worked together." She takes a step closer to me. "What if something did happen to you? Hmm. Then what? What would we do? How would I know?" She jabs me in the chest after each question. My eyes widen at her. I look over her shoulder and meet Obsidian's eyes. He looks just as lost as I feel.

"Finley, love," Stolas says, walking closer to her. She turns her head to look at him. There's a look of understanding on his face. What did he figure out that I haven't? "None of us are going anywhere. None of us would ever put ourselves in a position where we couldn't come back to you. We all love you too damn much to ever cause you heartbreak." Shit. That's what this is about? "It's okay to be scared, worried, and protective of us. We feel the same way about you."

"I don't know why this is affecting me so much," she whispers.

"I think it has more to do with the conversation you had with Nova, and maybe because he was alone," Stolas replies. Finley nods. She turns to look back at me.

"I'm sorry. Stolas is right. I was scared, especially when I saw Breaker, Cain, and Jett come from the house and you weren't back yet. I thought the worst had happened to you. It's not that I doubted you could do the job, I know you can, it's just..." she trails off. "It's just that if something did happen to you, you would have been alone. None of us would have been with you and we wouldn't have known. I just got you guys. I can't lose any of you."

"Oh, baby." I pull her back into my arms and kiss the top of her head. She looks up at me and I see the unshed tears in her eyes.

"Stupid hormones," she whispers. I smile.

"We'll figure out a way to be able to keep in touch if one of needs to go off and do something alone. I would feel the same way you are right now if the situation was reversed," I state.

"Really?" she asks.

"Yeah, baby, I would." She gives me a small smile and nods. I place a kiss on her lips before she turns to look at Obsidian.

"I'm sorry." Obsidian rolls his eyes at her, but there's a slight upturn of his lips.

"Just get over here," he says and opens his arms. Finley walks right into them. Obsidian leans down, placing his mouth by her ear. "I should spank you for what you did, but I won't. Not tonight anyway."

Finley pulls back and meets his eyes. "Promise," she says. Obsidian responds by tapping her ass, causing her to groan.

"Can we get out of here?" Stolas voices. "There's some shit we all need to discuss."

"Yes, please," Finley says. She grabs Obsidian's hand then one of mine and starts tugging us out of our little hiding place in the woods. We start to maneuver around the other shifters, trying to make our way out of the clearing, but we don't get far before Breaker steps in our path.

"Leaving so soon?" he asks.

"Yeah, I'm pretty tired," Finley says with a yawn.

"That's a shame. I was hoping to be able to spend a little time with you. We didn't get a chance to talk."

"Oh, well, I'm sorry. It's been a long day, but I'm sure there will be plenty of opportunities for us to talk. I really can't keep my eyes open much longer."

Finley leans more into Obsidian's side. She gives my hand a squeeze before letting go. Obsidian sweeps her up into his arms. Finley nuzzles her face in his neck, letting out a sigh of contentment. I shift my gaze over to Breaker who has narrowed his eyes at Obsidian. I turn my head to look at Obsidian and see that he has a shit-eating grin on his face. They both know what they're doing. Breaker clears his throat.

"Yes, I'm sure there will be," Breaker says between gritted teeth. "Have a good night, Finley." Breaker stalks off.

Stolas lets out a chuckle. "I thought he was going to have a coronary." Obsidian shrugs and Finley smiles.

"I know it probably wasn't the smartest thing to do, teasing him, but I'm not his. I never will be, and he needs to learn that I'm already taken, and Packmaster or not, I will never want or be with him," Finley states.

"We know that, but he's not all there in his head, and we don't know if he's going to lash out," I say.

"You can put me down," Finley says to Obsidian.

"No, I like you right where you are." He starts to walk back toward the bed and breakfast. Finley huffs, but wraps her arms around Obsidian's neck. Stolas and I follow behind them.

"Verkor, you're right, but you're also crazy if you think that he's just going to let me walk away. If he doesn't attack now, he surely would have when we tried to leave," Finley states.

"We shouldn't be talking about this out in the open," Obsidian growls.

"We'll be back at our room soon, and we can talk there," Stolas says. We all nod.

"Can we stop for food first? I'm starving." Finley's stomach growls just to punctuate her sentence. We all chuckle.

"Of course, love. What would you like?"

"Meatballs with melted provolone cheese on top, and fries. Lots of salty fries."

She moans just thinking about it. The sound goes right to

my cock. I swear, if we didn't have things to talk about, I'd strip her bare the moment we got back to our room. Maybe if I play my cards right, I'll still make that happen. Finley looks over Obsidian's shoulder and winks at me. Oh, yeah. I'm definitely going to make that happen.

CHAPTER 14

FINLEY

Dinner hit the spot. I'm leaning back against the headboard with Verkor sitting next to me, rubbing my belly. Stolas and Obsidian are perched on the edge of the other bed facing us. We decided to wait until everyone ate before discussing everything we found out. So, I told Verkor the story of Nova and what she said and Verkor relayed that I was right about the safe, but he couldn't and didn't have enough time to find the combination. He also mentioned what he overheard between Cain and Jett. Now, we're sitting here trying to figure out our next steps.

"I don't think we're going to get another chance at getting inside the pack house until the night of the Super Blood Moon party," Verkor states. He's rubbing circles with his thumb over the back of my hand.

"I think our only option is to have Breaker hand it to us himself," I say. All of their eyes land on me.

"How do you propose we do that?" Obsidian asks with a glare.

"By playing into his fantasy." All three of my mates growl at me. I roll my eyes. "Obviously, nothing is going to happen. I just need to see him again so I can suggest playing my violin at the party. It can be my gift to him for inviting us. The spell should definitely work on him because he's not extremely powerful. He's a normal shifter in a position of power. Breaker and everyone here should just fall into the trance. Once the spell works, I do what I would normally do and ask him to hand it over. Then we high tail it out of here and back home."

"That's not a bad idea," Stolas agrees. "The party will be the perfect cover as well, but remember the poem said we will have to prepare to fight. I don't think we're going to simply be able to leave."

"Ugh, I forgot about that," I groan. "So, at some point we're going to have to fight, but we're still going to need to escape fast afterward." They all nod their heads.

"So, we do what we did in the Hell Realm," Obsidian states. "We leave our belongings hidden somewhere near the gateway and grab it on our way pass."

"Okay, but there's not much between here and there. Where are we going to store the bags?" I question.

"We're going to have to run by the bed and breakfast on our way to the gateway. There are bushes out front that will conceal our bags. We'll just have to make sure no one is watching when we hide them," Obsidian responds.

"Okay, that works. Back to what I was previously saying, I still think playing my violin and asking for the last piece of the map will be the easiest way to obtain it."

"I don't like the idea of you going anywhere near him, but it's the best we have right now," Obsidian huffs. I smile, because I know I won. "We'll walk around tomorrow to see if we can draw him out. I would rather you talk to him in an open area with one of us around."

I nod my head. "That works for me. I would rather not be alone with him."

"Now that that is figured out, what are we going to do about the other issue?" Verkor questions.

"*I* don't want to do anything about it." All eyes turn to Obsidian. "Why should we be the ones to help and stop what is happening? We don't live here, and we're definitely not coming back here any time soon. Why do I have to help people who looked the other way when I needed it?" Obsidian spits out.

That last sentence is the real issue he has. It's not the fact he has to help people, it's the fact he will be helping people who didn't do the same for him. I don't blame him. In his eyes, they aren't worthy, and I can't say that I disagree with that, but still.

Obsidian turns away from us, going over to the window. He opens it just enough to let in some fresh air. Sounds of giggles and laughter drift up to us. I rub my hand over my belly, smiling to myself. Soon our home will be filled with the same sounds. I climb off the bed, move to stand next to Obsidian. Glancing out the window, I see a couple of little kids playing together. I couldn't tell you how long we stood, but it was long enough for Siddy to relax. He runs his hands down his face and groans. He gazes down at me.

"Fine, we'll figure out a way to help. Let's get one thing clear... I'm not doing this for shifters who didn't help me. I'm doing it for them," he points out the window toward the kids. "They are little kids who had nothing to do with the way I grew up and those kids need a better future than the current outlook."

I smile and nod my head. "What should we do?"

"I don't know, but we'll think of something."

"We could try to see if we can get Cain or Jett to flip on Breaker," Verkor voices. All of us whip our heads and gaze in his direction.

"I don't see that as an option," Obsidian states.

"It wasn't... until I overheard them talking tonight. Cain knows he's stronger than Breaker and easily could have been

Packmaster, but he gave the position over to Breaker instead of taking it for himself. Jett asked Cain if he regretted helping Breaker and he said yes."

Obsidian scoffs at Verkor words. "He probably regretted not taking the position himself. Why did he give to Breaker in the first place?"

Verkor shifts on the bed, angling his body more toward us. "Because he thought he was going to have more power by being Breaker's right hand man. He thought he would have been able to tell Breaker what to, whisper in his ear. He would have the perks of running the region, but not having to deal with the challenges."

"Well, it's evident that didn't happen," Stolas says. "But do you think you can get one of them to turn on Breaker?" Verkor shrugs his shoulders.

"I don't know, but it's worth a try," he replies.

"You're forgetting one thing." We all face Obsidian. "Even if we could flip one of them, the region won't be left in better hands."

"True, but it could be the first step in getting the proper people where they need to be," Verkor voices.

"Maybe," Obsidian says with a sigh. "When are we going to try this? There aren't many days left before the Super Blood Moon Party."

"We can go out and walk around tomorrow and hope to run into one of them," I suggest. "I doubt they'll be too far away from Breaker though."

"The chances of that happening are slim, and if we wait until the night of the party it will be too late," Obsidian groans.

"How about we table this topic for now and come back to it. We might think of something else when we're not trying. I do have a question though," Stolas remarks. "We know Breaker is torturing the challengers, but where is he doing it?"

I frown at Stolas' statement. It doesn't take long for it to click. "That door to the left," I respond. "When I asked about it he told me not to worry my pretty little head about it." I turn my attention to Obsidian. I hate that I'm about to do this to him, but I have to know what the room looked like. "Can you tell us what's in the room?" I ask softly.

I see Obsidian's body tense up. His eyes briefly meet mine before looking away. We all sit in silence waiting to see if Obsidian will answer me. The room is deathly quiet. I don't think any of us want to spook him. He's probably working there some things, mentally. I will wait here for as long as I need to because I won't push him unless he's ready.

"I don't know if it will be the same." Obsidian's voice is softer than I've ever heard it. I move my hand ready to comfort him, when he holds up a hand in my direction. I pause, waiting. "Let me get this out. I'll be fine."

I nod my head and move over to the end, perching myself on the edge. The bed dips and I feel Verkor moving up behind me. His legs land on either side of me, and his arms go around my waist, pulling my back to his front.

"I was put in there a handful of times." Obsidian clears his throat. "The first time, I was tied to a leg of the table in the middle of the room and whipped. I didn't get to see much of the room, only the wall directly in front of me." Obsidian turns his head, staring at the blank white wall. "It was covered in black padding from the ceiling to the floor. There were hooks spaced out every few feet with some form of instrument hanging from each. I couldn't have told you what half of them were used for." He sighs but doesn't move his gaze.

"The second time I was dragged inside the room, I got a better look. That black padding covered every wall. More hooks and instruments hung from them. I knew then what they used that room for. They tortured shifters. It's a scary thing to learn when you're just a teenage kid. It scared the shit out of me. I tried to stay away and keep to myself. I tried to avoid being sent in there, but sometimes I couldn't. I would take my punishment. I learned fast that if I screamed it gave them some sick satisfaction. I also learned that if I didn't make any noise the beatings were worse.

"The first few times it happened, I was waiting for some to bust through the door and help me. It seemed like no one could hear me scream. If they did, then no one wanted to be on the receiving end of what was happening to me, so they looked the other way."

Obsidian started to blur in front of me. I realized that tears were threatening to fall, so I let them. The more of his past he told me the more I didn't want to hear. I always thought I had it rough, and I did to a point, but the things that Obsidian has suffered... I can't compare my life to his. He's suffered more than most. I place my hand over my mouth trying to muffle the sob that is threatening to escape, but I couldn't. At the sound, Verkor pulled me tighter to his body, trying to comfort me. Obsidian and Stolas both look at me. Stolas has a worried look on his face and immediately gets up from the bed.

I watch as Stolas starts to shift. His tan muscular arms sprout black hair, and his hands turn into paws. My gaze moves to his face. His nose lengthens, ears form on the top of his head, and his silver eyes turn red. The rest of the shift happens quickly, and before I know it, where Stolas the man was once standing, is now Stolas the hellhound. My hellhound jumps up on the bed and lays his down next to me, pushing his body as close to mine as he can get. He places his head over my lap, nuzzling against my belly. I feel guilty that he came over here to soothe me when it's Obsidian that needs it, but I soak it up anyways.

I drop the hand from my mouth and thread my fingers through his fur. I wish I could wrap my arms around his neck and bury my face in his fur. But for now, this will work. I glance up to Obsidian who's still staring at me. I want to hold my other hand out and have him come over here to join the pile. I want him near me, but I don't do it. Obsidian will come over when he's ready. I won't force him.

Verkor breaks the silence. "What if you're right Obsidian, and no one did hear you. It sounds like the room was sound-proof. It would be easy for Breaker to kidnap the challenger and put him in the room until they killed them. No one would hear it."

"This is so messed up," I say. They all hum their agreement.

"Hey, not to make things worse, but did you ever ask Breaker what happened to your parents?" Verkor questions.

"Shit," I groan. "I knew we were forgetting something."

"It's fine. There's still plenty of time for me to get an answer. I forgot about it anyways. We were busy dealing with other things." He shrugs his shoulders. I sigh.

"We'll make sure we ask tomorrow, if we can draw him out. You deserve to know," I say. "Maybe you can distract Breaker long enough that someone can corner Cain or Jett."

"Can we talk about something else?" Obsidian asks running his fingers through his hair. He's done with this topic for now.

"Like what?" I question.

"I don't know, anything will do," he responds. "I'm just sick of talking about them."

"How about baby names?" I suggest.

The room gets so quiet that you could hear a pin drop. I move my upper body to the side to look behind me to see Verkor just staring at me without blinking. I have to try hard not to smile. My gaze moves over to Obsidian who has the same blank stare. I can't help the smirk that crosses my face. Stolas, who's still in his hellhound form, moves his head from my lap and shifts back into his human one. He ends up sitting next to me on the bed, giving me the same look as the others, and I can't hold back anymore. I burst out laughing. It takes me a moment to get myself together.

"Why do you all look like that? It's just a name," I say.

Stolas starts shaking his head at me. "It's not just a name. We can't saddle the kid with a horrible one. Do you have any in mind?"

I shake my head. "No. I wasn't sure how we were going to go about this."

"What do you mean?" He tilts his head to the side.

"Are we all going to agree on the name? Are only you and me picking the name? Can Verkor and Obsidian make suggestions? How are we doing this?" I question.

Stolas looks over my shoulder to Verkor, who hasn't stopped holding me, then over to Obsidian. He just shrugs his shoulders as if to say it's up to you.

"We should decide together, and everyone gets an input," Stolas answers. "I may be the pup's biological dad, but we are all in this together and we should do everything together."

"Okay," I smile. I reach over and take his hand. "Then how about if we all come up with a boy and a girl name we like, and we vote on each name. The names with the most votes win. This has to include middle names as well."

"That sounds perfect," Verkor says from behind me. I meet Obsidian's eyes and he nods in agreement.

"We can do this after we get this last piece of the map," I say with a yawn.

"Tired, love?" Stolas asks.

"Yeah," I say with another yawn.

"Well, let's get you into bed shall we," Stolas says.

He rises from the bed, walks over to the head of the bed, and pulls down the comforter. Verkor places a kiss to the back of my head and releases me. He gets up from the bed, and I move over so Stolas can turn down more of the blanket. When he's done, I roll over and position myself in the middle, because I know at some point two of them will be in the bed with me. Not that I'm complaining. Double the cuddles and the warmth.

Verkor moves from the bed and walks over to the closet. Stolas tucks the blankets around me, leans down, and gives me a kiss.

"Night, love," he says.

"Night, Stolas," I whisper. I smile and snuggle down deeper into the blankets. I know it doesn't take me long before I'm out.

CHAPTER 15

STOLAS

I wake up to a warm body pressed up against mine. Finley. Her leg is over mine and her hand is on my stomach. Her head is on my chest and I can feel the warmth of her breath when she exhales. One of my arms is wrapped around her, keeping her close to me, with my hand resting on the side of her belly.

She's starting to show more these days, and I puff my chest out a little bit. Hell yeah, I'm proud. Finley is sexy as hell and watching her grow with our child is making her more so. It's hard for me to keep my hands off her. I want to touch her all the time. My hellhound wants to rub his scent all over her. When his head was pressed up against her belly last night, we heard the strong heartbeat of our pup.

Absentmindedly, I start rubbing my hand on her belly. Finley sighs and snuggles against me, and I smile. This is the best feeling in the world and I'm going to soak up every minute of it. There is a slight flutter across my hand, and I pause. I wait for what seems like forever to see if it happens again. Right when I'm about to resume the rubbing, I feel the movement again.

My eyes widen, when I realize that I'm feeling my pup move. I spread my hand out as wide as I can and wait. This time I don't have to wait long before I feel something move against my palm. I know I'm smiling from ear to ear. I want to wake up Finley, but I also want to enjoy this moment.

"What has you smiling already this morning?" Obsidian says with a groan. He's not a morning person. I turn my head in his direction.

"If you promise to be quiet and not wake Finley, I'll tell you," I respond. That has him peeking at me from one eye. "It'll be worth it."

"What are you two yapping about?" Verkor whispers. I look the other way and see him spooned up against Finley's back.

"He wants to know why I'm smiling already this morning." Verkor lifts his head to look at me.

"Why are you?" he asks.

"It's something I have to show you. Since Obsidian still hasn't gotten out of bed, and you're closer, I'll show you first." I move my hand from Finley's belly and cup her ass. I turn on my side facing her. I reach over her and hold out my hand to Verkor. "Give me your hand." Without any reservation, Verkor places his in mine. I move his hand and place it on her belly. "Spread out your fingers." He does.

"What am I supposed to be feeling?" he asks softly.

"Just wait for it," I respond.

His brows furrow as he waits, but I know the second he feels the baby move, because shock and awe filter across his face.

"Holy shit," Verkor says with a smile.

"Right," I say while nodding my head.

"Okay, I need to know now," Obsidian states.

The bed next us creaks and a second later Obsidian is leaning over me. Verkor moves his hand and uses his other to prop his head up. The hand he just had on Finley's belly reaches up and brushes some of her hair from her face.

"Give me your hand," I say. He does, and I place it on her belly. "Spread out your fingers." Obsidian listens for once. "Now wait." He frowns at me, not understanding where I'm going with this, but he will. The moment it happens, I chuckle because his head whips in my direction.

"Holy shit," Obsidian whispers. I smile and nod.

"Yup," I say popping the 'p'. Obsidian looks down at his hand, then to Finley's face, then back to his hand. There is nothing but love, awe, and respect on his face for her.

"Are you boys quite done fondling my belly, because I need to pee," Finley's voice breaks through the silence. There's a teasing note to it.

"How long have you been awake?" I ask. She tilts her head back to look me in my eyes.

"Since you started rubbing my belly." She gives me a smirk.

"Why didn't you say anything?" She gives me a half shoulder shrug.

"It was cute." Finley uses my chest to help her sit up. She leans back against the headboard. We all watch as she lifts her shirt over her rounded belly. "I swear I'm getting bigger by the day."

"I think that's what's supposed to happen," I tease. She taps my arm.

"I know that. It's happening so fast. I mean we just found out a little more than a month ago, and I was already almost three months pregnant." She places her hands on her belly, and rubs. "I'm four months pregnant now. We only have three more to go before this little one gets here. We don't have a house, no baby items, no names. We haven't talked about where I'm having the baby.

"We still have to get this piece of the map, put it all together, follow the damn thing, and deal with whatever the outcome is, all before this baby is born. I don't think we're going to make it. Oh my God, we're going to be parents in three months." Her eyes widen at the revelation. I reach over and cover one of her hands with mine. Verkor does the same with the other. Obsidian crawls up the bed and sits in front of Finley, placing his hand on all of ours.

"We are, but I can't wait," Obsidian says. "It doesn't matter if you have the baby before we complete this journey. We'll still get it done. We'll just have one extra person. I'll make a deal with you. After we get this piece of the map and we return home, all of us will sit down and have a long talk about everything. We probably should have started the second we found out you were pregnant, but between the four of us we'll get it done."

Finley sighs. "You're right. Focus on one thing at a time." A small smile crosses her face. "It is something amazing." She moves her hand from under mine. I place my hand on her belly, Verkor and Obsidian try to do the same, but there isn't any more space. So, Finley moves her other hand, letting Verkor put his hand there in her place. Verkor and I shift our hands up, giving Obsidian a small space below our hands. All three of us hold them there feeling our baby move. It's a special and magical moment. Something none of us will forget.

OBSIDIAN

"What is our plan for today?" Finley asks.

I didn't want to let her up. I would have rather cuddled on the bed with her and felt our baby move, but she had to go pee, so I had to let her up. Now, she's standing in the bathroom doorway, putting her pink hair into some messy bun thing. She pulls a few strands of her hair out in front of her ears, and tugs on the hem of her pink t-shirt.

"Ugh, I'm going to have to start wearing your guys' shirts soon."

"Babe, your shirts look fine," Stolas says as he walks over and places a kiss on her cheek.

"They keep riding up," she huffs.

"Only a little," Verkor says.

"Whatever," she says and rolls her eyes. "So, what's the plan for today?" She sits on the edge of the bed, putting her boots on.

"We have to draw Breaker out, or we could just walk up to the pack house and see if he'll answer my questions. You know I'm not one to play games," I state.

"We can do that. He owes you those answers anyways. Plus, I need to propose my idea of playing my violin for him," Finley replies. "What are the rest of you going to do?"

"I was going to follow you guys, hide in the shadows, make sure you're okay," Verkor responds.

"And what about you, Stolas?" Finley asks.

"I was going to walk around and see what I can find out about this Super Blood Moon party. I think it's weird that no one is going crazy over it. Where are the decorations, why isn't the town more active with preparations? This is supposed to be a rare occurrence. The shifters should be hype over this," he says.

"Oh, it slipped my mind. One of the other things I heard was Cain asking if Breaker had picked anyone yet for the party," Verkor states.

"What the hell does that mean? I question. Verkor shrugs.

"I don't know, but it doesn't sound good."

"Maybe we can see if anyone is willing to talk about it," Finley states. I snort.

"Doubt it," I respond. "Just add it to the list questions we have."

"Well, since we have no idea what that means, I don't want

anyone to go anywhere by themselves," Finley says, crossing her arms over her chest, glaring at each of us.

"How about if I go with him and then we can find you and Obsidian and both keep an eye on you?" Verkor interjects. She uncrosses her arms and lets them fall to her sides.

"Okay," she says softly. Verkor walks over to her giving her a kiss. Stolas follows right after.

"We should go now," Verkor states. Both him and Stolas walk to the bedroom door and leave. A sigh escapes past Finley's lips.

"Ready to go?" I ask. I stand and move over to the bed she's sitting on. I hold out my hand to her, and she places hers in mine. I help her from the bed and interlace our fingers together.

"As I'll ever be."

CHAPTER 16

OBSIDIAN

After being back home for a few days, I can absolutely say that I don't miss a single damn thing about this place. Being back has filled me with more tension and anger than I thought possible, but with Finley at my side, I've been dealing with it better than I would have. The flashbacks I've been having are worse. It makes me feel weak when I worked hard to never be or feel that way again. I tried hard to push everything that has happened to me out of my mind, shoving it in a box to never to be opened again. It worked fine until I stepped through that gateway. Okay, not fine but I was able to deal with it better. I'm starting to realize that it's not so much the place that's affecting me, but the people.

Even now, I'm able to walk through the streets, and not have my memories trying to invade my mind. I don't think that would be possible with the help Finley and her forcing me to come here and confront my past. I may not be ready to let go of all of my past, but I feel like I have let some of it go. I look over to my mate, who's taking in everything around her. I'm so damn lucky to have her. As if sensing that I am looking at her, Finley turns her head in my direction.

"Are you okay?" she asks. She furrows her brows and tilts her head to the side, concern reflecting in her face.

I could lie to her but decide not to. "Not really, but maybe I will be after this is all said and done."

She squeezes my fingers on the hand that I'm still holding. "Whenever you're ready to talk about anything, you know that I'll be here for you. We all will."

This is one of the things I love about her. She's showing her support but doesn't push for more than I'm willing to give even though I know she must have a million questions running through her mind.

"Aww, how sweet," Breaker's voice cuts in from behind us. Well, it looks like we don't have to go to the Packmaster's house. Finley and I turn to face Breaker, who of course has Jett and Cain at his sides. "Taking a little stroll?"

"We were on our way to see you," I respond. "Oh, and my old house. Speaking of..." I say getting right to the point. "I meant to ask you last night where my parents are."

Breaker's smug face breaks out into a smile. "Oh, yes. I was wondering if you were going to ask me about them. Your father put up quite the fight. Your mother not so much." I clench my teeth together to keep from attacking him. If I do, then he'll never tell me what I want to know. Even though my parents weren't the greatest and I don't hold any love for them, they are still my parents and I have a right to know.

"Where are they?" I ask between gritted teeth. A sick look crosses Breaker's face and I know that at least one of my parents is dead.

"Should I tell you, or make you wait longer? I mean, you haven't been home in years so they can't mean that much to you," he says flippantly.

I feel a growl rise in the back of my throat. I feel the burning need to shift and tear him apart. A small hand lands on my forearm. I look down at it and then to Finley's face. With her eyes, she's saying it all. Pick your battles; don't give in to him. I take a few deep breaths while looking into her gray eyes and I feel myself calm down enough to turn my attention back to Breaker.

"How much they mean to me isn't the question, what you did to them is. Where are my parents?" My anger is starting to come through my voice. There's an edge to it.

"Tsk, tsk," Breaker says, waving his index finger in the air side-to-side. I want to reach out and break the damn thing. "Maybe if you showed me some respect and asked nicely, I would tell you." He takes a step closer to me. I pull Finley into my side.

It would be three against one, if he tries to do anything. The difference this time around is that I won't be the one on my knees being beaten.

"Breaker, will you please tell Obsidian what happened to his parents?" Finley states. Breaker turns his gaze on her. I watch and internally seethe at him eye fucking her up and down.

"Finley, you look lovely this morning, but then again you always do," Breaker says, then smiles and winks at her. Finley snorts. She's not buying what he's selling.

"Thank you," she replies.

"I'll tell him, only because *you* asked so nicely," Breaker states. He doesn't take his eyes off of her and it's pissing me off. I let go of Finley's hand and step in front of her, blocking his sight. "Now, now, Obsidian, is that any way to be?" A smug grin appears on his face. "I was only talking to her."

"And I've let you, but enough is enough. I've let you do other things that other shifters wouldn't have. So, consider yourself lucky because it would be in my right to kill you."

Breaker's eyes narrow at me, and I watch as his fist clench at his sides. Jett and Cain, who I've ignored this entire time, step forward, one on each side of Breaker.

"Is that a threat?" Breaker growls.

"No, it's a fact," I growl back.

I see the moment he's going to attack me. His muscles bunch and he twitches a second before he launches at me. His fist doesn't connect because I move to the side and away from Finley. I make sure my back is facing the wall of the nearby building. This gives my back coverage. Plus, Jett and Cain can't sneak up on me from behind. That's something that they liked to do when we were kids. The thing is they don't know what I've been up to since I've been away. I learned how to fight, how to take care of myself, because I realized early on that no one else would, not even the ones that were supposed to.

Breaker tries to throw a punch at me again, but I throw up my arm and block it. He does this a few more times, before I throw a punch of my own. But unlike Breaker's, mine connects. His head snaps back. I love the sound of my fist hitting his face. I've waited years for this. Realms that felt great.

"You mother fucker," Breaker yells.

I guess if he wants to get technical I am. Finley is pregnant. I'm not going to take offense to that. To show him his words don't affect me, I shrug my shoulders at him.

"Is that all you got? I really expected more from the Pack-master." My words have the desired effect.

"I'll show you," Breaker sneers, before attacking me again.

He partially shifts his hands, so his claws come out, and he takes a swat at me. I move to the side right before his claws can get me. I partially shift my hands as well, but the best part is my hands turn into Abaddon's. I'm sporting some long, wicked, yellow claws. When I swipe out toward Breaker, he doesn't move far enough out of my reach, and I leave deep scratch marks along his chest. Breaker lets out this high-pitched screech.

"No! Get your hands off of me!" I hear Finley yell. For a moment, I take my eyes off Breaker to spot Finley over to the side with Cain's arms around her, while she struggles to break free, and I see red.

"Must protect our mate," my shifting essence roars in my head.

I whip my gaze back to Breaker and charge him. I lower my shoulder ramming it into his stomach. I wrap my arms around him and lift him from the ground. Breaker takes his claws and digs them into my back, but I push the pain aside. I use my strength and slam Breaker down on the sidewalk. I hear the sick sound of his head connecting with concrete. I don't waste any time checking to see if he's still breathing. Instead, I turn my attention to Finley.

She's kicking her legs wildly, and one of her feet hits Cain's knee because it buckles, and he loosens his grip on her, but not enough for her to get away. Jett is standing off to the side looking rapidly between me, Breaker, and Cain before taking off at a run. It's the smart choice, for now.

"Let. Her. Go," I say slowly with a deep menacing growl.

Cain looks in my direction, his eyes widen. The shock is plain on his face. Finley stops struggling and looks at me. Cain places her on her feet and releases her. Finley runs over to me, and I push her behind me. I let out a loud roar, and I hear Cain whimper. He doesn't even spare Breaker a look before taking off in the same direction as Jett.

"Hunt. Kill," my essence voices.

"We will after we check on our mate," I respond. That seems to pacify my essence for now. We will enjoy it when we get to rip them all to shreds. And we will, because no one touches what's ours.

I turn to face Finley. I look over her body, not seeing any physical injuries. She's not bleeding that I can see. I sniff the air and don't scent her blood. I shift my hands back to normal and open my arms. Finley walks right into them. I pull her close, bury my nose in her hair, and growl. She's covered in Cain's scent and I don't like it. I start rubbing my face on the top of her head.

"Obsidian?" she says my name like a question.

"I don't like it," I state.

"Don't like what?" she asks.

"You smell like him and I don't like it," I reply.

Finley nuzzles the one side of her face on my chest, then turns her head and does the same on the other side. She plasters herself against my front and starts rubbing her body on mine. I moan, because now I want to do other things with her. She tries to pull back but I won't let her.

"I just want to do the same to the back," she voices. I let her turn within the circle of my arms. Finley pushes back against me and starts rubbing. I growl. My face goes to the crook of her neck and my hands rest on her belly. I inhale deeply.

"Much better." I place a kiss on her neck and then one behind her ear. I nip on her earlobe. "But now I have other things on my mind," I whisper in her ear. She shivers.

Finley doesn't get a chance to reply because there is a groan from Breaker. I sigh. At least I know I didn't kill him. In a way that's a good thing because then I would be Packmaster and that's something I don't want. On the other hand, it sucks because I know he's going to be pissed.

Finley and I turn to face Breaker and watch as he stumbles to his feet. It takes him a few tries because he falls a couple of times. He puts a hand to the back of his head and comes away with blood. There's some on the concrete too. Breaker glances around him and stops on me and Finley. He narrows his eyes at me and bares his teeth.

"This isn't over," he snaps. I didn't think it was, but I don't say anything. I narrow my eyes right back. Bring it. Breaker snarls before taking off.

"Well, this sucks," Finley says.

"Why?" I ask. She steps out of my arms and faces me.

"One, because you still don't know what happened to your parents. Two, he's severely pissed now, and there's no telling what he will do. And three, how the hell did he not die from getting his head bashed into the concrete?" She gestures to the spot where Breaker's blood is.

"Let's find Verkor and Stolas. Once we do, I'm going to have a little chat with Breaker," I growl. Finley places a hand on my arm.

"You can't go see him alone." Her grip tightens.

"I won't. I'll take Stolas with me."

"Did someone mention my name?" Stolas' voice rings out from behind me. I turn and stand beside Finley as we watch Stolas and Verkor walk toward us. They stop in front of us.

"Obsidian wants you to go with him to hunt down Breaker and finally get some answers about his parents," Finley states.

Stolas nods. "We can do that, right after we tell you what we heard about the Super Blood Moon party."

STOLAS

"Should we wait until we get back to our room before having this conversation?" Finley questions.

"Look around, love, there's no one out here." I open my arms wide and turn in a circle. "This is the quietest town I've seen where a party is involved, especially one that's revolved around some super rare event. This town should be crawling with people, but they're hold-up inside."

"I take it you know why?" Obsidian asks, holding her arms over his chest.

"Not fully, but we," I point to myself and Verkor, "overheard a couple of people talking about it at the grocery store. They were saying that they were hoping that no one in their family was picked for it. The person that they were talking to agreed."

"Okay," Finley draws out the word. "But how do you know they were talking about the party?" Her eyebrows furrow.

"Because they mentioned staying out of sight until then. The other person said that they only leave their house when it's absolutely necessary, and the other person agreed," I state.

"This confirms what Cain and Jett were talking about. Breaker picks someone for this party, but what is he doing with them?" Verkor interjects.

"My guess is he isn't having dinner with them," I joke. Finley rolls her eyes.

"Not unless torture is a form of dessert," Finley quips.

"We didn't have much luck. Whenever we tried to ask them what they were talking about, they clammed up and refused to talk to us," I say. Obsidian snorts. "What?" I ask looking at him.

"Did you really think that they would talk to you? You're an outsider. They don't know you. For all they know you would have run right to Breaker and told him everything they said." Obsidian runs his fingers through his hair.

"Okay, but what do we do now? We're supposed to be using that party as our cover."

"I don't know, but if we don't find out what it is beforehand, we'll know that night," I say.

"But that won't do anyone any good. Whatever is happening, it could be too late by then," Verkor replies.

"Maybe not. We could still stop whatever from happening. We'll just be going in blind."

"We can stop the cycle, or whatever is going on. By letting this continue when we could help makes us no better than they are." Obsidian narrows his eyes.

"Let's hope that we're not wasting our time. We're trying to help a bunch of heartless, selfish people." Obsidian turns, walking away. Finley lets out a sigh.

"Can one of you go with him? I don't want him to walk around out here alone. He pissed off Breaker before you guys showed up, and there's no telling what he could do," she says softly.

"I'll go, love," I say. I walk up to her and wrap her up in a hug. I look over my shoulder to Verkor. "Get her back to the bed and breakfast. I'll bring Obsidian back when he calms down." Verkor nods and releases Finley. I place a kiss on her forehead then take off after Obsidian.

He's not too far ahead of me when I catch up. I don't say anything. Instead, I wait for him to be ready to talk to me. I learned a long time ago it's best not to push him to open up. He'll just close himself off more and it takes longer to be able to reason with him. We walk in silence for a while before I hear him sigh.

"I know she's right," he says. I glance over at him before looking ahead again. I still don't say anything. I'm letting him work through his thoughts. "It's not that I don't want to help, it's just hard for me to want to help them, these shifters."

"You're more than this place," I finally say. Obsidian stops and looks at me. I face him. "You got out of here. You've been gone and free of this hell since you were eighteen. These people," I wave my hand around, "...they're still stuck here; they feel stuck here. They still had and have to deal with whatever torture and hell is going on here. Some of them may resent you for it. You know that someone here is going through the same things you did."

"I know that," he growls. "In order for me to help them, the quickest way would be to kill Breaker and I don't want to be stuck here as their new Packmaster."

"Who said it had to be you that kills him?"

Obsidian puts his hands on his hips. "Who else is going to do it? Obviously, no one can challenge him because they die the night before. How are we going to stop that from happening?"

"True," I say, patting Obsidian on the shoulder. "But who said you can't injure Breaker to the point where he can't fight back, and someone else can, someone worthy, can finish him off." I grin at him.

"Your idea isn't half bad," he rubs his hand over his beard. "After we get the last piece of the map, I can fight him, and let the shifters elect someone they trust to lead, deliver the killing blow."

"Exactly. Now, how about we go have that talk with Breaker and see about what happened to your parents." Obsidian nods. We turn and start walking in the direction of the pack house. "Do you think he's there?"

"I don't know where else he could go," Obsidian replies.

"What did you do to him anyway?" I ask.

"Lost my temper."

"Shocker," I tease. He glares at me and I chuckle. "Go on. Why did you lose your temper?"

"Because once again, I let Breaker get under my skin. Our plan worked on drawing him out. He ran into me and Finley walking around. It wasn't like we were trying to hide. He stopped us and I got right to the point." I knew he would. It's one of the things that I like most about Obsidian. He's never afraid to be direct. "I asked him what happened to my parents, and he told me that my father put up a fight, but my mother didn't. He still didn't tell me where they are or if they're alive, but that's my fault.

"Finley asked him to tell me, and he was going to, but I hated the way he was looking at her. So, I stood in front of her to block his view. He said something about respecting him and I threw it in his face that I could kill him because he kept coming after my mate. I saw him tense up right before he attacked. I was defending not only myself but Finley as well." My anger starts to rise as Obsidian continues to talk. "While I had ahold of Breaker, Cain grabbed Finley, and I saw red.

"I charged Breaker and laid him out and turned toward Cain and Jett. Cain let Finley go when he saw their Packmaster was out cold on the concrete. He and Jett took off. Breaker came around a few moments later and took off too."

"I see no problem with you getting mad," I say through gritted teeth. "I'm getting really sick of Breaker's fascination with Finley."

"You and me both," Obsidian states.

OBSIDIAN

The walk to the pack house was fast as I told Stolas what happened. Now, we're both standing on the front porch. Stolas glances over at me and nods. I know he'll have my back if needed. I turn my head to the front door and pound on it. It doesn't take long for someone to answer.

"What the hell are you doing here?" Breaker sneers at me.

I watch as he lowers his arm from the back of his head. There's a bloody rag in his hand and I grin. It makes me happy knowing that I hurt him.

"I'm here to finish our conversation. You're going to tell me what the hell you did to my parents." I shove my way inside the log cabin. "And I'm not leaving until you do." I turn facing him, crossing my arms over my chest, and glare at him.

"I could just have you thrown out of here," Breaker states.

I narrow my eyes. "Go ahead and try," I say menacingly. Stolas walks over toward me and stands shoulder to shoulder with me, showing a united front. "It seems to me that you're the only one here. I saw how fast your Beta and Omega ran when they saw you bleeding on the sidewalk." Breaker growls at me. I love that I'm getting under his skin. "Now, tell me what the hell you did with my parents and I'll leave you alone... for now."

"I didn't think you would care. Everyone knew what your father was doing to you and that your mother let him," Breaker snarls.

"What did you think was going to happen?" I take a step toward him. "That I would come here and thank you?" I laugh. "You may have done me a favor by getting rid of my father, but I still want to know where they are."

"I killed them both," Breaker growls. "I killed your mother first and made your father watch." *Keep it together,* I tell myself. "Imagine my surprise when it didn't affect him at all. He almost seemed relieved. I had no use for him either, so I killed him too."

"Where. Are. Their. Bodies?" I say each word slowly while walking toward him. I want to see them for myself. A sick and twisted grin crosses his face.

"I burned them." Every muscle in my body tenses. I want to beat his damn face in. "I used them as incendiary at a bonfire. I just tossed their dead lifeless bodies on top and watched them burn."

I take a step toward him, but Stolas steps in front of me, blocking my view.

"So, what you're actually saying is that you have no way to prove that you did kill them. For all we know, they could have left and never came back," Stolas states.

"Oh, no. I have proof. You can ask anyone. Everyone was there. It happened at our last Super Blood Moon party." Breaker curls his lip.

I growl and take a step toward him, but Stolas puts his hand up, stopping me.

"You're pathetic. Why are you doing this? What do you get out of torturing people? You can't tell me that all these people did something to you," Stolas states.

"I like the feeling that it gives me. It's a rush, a high, and I enjoy it."

I've had enough of him and his voice. This is all a sick game to him, and I don't want to listen to it anymore. I step from behind Stolas and get right in Breaker's face.

"One day someone will come along that is stronger than you. What are you going to do then? There will come a day when you fall and die. You are nothing without your little group of thugs. You're deluding yourself if you think that they respect and like you. Trust me when I say all your friends will turn on you, and when they do, what are you going to have to show for it? A sad life and existence, and a handful of years in power just to be forgotten when someone better comes along."

Breaker growls at me but otherwise doesn't make a move. I can see it in his shifty eyes. He knows that I'm right. My chest puffs up knowing that I got under his skin. I grin at him. His mouth tightens but he keeps it closed. I step around him and right out the door.

It must be my lucky day because I run right into Cain and Jett the moment I step out on the porch.

"Just the two people I was hoping to see," I say with a sneer. Cain and Jett narrow their eyes at me. They widen their stance and cross their arms over their chest.

"What could you possibly want with us, berserker?" Cain spits out. I clench my fist at my sides. I would love to punch them in the face, but I must think about the bigger picture. I relax my hands and shrug my shoulders.

"A little birdie told me that you might not be happy with your current Packmaster. I could be persuaded to help, but I need to know everything about him. From the challengers ending up dead, to whatever is happening at the Super Blood Moon party." Cain and Jett laugh.

"Why would we go and tell you something like that? Even if we weren't happy with our Packmaster, there is nothing anyone can do. You saw the other night what happens when you go against the Packmaster. There's no way I would be stupid enough to put myself in that position," Jett responds.

"It's no skin off my nose. I was just throwing the idea out there, but since you don't want my help, and I'll be leaving again, soon, maybe you can answer one question for me." They side eye each other, before focusing on me. "What the hell did I ever do to you as kids that would make you torment me the way you did?" Both of their eyes widen at my question. "I think after all this time I deserve to know at least that much."

"Look, it wasn't you so much..." Jett trails off. Cain picks up right where he left off.

"Breaker has always been untouchable, being related to the Packmaster and all. He was always on the small side. I think even then he knew he would never have what it took to win a challenge to become Packmaster." Cain sighs.

"He saw us training one day and approached us. He wove this tale of how when he became Packmaster he would name us Beta and Omega. We would have all this power. All we had to do was protect him and do what he said. At first we didn't want to, but he threatened to tell Packmaster Axel if we didn't and we heard of the things he did when defied," Jett states.

"Okay, but what does that have to do with me?" I ask, frowning.

"It was after word got out what you were... he started to get worried. Tales of the strength of hamrammr are legendary. It's not like there are a lot of you running around. Anyway, Breaker got worried that you would try to take over as Packmaster. He didn't want that to happen. He was... is scared of you and what you could do," Cain says.

"It was no secret what your father and the Packmaster did to you, so Breaker thought he should add another layer. He figured he could beat you into submission." My essence growls in my mind as I growl aloud. "Like I said he threatened to torture us if we didn't help."

"So, let me get this straight," I say through gritted teeth. "You never actually had a problem with me; you were just doing what Breaker wanted." They both nod their heads. "And you continue to do so." Again, they nod.

"We fear for our lives if we stopped now," Jett responds.

"You both are nothing but pussy ass cowards. You could have grown a spine and dealt this long ago, but fear held you back." I take a moment to let those words sink in because wasn't I doing the same? Well, not anymore.

"If it helps, we're sorry for what we did," Cain says, remorse in his tone. Does it help? Not at this moment, but at least I know why now. I shake my head at them.

"I have to thank you." Cain and Jett are shocked at my words. "You are part of the reason I am who I am today. I have a great job, great friends, and my mate. I'm happy with my life. If I didn't live through what I did, my life could have been drastically different. I got out." A little bit of peace settles within me. "You'll both get what's coming to you," I say before walking away, because at this point, they're not worth my time or energy anymore.

CHAPTER 17

FINLEY

Verkor walks with me back to our room at the bed and breakfast, which I'm currently pacing. He's sitting on the edge of one of the beds with his elbows on his knees.

"Finley, they'll be alright," Verkor says. "Stolas won't let anything bad happen to Obsidian, and he'll have his back. He also won't let Obsidian do anything stupid."

"You don't know that. Breaker has to be pissed at what Obsidian did to him."

He sits up straighter, opening his legs. I walk between them and he places his hands on my hips, pulling me closer.

"True, but Obsidian can handle this now, plus Stolas is with him to back him up should Breaker, Cain, or Jett try anything," Verkor says while rubbing my hips.

"This whole region is just fucked." I place my hands on his shoulders. "It's going to take a long time to fix what's broken."

"I have to agree with you there," Verkor says. "Obsidian only went there to find out what happened to his parents. Once he gets that information, they'll come back. You know how much Obsidian doesn't want to be Packmaster. I don't think he would do anything where that would be a possibility. He doesn't want to be stuck here." I sigh, knowing that he's right.

"Fine, but what are we going to do until they come back? I have to get my mind off of them or I'm going to go back to worrying and probably start pacing the floor again," I say looking him in his blue eyes. Up close like this, you can see the specks of white in them. They remind me of a cloudy summer day.

"I can think of one thing that will completely get your mind off of worrying," Verkor says with a huskiness to his voice.

"Yeah, and what's that?"

I wrap my arms around his shoulders, fisting his blond hair at the nape of his neck. I move my legs, placing my knees on either side of his hips, straddling him. He leans in close, hovering his lips above mine.

"You're already on the right path, baby," he whispers.

The first pass of his lips across mine is soft and gentle, but then the kiss deepens and becomes more urgent. He nips at my bottom lip before plunging his tongue in my mouth. I moan against his lips and rock my hips. We have too many clothes on. I want to feel his skin on mine. I want to run my fingers through his soft feathers. I grip him tighter.

Verkor runs his hands up my hips and back. One of his hands moves up to my hair, and grabs it, tugging on the strands. I gasp, but my desire heightens. He pulls back and I take in a much-needed breath of air, but Verkor doesn't stop. His lips travel across my cheek and down my neck, leaving little kisses behind.

"More, I need more." I can hear the neediness in my voice. The desperation of wanting to feel his hands on my bare body.

Verkor rises from the bed with me in his arms. He places me on my feet, staring directly into my eyes.

"Then strip."

I bite my bottom lip to keep from moaning at his words. I

don't waste any time. I take a couple of steps back from him, but quickly take all of my clothes off, tossing them onto the floor. Verkor runs his eyes up and down my body. I love the way he does it, because it makes me feel sexy, wanted, loved.

"What about you? You seem a little overdressed." All Verkor does is smile at me.

"Well then, I guess I'll have to fix that. But first, I want you to get on the bed and spread your legs for me." Verkor steps closer to me. He leans down, placing his mouth next to my ear. "I want to watch you play with yourself while I strip for you."

He nips at my earlobe. I clench my thighs together. When I don't move, he smacks my ass. He steps to the side and watches as I crawl on my hands and knees from the foot of the bed up to the headboard. As I position myself on my back in the middle of the bed, I see Verkor grab the hem of his shirt and whip it over his head, dropping it to the floor. A second later, his onyx black wings emerge. My heart rate increases.

I love his wings. Verkor standing in nothing but his blue jeans, wings out in display, and his blond hair slightly messy from taking off his shirt and from my hands; my winter fae looks like a sexy fallen angel. I want to go to him and run my fingers over every inch of his muscled abs, but instead I do as he asks. I open my legs, giving him an unobstructed view of my pussy. He drinks in the sight of me and I feel empowered knowing that I have the same effect on him that he has on me.

I move my hands over my breast, pinching my nipples. I release a little gasp, but I don't stop moving. Verkor watches my hand as I travel down my body, over my baby bump, and stop right at the apex of my thighs.

"You're still wearing too many clothes," I say. Verkor's hands move and he quickly unbuttons and unzips his jeans, shoving both them and his boxers to the floor. He steps out of them and moves to stand at the foot of the bed.

"Touch yourself," he says. So, I do.

I run my fingers through my slit, feeling how wet I am. Using my own juices, I circle my clit, not quite touching it, but it has the desired effect. I close my eyes and moan, bucking my hips when I finally make contact with my clit.

My eyes snap open when I feel the bed dip. Verkor crawls up the bed and positions himself on his knees between my thighs. His hands go to my knees, spreading my legs further.

"Yes, keep going. Does that feel good?" Verkor asks, desire lacing his voice. I love seeing the lust in his eyes. "Would you like my cock inside you instead?" His hands start rubbing up and down my thighs, and I lose all ability to speak. I'm too focused on how his hands feel on my skin to form a coherent thought. I simply nod my head. "I want you to ride me, baby. I want to see those luscious tits of your bounce." I groan. I want him inside of me so bad. I rub my clit faster.

Verkor stretches his wings out, ruffling the feathers. There's a grin on his face. He knows exactly what he's doing. He knows how much his wings turn me on.

"Switch places with me." I stop rubbing myself and quickly get to my knees. But before I can move any further, Verkor grabs my hand and puts my fingers in his mouth, sucking my juices off of them. "Hm, tasty."

"Fuck me," I say. I'm half a second away from throwing him onto his back and impaling myself on his hard, erect cock.

"Oh, I plan on doing just that."

Verkor carefully lays on the bed because his wings are still out. He doesn't have to say anything. Once he's on his back, I straddle his hips, and run my hands over his chest and down his abs. My fingers dip into each crevice that defines them. I scoot back just enough to tease my opening with the tip of his cock, and both of us groan. Verkor's hands run up and down my body.

"Realms, you're so sexy," he says roughly. I love that Verkor is more reserved in his everyday life, but when it comes to the bedroom, my smart, sexy, quiet mate says the filthiest things. He taps my ass. "Now, ride me."

I grip his cock at the base and slowly, inch by glorious inch, I take him inside of me.

"Fuck," he exclaims. But that's exactly how I feel.

VERKOR

Nothing in any realm feels as good as my mate sitting on my cock with me buried deep inside of her. Her warm, wet heat encases me, and it feels like heaven. Finley's hands go to my chest and her nails dig in as she starts to bounce. I move my hands to her hips to help.

"Yes," she says breathlessly.

I want her to be closer to me. I want our chests touching. I wrap my arms around her and pull her down. She stops her movement, but I take over, thrusting my hips up.

"Oh, fuck," she screams. "Yes, just like that. More."

Finley moves her hands to my sides. They land on my wings that I still have stretched out. When her hands touch my feathers, she threads her fingers through them, gripping them tightly. I shiver below her. I love when she pulls on my feathers. She raises her chest up and off me but doesn't move her hands. Instead, she tugs a little harder on my feathers and I buck up faster.

Finley places her forehead on mine, and her pink hair envelopes us like a curtain. I feel like we're in our own bubble. It's just the two of us and nothing else matters. Our breaths mingle as she rocks back on me and I push upward.

"I'm almost there," she whispers. I pull her flush against me and kiss her as I thrust a little faster. I nip her bottom lip.

"Come, baby," I whisper and that's all she needs to let go.

I feel her walls contract around my cock. The sensation is too much and I empty myself inside of her. Finley's arms buckle. Her head lays on my chest and the only sound in the room is both of our heavy breathing. I run my hands up and down her back. Neither of us say anything. We're just lying there basking in the warm after sex glow. Finley doesn't stir until our breathing returns to normal. She lifts her head from my chest, trying to meet my eyes.

"That was awesome," she says with a smile. I grin.

"I told you I would take your mind off of things for a while." She giggles.

"That you did, and you did a very good job of it." She shifts up my body a little bit and places a quick kiss to my lips.

"You're okay, right?" I ask. "Are you okay with laying on me like this?"

Finley's eyebrows furrow. "Yeah, why?"

"I didn't want to put pressure on your belly, and I didn't want to be too rough." Finley smiles. She uses my chest as leverage to push up. Her legs still straddle me.

"I won't be able to lay down on you like this for much longer; it's already starting to get uncomfortable." She moves her hands to her belly and rubs. "There's no mistaking I'm pregnant now." Her belly does seem to be growing more rapidly. "We have three months to go. I'm not going to let me being pregnant change anything between us. If I get uncomfortable, I'll tell you and we can reposition or find something else that works." She glances back up and looks me right in the eyes. She's so damn beautiful. "I do have a question," she says, tilting her head to the side.

"What's your question?" I ask, moving my hands to her thighs, rubbing them.

"There's no denying that I'm pregnant. You can clearly see that, but it doesn't seem to be deterring Breaker any. Why would he continue to try to push the envelope? He hasn't even mentioned me being pregnant." I wrap an arm around her and use my other to push myself into a seated position. I scoot back with Finley until my back hits the headboard.

"I don't know, baby, but now that you mention it, that is odd. We can ask Obsidian when he comes back. There might be a slight possibility that he hasn't noticed, but I don't think that's it. I think he would continue to come after you and show you interest just because he knows how much it upsets Obsidian," I reply.

"Okay, but if we're going on that, wouldn't it get under Obsidian's skin faster if he mentioned the baby?"

"Oh yeah, but this is Breaker. From the little that Obsidian has told us, Breaker has been tormenting him for years. If I had to guess, I would say Breaker is waiting to use that against Obsidian. Holding on to the one thing that would definitely push Obsidian over the edge. From the few interactions we have had with Breaker, he'd use this as a last resort. Obsidian has done pretty well being here all things considered." Finley moves her hands to my chest.

"Even Stolas has been good, and we both know he said he isn't happy with Breaker and feels the same way Obsidian does," Finley states. I nod.

"Yeah, but they're not the only ones."

"Really?" she questions. I shift my gaze up to look in her beautiful gray eyes.

"Yeah. I hate him sending you gifts, or touching you, flirting with you. I don't like that he tried to take you from me, because that's exactly what Cain was going to do. You're a female, a non-shifter, he could easily overpower you. There would have been no need to grab and hold you." Her hands move up my chest and settle on my shoulders. "I don't think they thought Obsidian would attack Breaker. They're relying too much on how Obsidian was as a kid. He's not the same person he was back then. Now, they have to factor in that he has a mate and a child. Obsidian would fight to the death to protect the both of you." I move my hands up to cup her face. I run my thumbs over her cheeks.

"We all would. I may not show my aggression and dislike like Obsidian and Stolas with their growls, but don't think for one second I don't feel the same way they do. I couldn't tell you how many times I've thought about strangling the fuckers with my shadows." Finley smiles at me.

"I've thought about using them as a dart board. I could keep my skills fresh by practicing throwing my Chinese death stars and those cool knife hair chopsticks. Hell, I would probably use my regular daggers as well." I chuckle, because I can see her doing that.

"Now, there's an idea. I think Obsidian would join you."

"He would have to wait in line for his turn." I let loose a laugh and drop my hands from her face.

"I don't know if you've noticed but Obsidian isn't known for his patience."

"You don't say," Finley says with sarcasm dripping in her voice. I open my mouth to respond, but the door handle starts to jiggle.

"Bathroom now," I say sternly. Finley scrambles off me and runs to the bathroom, closing the door behind her.

I don't have time to get any clothes on, but I get off the bed, putting myself in front of the bathroom door. I call the shadows to my hands as the bedroom door flings open. My shoulders relax and I let the shadows go when I see Obsidian and Stolas walk in. I retract my wings, pulling them back inside me. Stolas spots me, takes one look at my naked appearance, and wiggles his eyebrows at me.

"I see someone was busy while we were gone," he teases. Obsidian's hands tighten on the bags he's carrying, but he doesn't say anything.

"Could you put some damn clothes on," he finally grumbles. "You're not the one I want to see naked." He glances around the room. His gaze comes back to me. "Where's Finley?" I walk over to the end of the bed, picking up my discarded pants, and quickly put them on.

"She's in the bathroom. I had her head there when I heard the doorknob rattling." Obsidian nods his head, pleased that I got her out of what could have been harm's way. "Let me go and tell her everything is okay."

"No need," Finley walks out of the bathroom still naked. We all groan. I just had her, but I want her again. "I have hellhound hearing. Plus, there's a hole in the door." I forgot about that.

Finley casually walks over to our pile of clothes on the floor, grabs my shirt, and puts it on. She looks sexy in my clothes.

"I see someone had some fun while we were out," Stolas says teasing her. Finley smiles and shrugs her shoulders.

"It was either that or wear a hole in the floor from all the pacing I was doing. I was worried that something was going to happen to you, and Verkor distracted me." Stolas inhales deeply.

"It seems like he did an excellent job," Stolas' voice goes husky.

This is one of those rare times where I wish I had a shifter's sense of smell. The room has to be permeated with the smell of sex, and from both Obsidian and Stolas' reaction, it must smell good. Though I'm guessing it has more to do with how Finley's arousal and release smell.

"Oh, he did," Finley teases. I puff my chest out a little. Finley looks over at me and winks. She turns her attention on Obsidian, who still has the bags in his hands. "Whatcha got there, Siddy?" She motions to the bags in his hands.

"Food," he replies. His voice is a little gravelly. He clears his throat. "We stopped to get food on the way back."

"Great, I'm starving. I worked up quite the appetite." Stolas laughs, I shake my head, and Obsidian rolls his eyes. He moves to the closest bed and puts the bags on it. "So, not to be Debbie Downer, but did you find Breaker?"

"Yeah," Obsidian says. He doesn't look at any of us. Instead, he busies himself with taking the food containers out of the bag.

"Did you get any answers?" Finley asks softly.

Obsidian doesn't respond right away. His head is down, and I can't see his face. I glance over to Stolas. He nods his head, but a look crosses his face, sadness. What Obsidian found out wasn't pleasant. Finley moves to Obsidian's side, placing a hand on his shoulder.

"We don't have to talk about this right now. Whenever you're ready, I'll be here to listen." Obsidian looks down at her and sighs.

"It's fine," he says. He moves and pulls her into his arms. "After Breaker first mentioned them, I had a feeling that they were either dead or locked up somewhere." He places his chin on the top of her head and closes his eyes. "He said my father fought but my mother didn't. He killed my mother in front of my father, trying to get a reaction out of him. When he didn't, Breaker killed him too." Obsidian grips Finley a little tighter. "I told him I didn't believe him, and I wanted to see their bodies, but he said he didn't have them. After arguing with him, he finally told me that he burned their bodies at the last Super Blood Moon party."

"That's horrible," Finley whispers. "I'm so sorry."

"It'll be okay," Obsidian whispers. "I'll be okay. I didn't have the best relationship with them, but still..." he trails off. "There's nothing I can do about it now." Finley pulls back and looks him in the eyes. They don't say anything. Finley hugs him again.

"You should have heard Obsidian's speech before he walked out. It was epic," Stolas smiles wide.

"What did you tell him?" I ask.

"Basically, that someone stronger than him was going to take him down, and that he's not going to have anything to show for his miserable life. That no one really likes him and the second they can they will turn on him," Obsidian replies.

"Oh, it was much better than that," Stolas says. Obsidian shrugs his shoulders. He's trying not to be bothered by it, but it still has to hurt.

"Is Breaker still in one piece?" Finley asks, stepping out of Obsidian's arm. She moves over to the bed and starts opening containers. Once she finds the one she wants, she grabs some utensils and sits on the other bed and digs in.

"Unfortunately," Obsidian responds. He grabs a container and some utensils and sits next to Finley.

"Is there anything you would like from your house?" she asks, shifting on the bed to face him. Stolas and I grab the remaining food and sit on the bed. The bed is still warm from where the containers were placed.

"No," Obsidian shakes his head. "I don't have many good memories there. You saw the state of my room. I didn't have much and everything that I left behind I haven't missed."

"You don't want any pictures?" Finley probes.

"No. They would just be a reminder of what I went through. Those pictures are lies anyway. We weren't happy as a family. I don't want to keep something that's fake."

"That's understandable. Well, once the baby is here, we can take our family pictures and they'll be happy, good memories. Our family isn't a lie. We love each other. We'll fill our new home with those."

A knock on the door startles everyone.

"I'll get it," I say. I rise from the bed and walk over to the door. I open it to see one of Breaker's enforcers standing on the other side with a white box wrapped with a gold ribbon in his hands.

There's a scowl on his face. One that probably matches my

own. I don't want to see him here anymore than he wants to be here. He shoves the box out in front of him towards me. I take it. Without a word, he turns and leaves. I stare after him for a moment before closing the door. I walk the box over the bed, setting it down. There's a small card tucked under one of the strands of ribbon. I pull it out and see Finley's name written in sharp, masculine writing.

"It's for you," I say, looking Finley in her eyes.

There are two growls at my words. I glance around and see that both Obsidian and Stolas are frowning. We know exactly who it's from. Finley scoots down to the end of the bed, sitting cross-legged in front of the box. She grabs the end of the ribbon and pulls, unraveling it. Finley lifts the lid from the box, placing it next to her on the bed. Opening the tissue paper, laying in the bottom of the box is a white dress. I hand over the card in my hand. She takes it and flips it open.

"Finley, it would do me a great honor if you would wear this dress Saturday night, and be my honored guest. Yours, Breaker." Another round of growls sound after Finley's words.

"I swear I'm going to kill him before I leave," Obsidian says between gritted teeth.

"I'll help you," Stolas growls.

"Can you wait to kill him after he hands us the last piece of the map?" Finley questions. There is exasperation in her voice. "Once we have that piece, you can do whatever you want to him. I won't stop you."

"I won't kill him, but I'll leave him broken enough that someone else can," Obsidian states, clenching his fist. I don't think anyone would object to that.

CHAPTER 18

FINLEY

After I received the gift box a few nights ago, the guys weren't happy and made sure it was known. I don't blame them. The last few days have been filled with us talking and planning for what's to come tomorrow night. That's really all we could do. No one would talk to us. When someone would see us, they took off. They were avoiding us. I'm bored and need to get out of this room and away from this place before I go insane.

"Are there markets nearby?" I ask, shoving a bite of pancake into my mouth. We actually got up for once and made it downstairs to the bed and breakfast's free breakfast.

"There used to be one on the border of this region, but I don't know if it's still there," Obsidian replies.

"Is there any way we can find out?"

"Why, love?" Stolas questions. "What do you need there? There are plenty of shops around."

I shrug my shoulders. "I know, but I think it'll be nice to get away from here. I think Obsidian could use a break. I just want to look around and see what they have. It's my first time here in the Shifter Realm, and we haven't been too many places and everyone here hides. Not that I blame them."

"We can check," Obsidian says. I smile and go back to eating.

It doesn't take us long before we're headed out. "How are we going to get there?" I ask.

"We can walk. The border isn't too far from the gateway. Just in the other direction," Obsidian replies.

We walk the way we came, passing by the same shops and buildings. Nothing has changed. There are no decorations for the party tomorrow night. There are no people milling about talking in excitement. It's like a ghost town. It doesn't take long for us to make it back to the gateway. The shimmer beckons me. A part of me wants to step back through and go home. I would like nothing more than to get Obsidian out of here, but the drive to complete what I started keeps me walking.

I look around and see nothing but trees. It's quiet and peaceful. I strain my ears trying to use some of the perks I have acquired since becoming pregnant and taking on some of the traits of a hellhound. I don't hear any sounds of normal animals.

"Is it always like this?" I question. "I don't hear anything." The guys and I pause on the well-worn dirt path. Obsidian and Stolas tilt their heads and listen.

"Hm. I didn't expect anyone from my region to be here, but you are right. This is unnaturally quiet," Obsidian states. "Let's keep moving. It might just be Breaker's area."

We travel in silence. Then out of nowhere, the sounds of birds, and scurrying animals through the leaves fills the silence. The more we walk; the more different sounds start to fill my ears. The tinkling of swords, laughter, the rustling of bags. We continue to walk, and the market comes into view. The excitement of seeing people bustling around starts to affect me. I bounce a little as we walk.

"This is how it used to be in Breaker's region," Obsidian says softly.

"Whose region is this?" I ask.

"Years ago, it was Malcom. I don't know if it still is," Obsidian responds.

As we walk the market, I take in all the stalls. There's a weapons stall where two men are sword fighting. There are numerous clothing and material stalls, as well as jewelry. All the shining gems catch my eye, but my stomach rumbles. I inhale deeply, smelling the tantalizing scent of cooking meat. I let my stomach and my nose guide me there. The guys keep pace with me as I weave through the people. Finally, we get to the stall where that delicious smelling meat is cooking. I swear I drool some. My stomach growls louder, and the guys laugh.

"Hungry, baby?" Verkor says, stepping up beside me. He places a hand on the small of my back and starts rubbing it. It feels amazing.

I look up to meet his eyes. "I'm always hungry." Verkor smiles at me.

"Let's get you something to eat."

The guy running the stall walks over to us. He's a big, burly man as tall as Obsidian. This guy's bicep muscles are as big as my head. I'm pretty sure the palm of his hand would cover my face. He has a barrel sized chest and a huge, thick neck. The man is bald but has the thickest, scraggly black beard. The most striking thing about this man is his piercing blue eyes. They're so blue they almost look white. They're a sharp contrast against his mocha colored skin.

"What can I get you?" his voice booms out. It's deep and gravelly.

"Whatever it is I'm smelling," I say. The man moves his gaze down. He does a once over on my body, then meets my eyes.

"You got it little lady. It'll be just a minute longer." I nod. He turns walking over to a grill.

He grabs a spatula and flips the chunks of meat a few times. Then he uses the spatula to press the meat into the grill. I can hear the sizzle of the juices. The scent of the meat fills the air and I moan. The man looks over his shoulder and gives me a blinding white smile. He turns his attention back to the grill and scoops the meat off and into a container. He moves over to a table where various other containers sit.

"I make gyros," he says. I frown.

"What is a YEE-ro?" I ask.

"It's a Mediterranean sandwich usually filled with lamb meat, tomatoes, onions, and tzatziki or cucumber sauce. I also make them with chicken, pork, and a vegetarian option," the guy replies.

"Oh, you mean a Ji-ro. I've had those before." The man lets out a booming laugh.

"No, little lady. The correct way to say it is YEE-ro," he says with a smile. I would be embarrassed but I can't because he isn't being rude in correcting me.

"Well shit, I've been pronouncing it wrong this whole time. It's YEE-ro." I can't quite roll my *r* as he can. His smile widens, and he nods his head.

"You got it. What would you like on yours?" he asks.

"Everything. Can I have extra meat? On the side, in a cup, I'm not going to be picky."

"I can do that," he states.

I watch, mesmerized as the man fills the pita bread with all the condiments available and wraps it in a piece of pre-cut aluminum foil before fulfilling my second request of extra meat on the side. He walks over the gyro in one hand and cup of extra meat with a plastic fork peeking over the top in the other. The sandwich and cup are warm against the palms of my hands, the smell is amazing, and I can't wait to tuck in.

"Twenty-five credits," he says. Verkor holds out his wrist and the guy grabs a scanner, places it over Verkor's bracelet, deducting the credits.

"Thank you," I say. I turn to the side, looking over to Stolas. "Will you hold my sandwich?"

"Of course, love," he says, holding out his hand. I go to place it in his waiting palm but pull it back at the last second. I narrow my eyes at him.

"If you so much as take a bite of this sandwich, I will use your balls as target practice for my throwing stars." Stolas holds both hands up, palms out, facing me.

"I promise not to eat your sandwich." I nod and hand it over. The stall merchant laughs.

I turn my attention back to him. "What?" I ask. He shakes his head and smiles.

"You're fierce. You're gonna make a great mama to your baby," he replies.

"You can tell that by what I just did?" I ask.

"Yeah. There is nothing fiercer in any realm than that of a mama in protection mode. Your mate is lucky."

"I know," says three different voices, one for each one of my mates. I look at the merchant and roll my eyes. He just smiles.

"Thank you," I say again.

"Anytime."

I nod and turn away from the stall. I take the fork, shove the first piece of meat in my mouth, and groan.

"This is so fucking good." I hear the stall merchant laugh at my words.

"Come on, love. Are you not going to share one bite with us? It's not fair that you tempt me by making me hold your sandwich," Stolas says, increasing his pace so he can walk next to me. I glance over at him from the corner of my eyes.

"I guess I could share a bite."

I stab another piece of meat with my fork. We pause in the middle of the path and I hold out the fork to Stolas. He smiles, wraps his lips around the fork, taking the piece of meat. He moans and winks at me.

"You were right this is good."

I do the same for Obsidian and Verkor. I watch as each of them wrap their lips around my fork then lick their lips. I suck in a sharp breath thinking of them using their tongues and lips on my body. Oh, how I wish I was that fork. They all wink at me when they're done, and I know that they're doing it on purpose. The asses. Just wait, I'll get my revenge.

I polish off the meat in the cup and the sandwich as we walk around the market. I stop at a stall that has anklets. They range from plain yarn, in a multitude of colors, to stunning metal encrusted jeweled ones. There are even toe rings. I run my fingers over a set of silver ones. The band that goes around the ankle is thick and there are marquise and pear shape diamonds that alternate in a pattern on the silver band. Small chains overlap in loops around the anklets. They are beautiful, but not the ones that my eyes keep going back to.

Oddly enough, it's the one's made of yarn. The intricate crocheted barefoot sandal is stunning. There are no words to describe the work. They tie around the ankle and two crocheted lines extend from the end of the ankle piece and turn into a loop for your toe. They're simple but beautiful and will go great with the white dress Breaker sent to me.

I almost groan aloud at the thought of his name. I don't understand what he's doing. There has to be more to this than just getting under Obsidian's skin. I glance over at Obsidian who has his back turned toward the stall, arms crossed over his chest, glaring at everyone and everything as he scans the crowd. I wonder if there is more to their story, to their history? If as sensing that I'm staring at him, Obsidian turns his head and locks eyes with me. His amber eyes soften, and I give him a small smile.

"Are you getting something from here?" he asks.

"I was thinking of getting these barefoot yarn sandals." I turn my head and point at the white ones I was just looking at. "The Super Blood Moon party is going to be on the beach. They'll look good with the dress. Plus, it'll be easier for me to dance and move around in the sand."

Obsidian frowns but turns to face the stall. His gaze sweeps over the items on the table. He looks over at me and a wicked grin spreads across his face. He leans down, placing his mouth next to my ear.

"If you wanted to wear cuffs around your ankles, all you had to do was ask, doll." I suck in a breath at his words. "The pair I'd put on you would only lead to your pleasure. You'd be screaming my name in ecstasy." He nips at my earlobe before pulling away.

My body sways toward him, wanting... no *needing* him to fulfill his promise. I clench my thighs together, thinking of him between them, using his lips, teeth, tongue, and finally his cock. My heart beats a little faster with the image of my thoughts.

"You okay, love?" Stolas asks, moving to stand beside me.

I glance up, meeting Obsidian's lust filled gaze. Hell no, I'm not alright, but now is not the time to climb my hamrammr like a tree and make him do all the wicked things I know he's thinking and wanting to do to my body. Instead, I clear my throat and try to calm my raging hormones. I glance over to Stolas and smile.

"I'm fine. I was just telling Obsidian I was thinking of getting these barefoot yarn sandals for the party."

Stolas cocks an eyebrow at me but looks over to the table and eyes the items. "I like those ones. He points to the white ones that I like."

"I was thinking about those too."

I look around not spotting the stall merchant at first. I could just five-finger discount them. Who leaves their stall unattended? There are plenty of people like me who steal. I pick up the white sandals, running my fingers over the yarn. It's softer to the touch than I thought they would be.

"You like those I see," a soft feminine voice says, startling me. I look up and see a beautiful raven-haired woman walking towards me from the back of the stall. Her hips sway with each step she takes. Her piercing green eyes seem to glow as she takes me in.

"I do. How much are they?"

"Fifty credits. I hand make them myself," she states as she stops in front of me.

"They're beautiful. I'll take them." I hold out my arm and she produces the scan and deducts the credits.

"Would you like a bag for them?" she asks. I shake my head.

"No, thank you." She inclines her head and walks away. I turn and look at the guys. I move to Verkor and put my bare-foot sandals in his pockets.

"Obsidian Variel, is that really you?" Obsidian stops dead in his tracks and turns around at the sound of the woman's voice. My mouth opens at the smile that graces his face. I don't think I've ever seen him smile like that. I glance over to the woman and see the same big smile on her face. Whoever she is, she has to be important.

OBSIDIAN

"Obsidian Variel, is that really you?" a voice from my past yells out. I stop dead and pivot right on the spot. A huge grin breaks out across my face. I charge forward, scooping the woman up into my arms. She giggles swatting at my shoulder. "Oh, put me down," she says with a smile. I do, making sure she's steady on her feet before stepping back.

"Gemma, you still look as beautiful as the last time I saw you."

"Don't you try to flatter me. You look good boy. Time's been good to you," she states, giving me a once over.

"That it has," I respond.

Gemma has aged a little from the last time I saw her. But one thing that never changes is the scar on the right side of her face, and guilt surfaces. It's because of me that she has it, not like she's ever blamed me. She told me she knew what could happen, but she did it anyway to try to save me.

Breaker was being particularly nasty to me one night. He cornered me on my way home. Cain and Jett were with him like usual. I don't know what Breaker's issue that day was, but he felt the need to take out his anger and frustration on me and with a knife. Breaker had already cut my arm, chest, and stomach. I don't know if I made a sound that alerted Gemma where we were, but all I saw was the knife in Breaker's hand come for my face, and him stating that he was going to disfigure me. The knife never cut me.

No, instead Gemma quietly stepped in front of me and took the knife to her face. Cain and Jett had let go of my arms and took off running. I face planted on the concrete, too weak and tired to save myself. I'll never forget her yelling at Breaker while she bled. She lost the sight in her right eye. Gemma helped me to my feet and together we walked back to her bed and breakfast. She cleaned and bandaged all my cuts before taking care of herself. I was so angry at her for stepping in the way, but thankful at the same time. Who knows how far Breaker would have taken things if she hadn't interfered. I should have taken her with me when I left. All those thoughts flee my mind when her hand touches my arm.

"I know what you're thinking, and you need to stop. I got out just like you did. It wasn't until years later that I did, but it still happened. I'm happy here." I nod my head and place my hand over hers.

"A part of me will always blame myself for you getting hurt, but I'm thankful for what you did."

"I know, boy. Now, who are those strapping young lads and that pretty woman standing behind you?" she asks, looks around me. I know she's changing the subject on purpose; for now I'll let her.

I glance over my shoulder and motion with my head for the others to come forward. Finley doesn't hesitate and walks right over to my side, gripping my hand.

"Gemma, I would like for you to meet my mate, Finley. Finley, this is Gemma. She's the one I was still hoping was running the bed and breakfast. She's the only one who ever tried to help me." I want to see what they will do. A smile spreads across Finley's face. She holds out her hand toward Gemma.

"Hi, it's nice to meet you," Finley says. Gemma bypasses her hand and pulls her into a hug.

"Well, aren't you a pretty little thing," Gemma says as she pulls back, holding Finley's shoulders.

"Thank you," Finley whispers. Gemma's gaze travels over Finley and stops on her stomach.

"Oh my. Are you pregnant? My little Obsidian is going to be a father," Gemma's voice gets higher the more excited she gets.

"Yes, and yes," Finley says with a giggle.

Gemma turns her attention to me. "I'm so happy for you." Tears well in her eyes, but she doesn't let them fall. Instead, she clears her throat, then narrows her eyes at me. "Are you treating her right?" she questions. I understand the underlying meaning. There's no way in hell I would lay a hand on my mate in any way that wasn't pleasurable.

"Of course," I say, meeting her green eyes. She nods.

She turns her attention back to Finley. "If he doesn't, you let me know, and I'll skin him alive myself." I move to step between the two, thinking that my mate would try to defend me, but no, that's not what my mate does. Finley beams a toothy smile at Gemma then looks over at me.

"I like her," Finley says with a chuckle.

"Of course, you would," I mutter, try to hide how happy that statement makes me.

"Don't worry Gemma," Finley says, pointing her finger in Stolas and Verkor's direction. "I have two more mates that would get first dibs on dismembering his body, if there's anything left, I'll let you know."

Gemma throws her head back and laughs. "Oh, she's going to keep you on your toes." I nod, because she's not wrong. She lets go of Finley, taking a few steps back. "What are you doing here?" she asks.

"We came here to get some things." I jerk my head in Finley's direction. "Someone is giving me the push to confront the things from my past."

Gemma looks over to Finley. I watch her eyes water. "Thank you," she whispers. She turns her attention back to me. "Good. Maybe now I'll see you more. I've missed you."

"I've missed you too. No matter how much I wanted to come see you, I couldn't bring myself to cross that gateway and come back."

"I know, dear. I don't blame you. You've been through more than any one person should have."

"Do you have a minute? I have a couple of questions that I would like to ask you." I should have done this a long time ago. I should have talked to her about everything, but I wasn't ready to hear it. I think I am now.

"Of course. Come this way." We all follow her to some picnic tables a few feet away. I sit next to Gemma, and Finley sits on my other side. Verkor and Stolas sit across from us. "What did you want to talk about?" she asks.

"For right now, just what seems to be going on around here. Why is everyone hiding? Eventually, I'll ask about my past and family," I reply. I can only deal with one thing at a time and finding out what is going to happen the night of the Super Blood Moon party is more pressing than my past.

"By now, I'm sure you've seen that things are worse than they used to be." I nod my head at her words. "Things changed the day that Breaker took down Axel. No one really understands how that happened. There's been some speculation that Breaker did something to weaken him, because the next day he challenged Axel and won."

"Do you know what he did?" I question. Gemma nods her head.

"Word got around he used magic to suppress Axel's power. It made him weaker than Breaker. All he had to do was deliver the killing blow. I was there that night. You know that attending the challenges is mandatory." I nod my head. "Breaker just toyed with Axel, running his mouth about how strong he is and all things he was going to change. Axel was so weak that he couldn't even stand on his own two feet and couldn't shift. Breaker kept pushing him over with his feet any time Axel managed to get on his hands and knees. Breaker shifted and tore out Axel's throat, while Axel was still in human form." I wince.

"What does that mean? I take it's not something good for the way Obsidian just reacted," Finley questions.

"You would be right," Gemma replies. "To kill another shifter who is not shifted themselves is a major sign of disrespect. It's a big no-no. You either both shift or you don't. In that moment, Breaker let us all know just how ruthless he was going to be as Packmaster. From then on, things got worse. I'm sure you've seen that." We all nod our heads.

"Breaker was issued a challenge, but he made the challenge for the next day. We all show up to it, and the challenger is already dead," Verkor states.

"Yes, he kills them beforehand, but he's not doing it alone.

He has his Enforcers or Cain and Jett, bring the challenger to the pack house. We all know about the torture room. I've spent most of my life trying to stay out of it. Anyway, the challenger is tied up in that room, beaten, and tortured to death. Then the next day, Breaker parades them around like he's proud of what he's doing."

"We saw proof of that the other day," I say. "How did you find out? We were merely speculating what was happening?"

"Nothing stays a secret. One of his Enforcers let it slip one night what was actually going on."

"Breaker is such a tool," Stolas interjects.

"You won't get any disagreements from me," Gemma says.

"Do you know why everyone is hiding?" Verkor inquires.

"Everyone there tries to stay to themselves. Less you're seen and heard, the better off you are. That doesn't always work." Gemma leans forward, laying her crossed arms on the picnic table.

"Why hasn't the entire region come together to overthrow him?"

Gemma laughs, but it's hysterical. It's that you have to be crazy kind of laugh. "I'm sure they thought about it, but fear is a powerful thing. Or haven't you noticed?" she says once she's done laughing. "If there is one thing that I'm glad has happened, is you getting the hell out of that place. I may not know a lot about your life now, but you seem to be doing well for yourself. Your mate and friends truly care about you. I can see it in their eyes."

"We do," Finley says, interlacing our fingers together.

"They're protective. You need people in your life like that. Realms know you didn't have that here. I know you said you didn't want to talk about your parents, but just know they got what was coming to them."

"Breaker told me he killed them. I was going to ask if that was true, but you're statement cleared that up for me." I look in

Gemma's eyes, there are tears threatening to fall. "I went to their house," I say. I shift my gaze away from Gemma. Finley squeezes my hand. "Everything looked the same. It was as if no time had passed since the day I left. When I walked through the front door, I was assaulted with the memories I worked so hard to forget." I look back to Gemma, purposely meeting her eyes as I say my next words. "I'm not sorry that they're gone. I'm sorry I wasn't here to see it. I'm sorry I wasn't here to do it myself. I'm sorry I didn't get to tell them how I truly felt about them."

Finley lets go of my hand and stands so she can wrap her arms around my neck. Finley lets go of me while I move so that my back is to the table. Grabbing Finley by her hips, I sit her in my lap. Her head immediately goes to my chest, nuzzling it. I lean down, burying my nose in her hair, breathing in her scent. I place a hand on her belly, rubbing back and forth. I'm rewarded with a little kick against my palm, and I smile into Finley's hair.

I glance over to Gemma. Tears are falling from her eyes, and the biggest grin I've seen is on her face. It doesn't take long before Stolas and Verkor are in front of me. Stolas is fidgeting. My guess is it has to do with Finley being upset. Stolas drops to his knees in front of Finley, rubbing his hands up and down her legs.

"Oh Obsidian, I'm so happy for you," Gemma says between sobs. Gemma leans over, placing a hand on top of Finley's head, and placing a kiss on my cheek. "You have grown into such a wonderful man, despite what happened to you. I'm proud of you. You didn't let this place consume you. You have risen and become so much more."

"That he has," Finley agrees.

"I have one more question," I say. "What's the deal with the Super Blood Moon party? We overheard someone asking if Breaker picked anyone yet."

Gemma sighs. "Breaker likes to take the strongest shifter,

torture him, then throw his still bleeding body in a bonfire. It's his way of keeping the others in line. I suspect that magic is involved, but I've never been able to confirm it. At the very least, it's his way to stay as Packmaster. No one will challenge you if you just keep killing everyone before they can kill you."

"Breaker is truly a psychopath," Finley states.

"You're not wrong. That's why I got out. I left in the middle of the night and never looked back. This region is much better than Breaker's. The Packmaster here is caring, kind, and generous. He welcomed me with open arms. I told him what was going on and he said he would protect me if Breaker ever came looking for me. So far, he has kept his word. I even have a bed and breakfast that I run here. Next time you're here, you'll have to come by and see it."

"We will," I say. That's a huge step for me, saying that I will eventually come back here.

"And as much as I would like to keep talking to you, I have to get back," Gemma stands giving a kiss on the cheek. "It was good seeing you again. Don't be a stranger." She smiles, waves, and walks away. I'm glad I got to see her again. I'll be back... eventually.

CHAPTER 19

STOLAS

"Is there anything else we need to do here? Anything you guys want?" I ask, as we start to walk through the crowd.

"I need to go into the woods and see if there are any animals that I can get meat from," Obsidian states. "I have some in my pouch," he pats the bag on his side, "...but I'd like one or two more."

"I don't understand why you don't just shift into Abaddon. You said you haven't eaten any other meat and can still turn into him, right?" Finley questions. He nods his head.

"Yeah, but these are shifters and turning into a demon would be an unfair advantage. If I'm going to fight them, I'll do it as one of them." She nods in understanding. Obsidian stops and looks at me and Verkor. "Do you guys think you can keep her out of trouble for an hour?" Finley scoffs. Obsidian looks down at her. "Don't give me that. You get yourself into more trouble than anyone I know." She opens her mouth, but he raises his hand and sighs. "I don't trust anyone here and I want to make sure that you're safe. It'll be easier for you guys to blend in here at the market, in a crowd, than out on a dirt path waiting for me to come back out of the forest. There's no way I want you back in Breaker's region without me."

She sighs, knowing that he's right. "I'll be on my best behavior, I promise."

"We'll keep her out of trouble," I say, placing an arm around her shoulders, tugging Finley into my side. Obsidian rolls his eyes then looks at Verkor.

"Make sure they stay out of trouble."

"I will," Verkor states. Obsidian nods, leans down, and places a kiss on her forehead.

"I'll be back in an hour. Meet me at the market entrance," Obsidian states before turning and heading in that direction. Finley stares at me as Verkor steps up to my other side.

"What are we going to do now?" she asks. I look over to Verkor who shrugs his shoulders.

"Why don't we just walk around, see what they have going on here."

We walk around for about fifteen to thirty minutes, just taking everything in. Everyone in this region is excited and bustling around, preparing for the Super Blood Moon. This is what should be happening in Breaker's region.

"Wait here," I say to Verkor and Finley.

"Why?" Finley asks.

"I'm going to ask someone here about the Super Blood Moon party. I'm curious to see how they celebrate, or how it's supposed to be celebrated," I say.

"Do you think it would be better if I did it?" Finley questions. "I'm a woman, less threatening looking."

I snort. "Love, if they really knew you, no one would think that." Finley smiles and rolls her eyes.

"But still, I might be the better option."

She's probably right, but I want to keep her out of this as much as possible, which is hard to do with Breaker's obsession.

"Let me try, and if it doesn't work, I'll let you try." She huffs at my answer.

"How about we go over there and get some dessert?" Verkor says. Finley's eyes light up.

"Fine," she states.

Verkor offers her his arm. Finley loops her arm around his and I watch as he guides her a few stalls over. I look around trying to spot someone I could talk to but no one looks good.

"Fuck it," I say to myself. I walk up to the nearest stall and step up next to a person who's looking at some daggers. He glances over at me but goes back to perusing the weapons.

"You got something to say?" he questions.

"Actually, I have some questions if you'd be willing to answer them." He turns towards me, crossing his arms over his chest. The muscles in his arms bulge.

"It depends on what it's about." He narrows his eyes at me.

"It's about the region next to this one, Breaker's," I say.

"What about it?" he asks, raising an eyebrow.

"Have you ever been over there?"

"A handful of times. Got out of there as fast as I could. There's something strange going on over there."

"I noticed that too," I state.

"Why don't you cut to the chase and ask me what you want?" I like his no nonsense attitude.

"A friend of mine grew up in that region. He hasn't been back for some years, and he said things have gotten worse since he was last there. Anyway, we've been invited to the Super Blood Moon party tomorrow night, but no one there is acting like these people are. Everyone is hiding, no one's talking about it, no one's excited."

"And you want to know if I know anything about it?" he asks.

"Yeah. No one there will talk to us. They're all afraid of

their Packmaster and after seeing and hearing some things, I can't say that I blame them."

He chuckles. "Can't say that I'm surprised. Everyone in this region tends to avoid going over there. Word travels fast, especially when the shifters over there are trying to seek refuge over here. But, to answer your question, there's a rumor going around that more than a celebration goes down the night of the party."

My eyebrows furrow trying to play it off like I don't know what he's talking about. "Do you know what happens? My friend said it wasn't something that was celebrated when he was younger."

"Maybe in his region, but in mine it's always been celebrated. It happens so rarely that we use it to ask for good health, good harvest, and some ask for help financially or help getting pregnant. Whatever you may be struggling with in life, we use it as a way to ask for guidance and pray that it leads us in the right direction to achieve what we want."

"That seems harmless enough," I say. He nods in agreement.

"It is." He shrugs his shoulders. "I used to see it as a reason to party."

"Do you know what happens in Breaker's region? Why don't people celebrate it?" I ask.

"They used too, but rumor has it they use it as a way to kill the strongest shifter."

"Like a sacrifice?" I question. He shakes his head.

"No, more like to keep Breaker as Packmaster because he's weak and knows he wouldn't win a challenge."

"That actually makes a sick sort of sense. He was issued a challenge and mysteriously the challenger ended up dead before it could take place," I state.

"Doesn't surprise me."

I sigh. "Yeah, well thanks."

"No problem, man. I hope things turn around for them.

That region hasn't had the best luck with Packmasters." I nod my head in agreement.

He turns back to the stall going back to what he was doing before I interrupted him. I scan the crowd looking for Finley and Verkor. I look over to the stall I last saw them but they aren't there. I glance at every stall close to me searching for Finley's pink hair. Finally, I spot it off to the side. I start to walk in that direction, never taking my eyes off of her. I watch as she smiles at something Verkor tells her. Then she steps closer to him, wrapping her arms around him, hugging him close. Verkor encircles her with his arms, and the look on his face, I shake my head and smile. He's a total goner. I'm sure I have the same lovesick, dopey look on my face any time Finley is in my arms, or around me. I hang back for a moment, giving them some more time and space. I don't want to intrude.

Finley pulls back, looking up at Verkor. They smile at each other and he leans down, kissing her. I don't feel jealous but watching them makes me want to join. I wonder if Finley would be interested in being shared. None of us guys have talked about it, but I wouldn't be opposed. Out of Verkor and Obsidian, Verkor would be the one that would share. Obsidian is too possessive, too alpha. I'll have to bring it up to Verkor somehow, but it wouldn't hurt to test the waters.

I close the distance between Verkor, Finley, and myself. I walk right up behind her, placing my hands on her hips. I feel her stiffen, before relaxing. I press my chest to her back, effectively sandwiching her. I look over her shoulder and meet Verkor's eyes. He quirks one eyebrow. I smile and shrug my shoulders. He gives me a slight nod. I lean down, peppering kisses along her neck. Verkor does the same on the other side.

"Stolas. Verkor." Finley says breathlessly.

"Are you enjoying this, love?" She moans in response. "I'm going to take that as a yes." I press my hardening cock into her ass, which presses her tighter into Verkor. I place my mouth next to Finley's ear. "Have you ever thought about being between the middle of us?" I whisper.

"Yes," she replies. I grind against her a little more at her words. Both Finley and Verkor moan.

"What the hell are you doing?" Obsidian's voice bellows.

I look over at him. He's only a few steps away from us, fists clenched at his sides. Anger is plastered on his face and radiating from every pore of his body.

"We weren't doing anything, yet." I give Obsidian a salacious grin. He takes a step closer to me. "Relax, we weren't doing anything inappropriate. I would never put Finley in that position."

I kiss the side of Finley's neck one more time before pulling away from her. She whimpers, and I want nothing more than to go back to what we were doing, but behind closed doors and preferably in a bed. She looks over her shoulder at me and the lust, the desire, I see swirling in her gray eyes is calling me back in. The only thing that stops me is the sound of Obsidian's voice.

"I thought I told you to wait by the entrance," Obsidian growls. I look back to Obsidian. I didn't think his body could get any tenser, but it does. His body is practically vibrating with repressed rage.

"We got a little distracted," I say sheepishly. Which is the wrong thing to say, because Obsidian now looks a half a second away from trying to kill me.

"Siddy," Finley's sweet voice calls out. She walks right up to Obsidian. She lifts her hands, placing them flat against his chest. "We're sorry that we weren't waiting for you at the entrance. We lost track of time. Stolas went around asking for some information and Verkor was feeding me." She runs her hands over his chest. "I promise it won't happen again. If we agree to something, I'll make sure it happens." She wraps her arms around his waist, nuzzling her face against his chest. It takes a little while but eventually Obsidian relaxes and hugs her in return.

"When I didn't see you there, I started to worry. I thought the worst could have happened to you. I started storming through this place looking for you." Obsidian pulls back looking Finley in her eyes. "When I do find you, you're in the middle of some threesome out in public where everyone could see you. All of you were so distracted that I could have killed you." Obsidian runs his fingers through his hair, and then over his beard. "We have no idea if one of Breaker's men is roaming around. You can't let your guard down... ever." He looks over Finley's shoulder, meeting my eyes, then shifts his gaze to Verkor. I sigh because I know he's right, but I'm also sure he's going to yell at us more when he gets the chance.

"I did find out some information," I say, hoping to slightly make up for the fact that we could have placed ourselves in danger because we were thinking with our dicks and vagina instead of our heads.

"Tell us back in our room. Like I said, we don't know if any of Breaker's guys are here. It wouldn't surprise me if they were," Obsidian states. I nod.

"Did you get what you needed?" I ask. All of us start walking back to the bed and breakfast.

"Yeah," he answers. He reaches out grabbing Finley's hand, pulling her closer to him. The rest of the walk back to our room is down in silence.

VERKOR

The moment we stepped into the bed and breakfast, something felt off to me, like a crawling under my skin. As we walk over to the stairs, the feeling gets worse, and a soft thump sound comes from above us. We all freeze and look toward the ceiling. I meet Obsidian's eyes.

"Everyone be quiet as we go upstairs," Obsidian whispers.

He takes the lead, with Stolas following him, then Finley, and me bringing up the rear. I glance over my shoulder, quickly scanning the room to make sure no one is coming up behind us. We're all up the stairs in no time. There's another thump sound, but closer. Obsidian holds up his hand and we all pause on the landing. He turns to face us.

"Stolas with me. Verkor you stay here and guard Finley. Make sure no one creeps up on us from behind," Obsidian whispers. I nod. I see Finley getting ready to argue, but I place my hand on her shoulder, giving it a little squeeze. Now is not the time.

Obsidian and Stolas continue down the hall, silently making their way towards our room. I guide Finley over to the nearest wall. It's better to have our back protected. I position us so we have a clear view if someone is coming up the stairs, but we'd see them before they saw us. Plus, we'll see if anyone comes out of any of the other rooms. We can also stop anyone who might get past Stolas or Obsidian.

I glance down the hall and see that Obsidian and Verkor are stopped right outside of our room. Obsidian's fists clench at his sides. Someone is in there. Both Stolas and Obsidian let out low growls, before charging into the room. You can hear the signs of a struggle. A thump, the sound of glass breaking, and scuffling.

"I dare you to move," Obsidian's voice booms. A second later, Stolas' head pops out of the doorway.

"Come on guys," he says before disappearing back into the room. Finley and I make our way down the hall and into the room.

My eyes survey the room. Our bags were dragged out of the closet and our clothes thrown all over the room. The lamp that was on the nightstand, now lays broken on the floor. Finley's violin case is open on the bed. She immediately goes to check on it. Stolas is leaning on the wall by the closet, while Obsidian has his eyes locked on some guy in a chair. He's small and scrawny with beady little eyes. His hair is unkempt and so are his clothes. His face is bruised and there's blood pouring from his nose.

"What the hell were you doing in our room?" Obsidian growls. The guy looks like he's going to argue with him but thinks better of it when Obsidian leans down, getting right in his face.

"I-I was sent here," the guys stammers.

"By who?"

The guy gulps before answering. "Breaker." Obsidian stands, taking a few steps back before releasing a roar. The guy whimpers and throws his arms up shielding his head.

"Why?" Obsidian questions. The guy peeks from between his arms before lowering them.

"To-to see if I could find anything in your room. He wanted to know if there was some other reason you came here."

At this, Finley moves and goes right to her bag, but it's empty. She rummages through our belongings that spilled out all over the floor, until she finds a thin black envelope. It's the size of a piece of paper. She opens it and releases a sigh. She looks over at me and nods. The map is safe. We should have known better than to leave it behind.

"Did you take anything?" Obsidian growls. The guy shakes his head furiously.

"No-no. All I found was some daggers and a bag with some jewelry in it."

"Did you take the jewelry bag?" Finley asks as she walks over to the guy.

"It-it's in my pocket," he replies. Finley goes to search the guy, but Obsidian stops her, grabbing her wrist. She looks back at him, narrowing her eyes.

"Let Stolas look," Obsidian says. "We don't know if there is something else he's hiding." She nods, taking a step back to stand next to him.

Stolas moves from his spot by the closet and stops in front of the guys. "Stand up," Stolas says. A plume of smoke pours from his nose. He's pissed.

The guy stands. There's not much to check. He's wearing a holy shirt and jeans that look two sizes too big. I watch as Stolas pats him down, stopping at the guy's back pocket. Stolas pulls out the small black velvet bag that Finley uses to carry around jewels that she barters and trades with. Stolas doesn't stop until he has patted the guy completely down, finding nothing else on him. Once he's done, he steps back, handing Finley her bag and goes back to his position by the closet.

Finley looks through the bag. "Everything is here," she states.

"How long were you in here?" I ask. He got Finley's jewel bag, but not the map? The guy looks over at me, noticing me for the first time. I haven't moved from blocking the door.

"I-I don't know, maybe ten, fifteen minutes," he replies.

"Did you see anything else of interest while you were searching?" I question.

"No-no."

I don't believe him. I think he saw the torn paper, but when he saw there was nothing on it, he thought it was useless. I know the second that he leaves here he's going to run right to Breaker and spill what he saw.

"What did Breaker promise you in return?" Obsidian interjects.

"He told me that my debt to him would be paid for after this, and I wouldn't have to run errands for him anymore." Obsidian starts to laugh, and I mean laugh to the point he's hunched over with his hands on his knees. Once he gathers himself, he looks the guy right in his eyes.

"Oh, you're so stupid," Obsidian states. "Do you really think that Breaker is going to let you go?" Obsidian shakes his head. "No, he was hoping one of two things would happen. Either we found you and killed you, or you found something of interest here, took it back to him, and then he would kill you. You are expendable to him, everyone is. We're not going to kill you, but Breaker will when you go back empty-handed. I would tell you to run, but I bet you someone is waiting and watching for you." The guy starts to shake with fear. "If there's a back way out of here, you better take it and run as far and as fast as you can. Now." The guy doesn't wait another moment. I step to the side letting him leave. I close the door once he's gone.

Stolas and Finley start picking up our clothes, inspecting them for damage. The whole room is quiet, none of us talking, until I break the silence.

"Does anyone else think that it's weird he just wrote off the map like it was nothing?"

I walk over to where Finley is sitting on her knees folding clothes. I hold out my hand to her. She doesn't need to be doing this. There are three of us here. She places her hand in mine and I help her to her feet. I guide her over the bed.

"Sit, I'll get it, baby."

"I'm more than capable of folding clothes and cleaning." Finley narrows her eyes at me and crosses her arms under her chest.

"I know that," I say. "But you and I both know that Obsidian is just going to redo everything."

It's my excuse just to get her to rest. She's still doing jobs when we're not hunting down map pieces, and she barely lets any of us go with her. We're always worried something is going to happen to her. We all know she can take care of herself, but we're her mates and it's ingrained in our very souls to protect her. Besides, we still have to go over our plans for tomorrow night, and I know she mentioned playing her violin. I don't want her to over stress herself. It's not good for her or the baby.

"Fine," she huffs, breaking through my thoughts.

I go over to where she was cleaning and take over. I've been working with Obsidian long enough to know I can just fold the clothes and gather the supplies, placing them in neat piles, and he will still refold them.

"To answer your question," Obsidian starts. "I don't think he knew exactly what he was looking at. The map is empty, and a corner is missing. When you look at it, it looks like the corner was torn off. Still, with it being in an envelope and not just laying around, you would think that he would have realized that there is something special about the paper."

"Yeah, but he didn't look like he was the brightest crayon in the box. I mean, he took the jewels because he knows he can sell them and get money from it. Without actually knowing that the paper he was looking at was a map, he probably didn't think he could get something from it," Stolas says.

"Do you really think Breaker sent him here?" Finley asks.

"I do," Obsidian nods. "I'm surprised he waited this long."

"I don't think there was any other time he could have done it," I state. "Since we've been here, we haven't been gone from this room more than a few hours. Today was the first day we weren't close by."

"Do you think that he has someone watching us?" Finley questions.

Obsidian shrugs his shoulders. "He could, but if that is the case, then he could have sent that guy in here the second we walked back toward the gateway."

"Do you think Maxwell could have told him? I mean, does anyone else think it's weird that we haven't seen or heard from him since we arrived?" Finley asks.

"Someone has to be here, there's breakfast food available in the mornings," Stolas says.

"Yeah, but that could just be the cook doing his job," I reply.

"You don't think Breaker did something to him, do you?" Finley inquires.

"I don't think so. I think he would want to keep him here to keep an eye out on us. If he got to him, it would be for his benefit. He clearly knows where we've been staying, because he keeps sending you gifts," Obsidian growls. None of us are happy about that. "He has a virtual spy with Maxwell."

"Do you think he would sell you out?" I ask.

"I think he would for the right price or if there was something else Breaker was threatening him with," Obsidian replies.

I groan, running my fingers through my hair. I stand, leaving the neat piles of clothes and supplies on the floor. I sit on the edge of the bed with Finley, and Stolas sits on the bed across from us. Obsidian makes his way over to the piles, grabs our bags, and starts sorting through everything. The second that he starts to refold the clothes, a snort escapes Finley. I look over at her, meeting her eyes.

"You were right," she states with a smile and a shake of her head.

I smile back and lift a shoulder. I know Obsidian like the back of my hand. We've been friends for years now. You get to know the little things about people the longer you know and work with them. It's the same way with Stolas.

"The longer you're around us and working with us, you'll start to pick up on those things as well." She nods her head.

"Well, if there is anything that we have learned in all our years doing what we do, is that someone can almost always be bought for the right price," Stolas interjects. He's not wrong. We've seen it happen more often than not. "Since this isn't getting us anywhere, how about I tell you about the rumor circulating at what Breaker does at the Super Blood Moon party."

· · ·

OBSIDIAN

My anger about not seeing them at the entrance to the market has finally subsided. At first, I thought maybe I was early, but when I checked the time, I saw that I was late by ten minutes. Panic started to fill me. The worst thoughts filtered through my mind, and I had to take a few deep breaths not to go on a rampage. I made a plan to search the market first, ask if anyone saw them, and if they weren't there, then I would go on a murderous rampage.

Imagine my surprise when I found them in some corner practically having a threesome out in public. Okay, I can admit to myself that they weren't having a threesome, but they were a little too handsy and none of them were looking at their surroundings. They were too preoccupied with each other and that is when danger can strike. I was pissed that they would risk their safety.

I grab the nearest bag by me, which is Stolas', and I start to refold, repack, and organize his things. I'm a little obsessive over it, but this will also tell me if anything was taken, damaged, or needs to be replaced. Plus, it keeps me from tearing through the town. I can focus my time and energy into this.

"So," Stolas' voice captures my attention. "I talked to this guy who lives in the region next to this one. I asked him if he knew why no one here in Breaker's region was happy and excited about the Super Blood Moon party, and why it is that they celebrate because my friend who lived here as a kid said they never did before."

"What did he say?" Verkor asks.

"He said this area used to celebrate it; I'm guessing a long ass time ago because he said his region has always celebrated it. They use it as time to ask for help and guidance if they are struggling. They pray for good health, good harvest, maybe for a job to help ease their financial burdens, that sort of thing. He said the rumor going around about this region is that they use it as a time to kill the strongest shifter."

"That's what that guy in the next region said," Stolas interjects.

"That's what I asked. But he said they do it as a way to ensure that Breaker stays Packmaster because he's too weak to win a challenge."

I snort at this because we already figured that out. A challenge was issued, and that person mysteriously turns up dead before it takes place. It's not hard to put two-and-two together. I finish with Stolas' bag and start on Verkor's as the conversation continues.

"Okay, but how is he picking them? Why bother? If they challenge him, he ends up killing them anyway," Finley inquires.

"Maybe it's a way to keep the shifters here in line. Why would anyone want to risk fighting him when they know what the outcome will be?" Verkor asks.

"There has to be more to it than that," Finley says. I look up, glancing at each of them. They all have a look of confusion on their faces. "I guess we could always ask him." I laugh.

"Doll, what makes you think he would tell us anything?" I ask.

"He would tell us anything we wanted if I can get him in a trance. You saw what happens to people when I play. I could ask them to do anything and they would willingly. So, while we have him giving us the last piece of the map, we can ask him questions and he would spill everything," she states. It's not a bad idea, but one of us will have to be there with her.

"On that note, what is our plan for tomorrow?" Stolas questions.

I go back to packing Verkor's bag, because I need to keep busy. I know Finley is going to suggest playing her violin and as much as I hate the idea, it's our best option.

"I'm Breaker's guest," Finley states. "I'll wear the dress he sent and my boots there and try not to raise any suspicions."

"That will be hard to do, because we all know that the shifter that was here isn't going to make it through the night, and he will know that we know he sent someone looking through our things. If you go in there and pretend like nothing happened, that might make him more suspicious than you questioning him on why he did it," I interject. I finish up with Verkor's bag and start working on Finley's.

"What should we do?" Finley probes.

"I think you have to be the one to question him about it as much as I hate the idea," I utter. "If anyone but you does it, he'll take it as a challenge. If you do it, he might be more willing to give you an answer. Plus, you can use that opportunity to ask if you can play your violin. I doubt he would deny you anything," I say with a bite to my voice. I really hate all the attention he's been giving her. I want to rip his throat out. I want to feel the warmth of his blood coat my hands and watch as the life leaves his eyes.

"Okay," Finley voices, bringing me back from my spiraling dark thoughts.

"One of us will have to be nearby. I don't want you anywhere by him alone," I state.

"Agreed," Finley says.

"So, Finley will go up to Breaker, ask why he sent someone looking through our things, ask to play her violin, put everyone in a trance, then..." Stolas trails off.

"Then we tell everyone to stay where they are, and I ask Breaker to take me to where he's keeping the map. On our way we can ask him anything we want, and he'll answer," Finley says.

"Don't forget that line of the poem," Verkor states. We all look at him. "We're going to have to prepare to fight."

"Right," Finley sighs. "Once I have the dress on, I'll see where I can hide some daggers or blades. Obviously, Stolas can shift into his hellhound, Verkor can use the shadows, and what are you going to turn into, Obsidian?"

"I found a bear. There were other animals, but they were too small," I respond.

"I still think you should just shift into Abaddon," Stolas states.

"I could, but what would be the fun in that," I say, grinning. "Besides, I only need to fight Breaker long enough that he won't be able to fight back. I'll drag his body out in view of everyone and let one of them finish him off."

"Well, okay then. What are you guys going to be doing when I have Breaker take me to the map?" Finley questions.

"We'll be with you," I say. She opens her mouth to argue, but I hold up my hand, stopping her. I shake my head. "Don't even suggest that we let you go anywhere with the piece of shit alone. You'd have to be out of your damn mind if you think that we would allow that."

Finley narrows her eyes at me. "All of you can't come with me. Someone has to stay behind."

"Why?" Verkor asks. Finley looks at him, opening and closing her mouth. "You can't come up with a good reason," he states.

"You're going to spell everyone and you're going to order them to stay put," Stolas interjects.

"Yeah, but how long everyone stays in the suggestive state varies. Some break out of it faster than others," Finley declares.

"So," Stolas states with a shrug of his shoulders. "One of us will go in the house with you and the other two can stand guard outside of the door. We can head off anyone who tries to get in."

"It's not a bad idea," Verkor agrees. Finley's shoulders slump in defeat for a brief moment, but she quickly regains her resolve.

"Fine. Who is going in with me?" she inquires.

"I will," I say in a matter-of-fact tone. She nods.

"Are we done planning, because I'm tired and we all know something will go down tomorrow that's out of our control," Finley says rubbing her temples.

"Yeah, love, we're done," Stolas says softly. He walks over to his bag and pulls out one of his t-shirts before he strolls over to Finley, holding the shirt out to her. "Here, go get changed and I'll cuddle with you." Finley takes the shirt and nods. We all watch as she walks to the bathroom, closing the door behind her. Verkor lets out of breath. Stolas and I turn to look at him.

"Is something wrong?" Stolas questions.

"No," Verkor replies. "I'm just worried about her and the toll all of this is having on her, her body, and the baby."

"Why? Has she said something?" I ask. Verkor shakes his head.

"No, but would she?"

That's a good question, and one we don't get to remark on because Finley comes out of the bathroom.

"I'm so tired," she says with a yawn. I walk over to her, grabbing her clothes from her hands.

"Come on, doll. Let's get you into bed."

I follow behind her, watching her as she crawls into bed. Stolas climbs in on the side, pulling Finley into his arms. She snuggles into his embrace and sighs.

"Night guys," she says with another yawn. "Love you," she whispers.

I walk over to her side of the bed, lean down, and place a kiss on her forehead. She smiles. "Night, doll. I love you."

I straighten and move over to her bags. Verkor takes the spot I was just in, giving her a kiss on the cheek, murmuring a goodnight and I love you. Stolas does the same. Finley's eyes close and in a matter of moments she's out.

She looks so peaceful and beautiful. I don't know how my angry ass got so damn lucky with her. I will do everything to keep her safe, even from my demons who haunt me. I hated the idea of coming back here. I didn't want to expose Finley to anything from my past. In some ways it's been good for me. I'm finally realizing that this place, even with all it's bad memories, should no longer hold so much over me. Did it shape me into the person I am tonight? Yes. But where would I be if I had caved into everything they did to me?

I didn't let them break me then, and I refuse to let the memories and the games they're playing break me now. It's time I let go of all this. I have so much more to look forward to. I have a mate and a baby on the way. I have two best friends, a roof over my head, and a job I love. It's time I start thinking and living that way. It's about time I let all of this go and leave it all behind me. At this moment, I finally feel free of this place and its people. It feels like a huge weight has been lifted off my shoulders. It's the best feeling in the world.

CHAPTER 20

FINLEY

I woke up to find myself in the middle of a hot man sandwich and it's not something I'm mad about. Stolas is on one side and Verkor is on the other. My mind drifts to yesterday at the market when they were both touching and kissing me. I would love to pick up where we left off, but we have a lot to do today. So when we get home, it's high on my list of priorities. As much as I would love to stay in this meat sandwich, my bladder is screaming at me.

I untangle my legs from theirs and gently move their hands from my hip. It takes a little bit of wiggling, but I manage to get from between them. I crawl on my hands and knees to the foot of the bed and climb off. I glance over to the other bed and see that Obsidian is already awake. His back is against the headboard with his feet stretched out in front of him. His arms are crossed, resting against his tattooed chest. I lick my lips at the sight of him half-naked in bed.

"See something you like, doll?" he asks.

His voice is husky, either from just waking up not long before me or from lust and desire. Obsidian is sporting some serious bedroom eyes. They're slightly hooded and devouring my body from head to toe. That look sets my body aflame. I give him the same look in return, because I can't be the only one this flustered and turned on first thing in the morning.

"Always," I reply. A sexy half grin crossed his lips. "What are you doing up so early?" I ask, changing the subject before I jump him. I walk over to the bathroom door, pausing with my hand on the door handle as Obsidian answers my question.

"Thinking about today," he replies.

"Give me one second," I say.

I go into the bathroom and do what I have to do. When I'm done, I open the door to see that Obsidian hasn't moved and Verkor and Stolas still aren't awake. I wonder how long they stayed up after I went to sleep. I crawl into bed with Obsidian, snuggling up against his side. He wraps an arm around my shoulders, pulling me closer, then kisses the top of my head.

"Are you worried about what's going to happen?" I ask.

"I'm mostly worried about you," he responds. "There are a lot of what if's running through my mind. I thought I knew how Breaker and the rest of them were going to react when I came back, but I was wrong." I start tracing the outline of one of his tattoos but continue to listen to him. "I of all people should know how much someone can change as they get older. I'm not that same little kid that used to live here, and I should have known they would change as well. Clearly, not for the better."

"Is this what has you worried?"

"Yeah," he says with a sigh. "The majority of our plan rests on your shoulders and I don't like it. We don't know if Breaker will succumb to the spell. If he does, then great, but if he doesn't..." Obsidian trails off. I move my head back so I can look him in the eyes.

"If it doesn't, we'll find another way. We'll get what we came for. We were destined for this." Obsidian raises an eyebrow at my words.

"I thought you didn't believe you were the descendant of the Supreme Ruler?" he questions.

"At first, I didn't. But, the further along we get in this journey and the closer we get to having completed the map the more I've started to think it's a possibility. I mean, we could be wrong and we're just some lucky ass people who were in the right place at the right time, but... what if it's true?" I move my head back down, going back to outlining one of his tattoos.

"If it's true, then we will deal with what comes with that when we have to," he replies. I nod my head against his shoulder.

"Guys, it's too early for all this serious talk," Stolas whines.

I look over and see him lift the blanket over his head. I giggle. Verkor shifts, stretching as he does. The blanket covering him moves down a little bit, putting his toned chest on display. I am one lucky ass girl. My men are hot. I meet Verkor's sleepy gaze. He grins at me and winks. I roll my eyes but smile in return. They know they're hot and what seeing their naked bodies do to me. Verkor gets out of bed and makes his way to the bathroom. Stolas rolls over, moving the blanket from his head.

"Why are you way over there, love?" he asks. He lifts the blanket. "Come back over here."

"We need to eat and get ready for later," Obsidian states.

"Ugh, just a few more minutes," Stolas huffs, dropping his arm and blanket back down onto the bed.

"Did you stay up late last night?" I ask. I push myself up onto my knees by using Obsidian's chest.

"Yes."

"Why?" I crawl over Obsidian, but before my feet can touch my floor, a smack lands on my ass. I look over my shoulder and meet Obsidian's amber eyes. There's a half smirk on his face.

"You can't put your ass in the air like that and not expect me to smack it," he says nonchalantly.

It's not the slap to my ass that has me looking back to him. It's the fact he knows how much I like it. I clench my thighs together, trying to assuage the ache growing in my pussy. Obsidian's face changes from the *I want to devour you* look, to the *what are you going to do about it* one. I would love nothing more than for him to tie me up and to feel his cock inside of me, but we don't have time for it.

A soft growl comes from the other bed. I turn my attention to it and see Stolas gazing right at me. I know he can smell my arousal. He's looking at me like a snack, and all it does is heighten my desire more.

"What did I just walk into?" Verkor's voice rings out in the silence of the room.

I finish getting off the bed and gaze in Verkor's direction. Seeing him leaning against the bathroom doorway with his arms crossed over his naked chest, and his sweatpants riding low on his hips, only adds to the sexual tension already in the room.

"Oh, you know just making Finley all hot and bothered," Stolas states with a huskiness to his voice.

"Oh, are we doing that as a team now?" Verkor asks.

I suck in a sharp breath. I know Stolas and Verkor have mentioned wanting to share me at the same time, but they can't mean now. We have so much to do and prepare for, but I want them. All of them.

I glance around the room, meeting each of them in their eyes. Desire and lust are burning in their gazes. Verkor's eyes travel up and down my body. Obsidian has a wicked grin on his face that promises nothing but pleasure. Stolas licks his lips, staring right at the apex of my thighs. I lavish at the attention they're giving me.

"I never took Obsidian as a team player," I say. "At least not in the bedroom."

"Mm, I could be persuaded. I would definitely have to be in charge. I'm sure the guys know what I like in the bedroom. I haven't kept it a secret." Obsidian rises from the bed, and Stolas does the same from the other. The space between the beds is suddenly crowded. Obsidian leans down, whispering in my ear. "Would you like that, doll? Would you like to have all of us touching, kissing, and tasting you?"

I feel my heart pounding in my chest at his words. Hell yeah, I want that more than anything, but if we start that now we won't be leaving this bedroom.

"Oh, I would love that, but now isn't the time or the place to do this," I say, trying to be the reasonable one.

"Probably not, but it's tempting," Verkor says walking closer to the rest of us.

Oh, it's tempting alright. Especially now with all of them surrounding me. I'm half a second away from throwing caution to the wind and giving in to the three-half naked muscular men. But one of us needs to keep our group on track and that looks like it's going to be me.

"Well, how can I resist with such visible stimulation on display?" I reach out, running a finger down Obsidian's bare chest. "I would love spending the day in bed with all three of my mates," I say huskily. I shift slightly, reaching out toward Verkor. I rub my thumb across his nipple, watching it pebble under my touch. "I don't mind staying here longer." I turn my attention to Stolas. I place both of my hands on his chest, running them up and down. "But when we're done, you guys have to help me come up with a new plan on how to get the map from Breaker." That seems to snap them out of their lusty haze, but I keep going. I reach for the hem of the shirt I'm wearing. "How are we doing this?" I don't get far before a pair of hands land on mine.

"We get it," Verkor says, stopping me from lifting my shirt further. My more reasonable mate. I nod at his words.

"Don't get me wrong, this is *so* going to happen, just at our home and when we don't have to worry about crazy Packmasters," I say.

"I'll go and get us breakfast," Stolas states.

"Let's all go. I want to see how everyone is acting today. It's supposed to be some big party happening tonight, everyone should be out getting ready for it," Obsidian responds.

"Well, I call dibs on the bathroom first," I voice, pushing Verkor out of the way.

I walk over to the closet, pulling my bag out. I rummage through it until I find a pair of yoga pants and a plain light blue t-shirt. I enter the bathroom and close the door behind me. I take a deep breath. This is it, if everything works out today then we'll have the last piece of the map. We'll have the map to the hidden treasure the Supreme Ruler left behind. We'll be on our way to maybe finding out where I come from. It's a scary but exciting thought. But I know that what we come across those three men in the next room will be there for me through it all.

STOLAS

It doesn't take long before everyone is ready to go. We're walking down the street with Obsidian in front and Verkor and I crowding Finley in between us. Not surprising, there is no one out on the streets. If anything, it seems quieter. It's eerie. It's like a ghost town.

"Do you think anything is open?" I inquire. Every shop and store we pass looks closed.

"Something better be open. I'm starving," Finley says.

"Let's try the diner that's up the road," Obsidian says. "Even if everyone is scared because of what tonight might signify, someone should still be open if they want to make money."

"What I don't understand is why everyone is hiding. If what

that guy said in the other region is correct, then hiding isn't going to help. Breaker is just going to pick who he thinks is the strongest and try to kill him," Finley voices.

"It could be the out of sight, out of mind thing. If I had to guess, I would think by hiding that they would be forgotten and passed over," Verkor replies.

"Do they honestly think that would work?" Finley asks.

"No," I say. "I think it has more to do with hoping and praying that they or their family member isn't chosen."

"I don't understand how they can live this way. It seems like they are constantly living in fear," she says softly. I hear her sniffle. I wrap my arm around her shoulders, pulling her closer into my side. She lays her head on my shoulder. "Goddamn these hormones." She wipes at her nose. I chuckle.

"Are you going soft hearted on me, love?" I ask with a teasing voice. I place a hand on her belly. A second later I feel a kick against my hand. "That's amazing," I whisper to her. She nods her head against my shoulder.

"I get to feel that all the time. The kicks are getting stronger by the day," she says. I puff my chest out. My hellhound preens in my mind. "Speaking of the baby," she raises her voice, making sure Obsidian and Verkor are listening. "We have an appointment coming up. If the doctor asks, do we want to know what we're having, or do we want to be surprised?"

"What do you want?" I ask.

"I want to know," Finley replies.

"I do too," I say.

"I want to know," Verkor says.

"I as well," Obsidian states.

"Okay," Finley says with a smile. "I can't wait to start getting stuff."

I smile at her excitement, but I also feel a little bad. We haven't gotten to really enjoy this epic moment in our lives.

"We will once everything calms down," I say. She nods in agreement.

We stop in front of the diner and watch as Obsidian opens the door. The bell above it jingles.

"At least they're open," Obsidian says. We walk inside but no one comes out of the back. We wait at the entrance for a few more minutes before seating ourselves.

"Are you sure they're open? Maybe someone left the door unlocked," Finley states as she scoots in the booth after Obsidian.

I inhale deeply, picking up the different scents in the diner. Cleaner is the heaviest scent, but I can pick out at least two people.

"There's two other people here," I state.

"One is peeking out the kitchen window," Verkor whispers. Subtly, I glance over to see a young girl regarding us wearily.

"We're not Breaker, so why is she hiding from us? We don't even work for him. Hell, none of us like him," I say in a raised voice.

It's mostly for the benefit of the girl and whoever else is in the kitchen with her. It takes a few more minutes before she gathers enough courage to come to our table.

"Go-good mo-morning," she stammers. "Wh-what can I-I get for you?"

This girl is terrified. Her hands are shaking, and she can barely write our order. We go around the table, saying what we want, and the second that we're done she takes off. She comes back a moment later with our drinks. She doesn't say anything. She places our cups down and takes back off for the kitchen. We don't see her again until our food is ready. The second she's done passing it out she's gone again.

"I get being afraid, especially if what that guy said in the other region is true, but this is just plain rude," Finley states. "We haven't given them any reason to make them think that we would hurt them." Her voice rises with each word and a plume of smoke escapes her nose.

"That's true, love, but I don't think you getting angry and blowing smoke is going to help the situation. Let's just eat so we can get out of here," I say.

The rest of our breakfast is silent. Once we're done, Verkor gets up from the table, walks over to the counter, and waits for the girl to come out of the back so he can pay for our meal. The wait for that is just as long as it took for her to come out and take our order in the first place. Once that's taken care of, we leave.

We walk around a while longer but the only other place that is open is the grocery store and there was the fewest amount of people working. It's like everyone is hiding. We walk by some of the houses and not a single light is on. There were a few curtains that I saw move, but that's it.

"Well, this is getting us nowhere," Finley states as we walk back toward the bed and breakfast.

We walk the rest of the way back to the bed and breakfast in silence. I keep an ear and eye open, but other than it being quieter than normal, I don't spot or pick up on anything. I glance over to Obsidian and see him scanning everything around us. The scowl on his face deepens. As if sensing that I'm looking at him, Obsidian turns his gaze in my direction. Our eyes meet over Finley's head. He gives a slight shake of his head. He doesn't want to say anything out in the open. I was wondering what he sensed that I didn't?

I inhale deeply, not smelling anything but the usual scents of myself, the others, and outside. Obsidian has the best sight and smell out of all of us. It wouldn't surprise me if he caught something.

Verkor holds open the door, and we all file inside. The silence in the room is broken by Finley yawning.

"Tired, love?" I question. Finley nods.

"Yeah," she says yawning again. "I must be," she yawns again, "...in one of those growth spurts things the doctor mentioned."

"Why do you say that?" Verkor asks, as we walk up the stairs and head to our room.

"Because my muscles and back are sore." She barely gets the words out before yawning again.

"Luckily, this is the last piece of the map. I don't think we can wait a month before following where it's going to lead us," Verkor states. He opens the door to our room and helps Finley get into bed. Her head barely hits the pillow before she out like a light. I shift into my hellhound, jump on the end of the bed and curl up next to Finley's legs. The bed dips form Verkor sitting down on the side of the bed.

"I think you're right. Once this is over and we get back home. We'll take a week, two at the most, to rest before following the map." Verkor nods and I huff my agreement, releasing a little smoke from my nose. Verkor and Obsidian take off their shoes and cuddle up next to Finley. I yawn, closing my eyes, and fall asleep within seconds. My last thoughts before drifting off to sleep is to make sure we keep Finley safe.

CHAPTER 21

FINLEY

The nap earlier did wonders. I woke up feeling refreshed and ready to tackle our plan. I just finished putting my pink hair up in a high ponytail and pulling pieces out by my ears. I give myself a little twirl in the white dress Breaker gifted me. As much as I don't like him, he does have great taste in clothes. I run my hands over the lace covered top. I run my hands over my belly. There's no hiding I'm pregnant in this. The top is to form fitting. I turn to the side and in the mirror, you can see the faux satin ribbon corset back, and my protruding belly. The thin straps of the dress are beaded. The top is simply gorgeous, but my favorite part is the bottom of the dress. I twirl again, watching the flute pointed, white chiffon bottom flare out around my legs. I put on the white crocheted barefoot sandals I bought at the market. I have to say, I love how it looks. It's simple, but elegant.

I meet my gray eyes in the mirror, pleased with the fresh, easy makeup I applied. I don't wear a lot as it is, but we're going down to the beach, and there's supposed to be a bonfire, water and heat just don't mix with makeup. A knock on the door grabs my attention. I'm done getting ready besides my boots, which I plan to take off to walk around in the sand. Luckily, the crocheted barefoot sandals are thin and lay flat and don't give any extra bulk. Otherwise, I couldn't have worn them with my boots.

I open the bathroom door to see Verkor standing before me. He's wearing a blue tank top with a blue button up shirt over top. The shirt is open, and the sleeves are rolled up to his forearms. I lick my lips. Why is a guy exposing his forearms like that such a turn on? I continue my perusal of him. He has on loose fitted black pants that are folded up at the ankle, and he's still barefoot. I could jump him right now. My eyes travel back up his body, meeting the smirk on his face, and the lust in his captivating blue eyes. Neither of us speak as we gaze into each other's eyes.

"Are you guys having a staring contest?" Stolas voice cuts through the silence. "Who's winning? I'm going to say Finley." Verkor sighs and rolls his eyes. I smile, because all of them have picked up that habit from me, and I think it's cute.

"We're not having a staring contest but wait until you see what our mate looks like. She's stunning," Verkor answers. My smile grows wider and I send a wink Verkor's way. I step up closer to him, pressing myself against his chest.

"Maybe once we get home, we can pick up where you, me, and Stolas left off at in the market," I say huskily.

Verkor groans, wrapping his arms around me. He leans down pressing his mouth to mine. He nips at my bottom lip, causing me to gasp. It gives him the opening that he needs to slide his tongue in my mouth. I grab his button up shirt, trying to pull him closer, even though I'm already plastered against him from chest to hip. Verkor is devouring my mouth like it's his last meal.

"Obsidian, you might have to stop them. I don't think either one of them has come up for air," Stolas voices.

"Finley. Verkor," Obsidian growls. "We have some pressing matters to attend to. We are on a timeline here. Places to be, people to kill."

I sigh, knowing that Obsidian is right. I pull back, meeting Verkor's eyes. "We'll finish this later."

I place a quick kiss on his lips, before he steps to the side. He smacks my ass as I pass him. I glance over at him and he winks. I'm sure we could pull a quickie off in the bathroom. I'm just about to go and drag Verkor into the bathroom, when a pair of muscular arms wrap around me, pulling me tight against a firm body. I inhale, and the distinct smell of grass and trees fills my nose, Obsidian. He leans down, placing his mouth next to my ear.

"I can smell your arousal Finley." Obsidian's voice comes out husky. I feel his lips against my neck. He playfully nips at it. "It's the sweetest scent, and if you keep that up, we won't be leaving this room anytime soon."

I suck in a breath at his words. My mind goes right into dirty thoughts of me riding Stolas, Obsidian taking me from behind, and Verkor in my mouth. It's something I desperately want to happen. Preferably, right now.

"Obsidian, you're not helping the situation," Stolas says with a groan.

I glance over at the bed he's lounging on, meeting his lust filled gaze. I can see he's just as affected as the rest of us by the bulge in the front of his pants.

"I know that everyone of us wants to continue this, but we all know none of us want to be here any longer than we have to," Verkor interjects. He's right.

Obsidian places another kiss to my neck before letting me go. I close my eyes and take a couple of deep breaths, trying to calm my raging libido. Once I have myself under some form of control, because let's face it my mates are just too sexy, I open my eyes. My gaze scans them. Verkor now has on shoes. Obsidian and Stolas are wearing something similar to Verkor, but Obsidian is in black and Stolas has on white.

Stolas rolls off the bed and onto his feet. He walks over to the closet and grabs my boots. Obsidian guides me over to the edge of the bed. Stolas moves until he's kneeling in front of me. He picks up my foot, running his fingers up my ankle and calf, and then back down.

"Are you sure you're going to be able to wear your boots and these anklets?" Stolas asks.

"Yeah. I'm not wearing socks and the anklets are pretty thin. Besides, I don't plan on wearing my boots the whole time. I'm going to take them off to walk barefoot in the sand. You know, I've never been to a beach before," I say. I feel all of my guys' eyes on me.

"I'm sorry that you can't really enjoy it this time, but we'll take you to a beach. Perhaps one in the Earth Realm. We'll make sure you get to relax and enjoy it," Stolas states. I glance up briefly meeting his silver eyes. He winks at me, then continues to put my boots on. When he's done, he stands, holding out a hand to me. "Ready?"

"Almost." I walk over to my bag Obsidian packed earlier, grabbing my violin, bow, and the map. After finding someone digging through our things, I don't want to take a chance leaving it behind. I turn and face the guys. "Are we going to leave our bags here?" I don't remember coming up with an idea on where to put them.

"I'm going to bring the bags down with us. There are bushes outside in the front. I can put them there. We have to come by here in order to get back to the gateway. We can grab them on the way. I don't want to stick around any longer than necessary," Obsidian states.

"This plan sounds a lot like the one we did in the Hell Realm," I note. Obsidian shrugs his shoulders.

"Why change something that worked," he says more as a statement instead of a question.

"Well, okay," I respond. "Obsidian, can you hold onto the map?"

"Of course, doll."

He walks over to me and I hand over the map. I watch as he puts in one of the pockets of his cargo pants. Obsidian moves over our bags, rummaging through his. He pulls out his pouch that holds his chunks of meat. He opens it and eats a piece before placing it back in his bag. As he stands, he picks up our bags. Verkor takes a step closer and takes two of the bags. Stolas holds his hand out toward me and I take it, lacing our fingers together.

"Let's get this show on the road," Stolas says with a smile. I smile in return.

VERKOR

It doesn't take us long to hide the bags in the bushes in front of the bed and breakfast and make our way down to the beach. I'm surprised by the amount of people I see. It's more than I've seen the entire time we've been here.

Near the bonfire sits Breaker and his posse. Everyone else is huddled together in groups, staying away from the Packmaster. There's soft music playing, but I don't see where it's coming from. A delicious smell is coming from one of the many grills that are going. A growl sounds from next to me. I look down and see a chagrin look on Finley's face. She rubs a hand up and down her belly.

"Realms, I'm starving," she says. Her hand goes to her lower back, rubbing it.

"Is your back hurting, baby?" I question. She nods looking up at me.

"A little. I'll be fine to play, but I'm looking forward to a few days' rest after this," she replies.

I raise an eyebrow and really look at her. Her belly has definitely grown. There's no mistaking that she's pregnant. Her doctor did say she would experience some growing pains. I'll have to remember to give her a massage once we're home.

"Finley, you look positively amazing," Breaker's voice cuts through the mostly silent party.

I look over at him and see him walking this way. I want to shield Finley by pushing her behind me, but I know I can't. He stops in front of her, eyeing her from head to toe. I hate it. I clench my fists at my sides. He doesn't deserve to look at my mate that way. His gaze stops on her belly and his head tilts to the side. Oh, this can't be good. I look over Finley's head and meet Stolas' and Obsidian's eyes. They both nod and take a step closer to her. I turn my attention back to Breaker. It's like he's just now seeing what was there this whole time.

"You're pregnant," Breaker says with shock in his voice.

I drop my foot back, getting in the fighting stance. I call the shadows to me, feeling them surround my hands. I'm ready, anticipating Breaker's next move.

"I am," Finley replies, tilting her head to the side. The look on her face screams 'and you're just now noticing?' It's not like we've been hiding it.

"Nice. A ready-made family. I can't wait to show this baby all the power it can have," Breaker says with an evil grin.

A loud growl rents through the air. I glance over and see Stolas straining to hold his human form.

"Like hell I'll let you anywhere near my pup." Stolas' voice is more of a deep growl.

"It seems like you've been hiding things from me." His voice is clipped. There's an edge of anger in his tone as well.

"We didn't hide anything from you. Everything was staring you right in your face," Obsidian growls. "You'll have to get through all of us to get anywhere near my mate and pup."

Breaker lets out a high-pitched laugh. "We'll see about that," he says. Stolas moves to take a step toward him, but Finley holds up her hand. Stolas stops, barely. She glances back at him and shakes her head. "What have you got there?" Breaker points to Finley's hand. She lifts it, showing Breaker.

"It's my violin. I thought I would offer to play for you, seeing as how you sent me such beautiful dresses." The tone of her voice is sickeningly sweet, which is completely at odds with the stiff way she's holding her body. A huge grin breaks out of Breaker's face.

"I love that. Come, Finley. Let's sit by the fire and chat for a little bit." Breaker turns and starts to walk back over to the bonfire.

Finley follows behind Breaker, stopping at the edge of the sand. She toes off her boots, leans down, and grabs them. We watch as she takes that first step onto the sand. All of us step next to her. She lifts her head and smiles at each of us before looking back down at her feet. I look down as well, seeing her wiggle her toes.

"How cold do you think the water is?" she asks, looking up toward the water.

"It'll be cold. I wouldn't go swimming, but you can dip your feet in it, then warm them up by the fire," Obsidian answers.

"What's the hold up?" Breaker calls out across the beach. Finley sighs.

"Just the sound of his voice ruins the moment," she says.

Her shoulders drop as she starts walking toward Breaker. We follow right behind her. Finley sits on a log adjacent to Breaker, placing her boots on the sand next to her. She searches around her for a place to set her violin down, and sighs. I know she doesn't want to set it down on the sand. I wish she would have brought her case, but she didn't want to lug it around and then end up having to leave it behind if we have to run out of here. I walk over to her and carefully take the violin and bow from her hand. She gives me a grateful smile. Obsidian comes over sitting next to her. Stolas stops and kneels in front of her.

"Would you like me to get you something to eat?" he asks. Finley's stomach growls at that moment. We all chuckle. "I'll take that as a yes," Stolas says with a laugh. He leans forward giving her a quick kiss, before standing and walking toward the grills. I move to stand behind her.

"I see you have all of them wrapped around your little finger," Breaker voices. Finley looks his way and shrugs her shoulders.

"They are my family. They would do anything for me, just as I would do anything for them," she says in a matter-of-fact tone.

"I like that kind of loyalty. It's rare," Breaker states.

My eyebrows furrow in confusion. Does that mean he doesn't trust those around him? It would be wise, especially if he knew what I overheard between Cain and Jett that one night. Hell, we're planning on taking him down tonight, he just doesn't know it. I hope things turn around for this region. It can be so much more than what it is now.

"Yes, it is," Finley responds, pulling me from my thoughts.

Stolas returns, halting the conversation. He hands Finley a plate piled with different kinds of meat, potato salad, and corn on the cob.

"I got you a little bit of everything. I wasn't sure what you wanted, plus I grabbed a bottle of water for you."

"Thank you, Stolas."

He sits down in the sand in front of her, turning until his back is pressed against her legs. The way we're surrounding her shows we're protecting her and if Breaker tries to do anything, he's going to have to go through us first.

I glance over to Cain and Jett who walk up and sit on either side of Breaker. Cain has a frown on his face, and Jett has a look of deep concentration on his face, like he's not even paying attention to what is going on around him. Breaker is intently focused on Finley, watching her every move. I hate it. I can feel my wings wanting to burst from my back. I want to use them to shield her from his prying eyes. I would like to rip his eyes out, but that has to wait until later. I suck in a sharp breath at my thoughts. I'm never the blood thirsty one, that would be Obsidian, but I can't deny the overwhelming need to protect Finley and our baby with every fiber of my being. I would do anything and everything I can to make sure they are safe.

"Okay, that was good," Finley says, placing her empty plate on the sand next to Stolas. She opens the bottle of water taking a huge gulp. "I need to let this settle before I do anything else." Finley leans back, and I step forward, closing the little bit of space between us. She rests her back against my legs and groans. "I think I ate too much."

Stolas chuckles. "You'll burn that off soon enough."

"Yeah, you're right," Finley giggles. She tilts her head back against my legs, looking up at me. With my free hand, I caress the side of her face and she smiles at me.

My heartbeat starts to beat faster as I gaze into her stormy gray eyes. I love her so much. I can't imagine my life without her in it. She's brought laughter, love, and happiness into our group. I was finally able to confront my past about my mother because she was by my side, lending me comfort and support. She's been doing the same with Obsidian.

He's taken being here in his hometown better than I thought he would. Finley has been here to bring him back when he gets lost in his flashbacks. I can honestly say that neither me nor Stolas would have been able to help him the way she has. Hell, there's no way either of us could have gotten him to come here in the first place. But one pink-haired, tiny female comes dancing into our lives, literally, and turns it upside down. I wouldn't change it for the world. None of us would.

Once we get this last piece of the map, we'll follow wherever it leads us. And we'll do it together.

CHAPTER 22

Obsidian

We haven't been here at the party that long and I'm ready to rip someone apart, more specifically Breaker. The bastard hasn't stopped staring at Finley since she's walked up to the beach. All it makes me want to do is gouge his eyes out. Maybe I'll get to do that later before I let someone else finish him off. I'll keep my fingers crossed. I've been watching Breaker just as intently as he has Finley.

Breaker's face goes from calm to angry in an instant, and I don't like it. I glance over at Finley to see what could cause a change in him, and I see her looking at Verkor with lovesick eyes. Normally, that type of thing would have me rolling my eyes, but I love when she looks at me like that. Is that why Breaker is angry? Is it because of the way she's looking at Verkor and isn't paying him any attention? A slow grin crosses my face. I love it. She doesn't even know she's getting under his skin.

"So, Finley," Breaker voices, trying to get her attention back on him. The thing he doesn't realize is that he doesn't have her attention, at least not in the way that he wants. She turns to look at him. "How long have you played the violin?"

Finley shrugs her shoulders. "Years," she replies.

"Do you enjoy it?" Breaker asks, trying to keep her talking.

"Well, I wouldn't keep doing it if I didn't," she snarks back. Then she sighs, and I know what must be running through her head. She has to be nice to him because we don't know what he's going to do, and we still need something from him. "Sorry," she says. "I love playing. It's the one thing that came naturally to me. It's my happy place," she says with a soft smile.

"You have to hear and see her play. I've never seen someone so in-tune with the music," Stolas states.

"She's a vision," Verkor voices. My gaze shifts to Finley whose cheeks are flushed.

"Well, I definitely need to hear and see you play then," Breaker says with a smile.

"I do have a question," Finley states.

"What's that?" Breaker smiles at her.

"Why was there someone in our room searching our things?" Finley comes right out and asks.

"I don't know what you mean," Breaker says with a shrug.

"There's no point in lying. The shifter we caught told us you sent him."

"You can't blame me for being suspicious. The Berserker never comes back home. Why now? There has to be something more than just showing his mate where he's from. So, I sent someone to look. Lucky for you, he didn't find anything."

"You could have asked," Finley clips out.

"I could have, but would you have told me the truth?" Breaker tilts his head to the side. I'm over this. I'm ready to leave.

Finley glances at each of us, and I see the question in her eyes. Are we ready? I give her a slight nod. We're ready for this. She looks over to Breaker and gives him a forced smile.

"You know what, it's done and over. How about I play my violin for you?" she says.

Finley uses Stolas' shoulders to stand. He moves slightly to let her get around him, and immediately takes the spot she vacates. She turns towards Verkor and he hands her the violin and bow. They search each other's eyes briefly before he releases the violin.

"Can we move the logs back from the fire?" Finley asks, directing her question towards Breaker.

"Of course." Breaker snaps his fingers as he, Cain, and Jett rise from the log that they're sitting on. Two shifters from nearby come rushing over. Breaker points to the logs and says, "Move these logs and put them over there." He points over to the side.

This gives Finley plenty of room to move around the fire and dance, and where the logs are being placed gives Breaker and his lackeys a good view of her front and center. Verkor, Stolas, and I walk over to where Breaker is sitting and stand next to him. We watch as Finley moves in front of the fire, facing Breaker. She glances at us before taking a deep breath. I watch as her shoulders slump, she's relaxing herself, even if she's anything but.

Finley gets into position, putting the violin under her chin and resting the bow on the strings. She stands with one leg in front of the other, crossed at the ankle. She slides the bow across the strings and the first cords of the melody drift through the air. A peacefulness settles across her features. I could sit and watch her play forever.

Finley moves her leg in an arc out in front of her, leaving a line in the sand from her path. Her leg comes to rest next to her other one. She sways her hips in time with the music. Finley turns, walking slowly around the bonfire on the tips of her toes.

I briefly take my eyes off of her to look around. I see more shifters gathering closer to watch and listen to Finley play. Good, the more we put under our trance the better off we'll be. I turn my attention back to my mate. She looks beautiful, almost ethereal, in the blood moonlight. Finley twirls twice, causing the bottom of her dress to flare out around her.

"I love the way her eyes dance in the fire light," Verkor says from beside me.

"She's simply gorgeous," Stolas states with awe in his voice. "I could watch her play all day." I hum at his statement because it echoes a previous thought I had.

"It seems to be working," Verkor utters.

I look over at him and notice that he's looking at Breaker and his posse. I shift my eyes and see that they are becoming spell bound by Finley. I grunt in response. Not wanting to spare another second on Breaker, I move my gaze back to Finley.

She's making another pass around the bonfire, coming close to me and the guys. Our eyes meet and she gives me a wink and smirk. I give her one in return. Finley starts to exaggerate her walk, dragging her toes in the sand, as she gets closer to Breaker. She stands nearby, just playing. The song ends quickly after that, but she doesn't waste any time before she starts playing another.

All of us are captivated by the sight of her. We're some lucky sons of bitches to have her as our mate. The second song isn't as long as the first, but Finley makes sure she's standing in front of Breaker as the song ends. Glancing around the beach, everyone near us is in a trance. I look at Breaker and his crew to see if they are completely under like the rest of them. It looks like they are.

"You know, I'm so glad that we aren't affected by the magic. I don't want to know what it feels like to be that way," Stolas says as he motions to everyone around us. I have to say I agree with that. No one likes to have their free will taken away.

"Are we ready?" I ask gruffly. Both Verkor and Stolas nod.

"Let's do this." I square my shoulders and walk towards Finley with Verkor and Stolas right on my heels.

FINLEY

I love how free I feel when I play, like I was born to do it. Music is my happy place. I can let everything go. It's a way for me to release my emotions. Even though I just played, I'm still filled with rage. It's directed to the person I'm standing in front of me... Breaker. All I want to do is rip his eyes out. I'm angry for Obsidian and the shifters in this region. I don't know how people can treat others this way. Why do people crave power? I don't understand. I hate the power I have over others when I play. I don't like taking away someone's free will, but the other option was force. I don't like to hurt someone unless it's necessary. I would make an exception for him, but I need something from him first. I plaster a smile on my face and look Breaker right in his brown eyes.

"Breaker, would you be willing to get something for me?" I say sweetly. He quickly nods his head.

"Anything."

My smile widens at his words. I move a little closer, bending over slightly to give him a view of the tops of my breasts. Breakers' eyes immediately go there. I have to restrain myself from rolling my eyes. Men, so predictable.

"You see, I'm looking for something and I think that you have it. It's a tan piece of paper and it's ripped. The page is blank on both sides. You wouldn't happen to have seen anything like that would you?" I bat my eyes at him. Breaker nods his head. I stand up straight, and bounce on my toes, making my boobs jiggle. I would clap my hands but can't with me still holding onto my violin and bow. There's a couple of growls that sound from near me, and I know without looking that it's my mates. "Awesome. I need you to take me to it."

Breaker stands and starts walking towards the woods. The guys and I follow right behind him. Verkor stops me right before we step into the woods. He drops my boots by my feet. I smile at him, grateful that he remembered to grab them. They are my favorite pair.

"Thank you." I quickly slip them on and continue to walk after Breaker.

All of us are quiet as we traipse through the woods. The walk goes by quickly and soon we're breaking through the tree line and into the backyard of the pack house. I scan my surroundings, not seeing or hearing anything. We continue to follow him up the steps and through the back door. We make our way through the kitchen and into the living room. Breaker leads us to the door that's under the staircase.

He pushes the door open and switches on the light. He walks around his desk and stops in front of the painting on the wall. Grabbing the corner, Breaker swings the painting open to reveal a safe in the wall behind it. There's nothing special about. It's just a standard wall safe with a dial for the combination lock. Breaker makes quick work of it and rummages through whatever he has in there. A moment later he turns towards us with a piece of the map in his hands. I beam a smile at him.

"Oh, you are a lifesaver. You have no idea how long I've been looking for it," I say sweetly, batting my eyes at him.

I hold out my hand toward Breaker and he places the last piece of the map in it. As much as I would like to revel in this moment, I don't. I hand the map to Obsidian, watching as he puts them in his pocket.

"Thank you, Breaker," I say. I turn to face my guys. "Let's get the hell out of here." They nod in unison. We file out of Breaker's office, but we don't get every far. The sound of growls come from all around us. "I guess the spell wore off."

"You think," Obsidian says snarkily.

"What the hell did you do to me?" Breaker bellows from behind us. I whip around at the sound of his voice.

"We didn't do anything," I say.

"Bullshit," he sneers. There's rage and hate filling his eyes. "Did you really think you were going to get away with this?" Breaker growls. "I should kill you all where you stand." Venom drips from his voice. He turns his attention to my mates. "I'm going to make you watch as I torture her. You're going to have to listen to her screams of pain and there's nothing you can do to stop it or help her. I guess it's my lucky day that not everyone was at the party yet." Breaker's high-pitched laugh bounces off of the walls, before he points to me. "Grab her."

Obsidian roars, the sound of it bouncing off the walls. I turn my head in Obsidian's direction to catch the tail end of him shifting into a giant ass grizzly bear. I'm distracted by watching Obsidian that I don't notice the two shifters that come up behind me. Before I can act, I'm wrapped in a pair of hairy, muscular arms. My gaze shifts around the room and I see that Cain and Jett have Stolas and Verkor preoccupied. I didn't even see them enter the room. My focus was on Obsidian and Breaker, that I didn't see Cain and Jett come in.

"Let me go," I yell. My violin and bow drop from my hands. I hear them hit the ground and wince. I'm probably going to have to get another new one.

I start to kick my legs wildly. It's the part of my body that's free, since my arms are trapped at my sides. Luckily, his arms are around my chest and not my belly. I lean forward as much as my upper body will allow, then I swing my head back, hoping to hit whoever has me in the face. I get lucky and I do. I hear the sick crunch of my captor's nose breaking. The sound is satisfying. Unfortunately, it didn't do anything but make him grunt. His grip doesn't loosen. But one thing is for sure, I'm not going down without a fight.

I double my efforts, trying to wiggle in the tight embrace. I kick my legs wildly, aiming for anything in range.

"Will someone grab her legs?" the gruff voice of my captor says from behind me.

His friend steps forward to do as he asks. I won't make it easy for him. I wait until he's close enough and I strike, kicking him square in the face. The friend stumbles back a few steps as he cries out. His hands go straight to his face. When he catches his balance, there is a promise of retribution in his dark brown eyes. The look is more menacing with the blood pouring from his nose and in between his fingers. I broke his nose too, and I grin.

"You stupid bitch. I'm going to enjoy making you scream," he sneers.

I laugh. "Did you think that I was going to make this easy for you?" I sneer.

"You know where to take her," Breaker's voice breaks through our banter.

I take the moment when the guy behind me is distracted by Breaker to slowly move my foot to my hand. I quickly grab the throwing star that I keep in the heel of my boots. I'm so glad Verkor grabbed them. I'm in the process of moving my other foot when the guy holding me jostles me a little.

"Would you quit moving?" He turns and walks toward the front of the pack house.

"VERKOR! STOLAS! OBSIDIAN!" I yell at the top of my lungs. Two loud, vicious roars fill the air. The guy holding me and his buddy both stumble a step at the sounds.

"What the hell was that?" I meet the friend's wide-eyes and worried expression.

"Oh, you done fucked up now." I grin as wide as I can as a giggle escapes my lips.

The friend looks over my head to the guy holding me. Behind us you can hear the sounds of a fight. Growling, yelling, screaming, and items being broken are the most prominent noises. Fear quickly replaces the worried look on his face.

"I don't think we should do this." The friend's eyes are darting around the room.

"It's too late now," the voice behind me rumbles.

"Do you hear that?" The guy in front of me points in the direction we just came from. "Whatever is in there with Breaker is bigger and badder than he is."

I smile in smug satisfaction. Hell yeah my mates are bigger, better, and scarier than Breaker and his goons. These two fools don't realize the danger they're in. My mates will rip them to shreds.

"The one guy was turning into a bear. Are you saying you can't hold your own against him? Bears are slower than wolves."

"Yeah, but you don't know what the other two shifted into." The friend runs his fingers through his hair.

"Look, let's just get her into the room and lock the door. We can take off after that. All Breaker said was to get her to the room. He didn't say anything about sticking around."

Brown eyes in front of me nods his head. The guy holding me starts to walk again. We don't go much further because we stop outside of the door in the front of the house. The door Breaker told us not to worry about. The door that leads to the room where I'm pretty sure Obsidian got tortured in when he was younger. The friend scurries forward to open the door. The room is pitch black as we enter. The door slams shut behind us. My heart rate increases. I can feel it pounding in my chest.

"Hit the lights," the goon holding me says. There's a small flicker before the lights come on.

My heart drops as I look at what's around me. There's a metal table dead center in the room. There's a drain towards the bottom of the table. I shiver looking at it. I know it's there for the bodily fluids to drain. The worst part is seeing a brown-haired man strapped to it. He's a decent size guy. Probably as tall as Verkor but with less muscle definition. He's kind of rugged looking with his plaid shirt, blue jeans, scruffy beard, and brown hair that could really use a trim. His face is a little bruised and swollen but it doesn't look like Breaker got too far in torturing him yet.

Glancing around the room, every square inch of the padded black walls are covered with some form of torture device, from floggers to whips to knives to things I've never seen before.

"Holy shit." The words are barely audible as they fall from my lips.

I start to struggle in the guy's hold, desperate to get free, not only to save myself but the guy as well. I feel a sharp sting in my hand. Shit, my throwing star. I forgot I was able to get one from my boot.

I move my hand to rest against my side. I move it toward his leg and strike, fast, stabbing him. The guy grunts and falls to one knee. His grip loosens and I'm finally able to break free. I turn to dart back to the door but the friend steps in front of it, blocking me.

My eyes quickly glance around the room, and they land on the knives. I rush over grabbing two off of the wall and brace myself. The guy I stabbed is back on his feet. Both him and his buddy take a step closer to me. That's as far as they get because the door crashes open and a hellhound, a massive ass grizzly bear, and my unseelie fae come barging in.

STOLAS

A FEW MOMENTS EARLIER

The sound of Breaker's laugh grates on my nerves. I'm tired of hearing his voice at this point. If Obsidian doesn't shut him up soon, I will. I remember the plan to not kill him, but I will help aid in his demise. All of us have our attention on Breaker, that we didn't see Cain and Jett waiting in the hallway at first.

It's not until they step toward us that we notice them, and it distracts us that we don't see the guys come in and grab Finley. We don't notice until Finley is screaming our names. I look behind me, to some mangy mutt put his grimy hands on my mate and pup.

"*We must kill him,*" my hellhound roars in my head.

"*Oh, we will,*" I reply.

I'm about to take off toward Finley when the commotion behind me pulls my attention. I see Obsidian, Cain, Breaker, and Jett all shift. Jett and Cain step in front of Breaker. No way in hell is Breaker going to be protected and make it out of here.

My shift takes over quickly. My paws leave scorch marks on the floor from the flames of hell that surround them. I don't call upon my flames often, but when I do, I mean business.

I leap in front of Obsidian, who shifted into a grizzly bear. I tackle the wolf closest to me... Cain. A whimper comes from him as my hellfire touches him. The smell of burning fur and skin fills my nose. He tries to use his back paws to scratch at my underbelly, but I'm bigger than he is, and his claws barely touch me.

I stand above him, teeth bared, smoke pluming from my nose. He tucks his tail close to his body, baring his neck. He thinks that I'm going to make this easy, after everything he put my friend through, everything he has helped do since we arrived. I'm going to enjoy ripping his throat out. I may even make a trip back into hell to see where they all end up. Obsidian might like going too. It would do him good to see them getting tortured the same way they have done him and multiple others.

I grip my teeth around his throat, picking him up. I shake my head furiously from side to side. Cain lets out another whimper as I fling him to the side. He lands in a heap on the floor. His breaths are shallow. I walk slowly over to him. Cain opens his eyes, and there's a slight twitch in his paw, but otherwise doesn't move. Blood is pooling underneath him from the tears my teeth have left in his neck. I lower my head looking right in his eyes and growl. I let go of my hellfire. Raising my paw, I use my claws to rake down his side and belly. I watch as the life leaves his eyes. His breathing stops. Cain is utterly still.

"Stolas, we need to get to Finley," Verkor says. He doesn't stay by me. He runs and moves over to Obsidian. There's a silent communication between them, and I see Verkor wrap Breaker in the shadows. We turn and head after the guy that touched our mate. Now it's time to make him pay.

VERKOR

A FEW MOMENTS EARLIER

All hell breaks loose the second Finley screams and some guy I haven't seen around puts his hands on her. Breaker and his goons shift first and Obsidian and Stolas follow. Stolas comes flying past me and attacks Cain. I jump into the fray and take on Jett. I call the shadows to me, lashing them out at him. They wrap around his legs causing him to fall on his side. I pull on the shadows, dragging the wolf toward me. Jett snarls, growls, and snaps his teeth in my direction. Calling upon more of the shadows, I use it as a muzzle. I kneel down next to him.

"I may not be a shifter, but I'm just as dangerous. Did you know very few unseelie fae can naturally use the shadows as magic?" Jett tries to curl his lips up but can't. "Everyone always assumes that I'm the weak link because I look human. I don't have the scent of a shifter. Just by looking at me you would never know I was more than human."

My wings ruffle under my skin. I let them break free. There's a moment of clarity in Jett's eyes when he sees my black wings. Only the members of the royal family in the Unseelie Court have onyx wings. Every realm but Earth knows this.

"The best part about this is I don't have to get my hands

dirty and no one will ever know I was here." The whole time I've been talking to him I slowly crept more shadows around his neck. "I'll make this quick because every second I'm wasting on you is another second something could be happening to my mate and child. And I swear, if anything happens to them, I'll cloak this region in darkness and kill you all."

I will the shadows around his neck to tighten. Jett starts to struggle against the bonds, but he doesn't get anywhere. He tries to double his efforts, but it only makes it worse. His struggling only lasts a few moments longer before he goes still. I loosen the shadows around him until I pull them back completely.

My shoulders slump. I hate this. It never feels good to take a life, but it's either mine or his. I would do anything to protect and get to Finley. I wasn't lying when I said I would kill everyone here if something happens to her or our child. I'm not normally like this, but I will help Stolas rain hell here if we don't get to her on time.

I stand and stretch my wings, ruffling the feathers, before pulling them back and putting them away. I scan the room and see that Stolas has finished off Cain and Obsidian is toying with Breaker. Since Stolas is closer, I run to him.

"Stolas, we need to get to Finley." I don't stick around. I need to get Obsidian. "Obsidian, we have to go. We have to get to Finley."

He turns his bear head toward me then back to Breaker. It takes me a moment, but I catch on. He doesn't want to leave Breaker behind. I nod to him and wrap Breaker up in my shadows.

"He'll be with us. He's not going to get away," I tell Obsidian. He nods and charges after Finley. Stolas is at our side.

OBSIDIAN

A FEW MOMENTS EARLIER

The moment that Breaker tells one of his followers to grab Finley, I see red. My anger gets the better of me and I immediately shift, dropping down onto the four paws of a grizzly bear. I wish I would have listened to Finley and shifted in Abaddon, but I wanted to do this the shifter way. I would love to see the look on Breaker's face as the King of the Abyss stared him down. I'm sure that's where Breaker is going anyway, and he'll meet him soon enough.

Breaker, Cain, and Jett waste no time shifting. Breaker is the smallest in his hyena form. Cain and Jett, both in their wolf forms step in front of Breaker. A growl sounds from next to me and the smell of sulfur is strong in my bear nose. Stolas has shifted into his hellhound form. He doesn't wait to attack. He leaps in front of me, tackling Cain. Verkor appears from the shadows beside me and attacks Jett, which leaves Breaker to myself.

I let out a roar and charge. I use my paw and swat at Breaker, causing him to smack into the wall. He lands in a heap but doesn't stay down. He gets up on his paws, shaking his head. He turns in my direction and runs straight at me. Breaker leaps into the air but I use my paws to bat him down. He stays down longer this time, but eventually gets on his feet.

I can hear Stolas' growls and the sounds of two animals hitting from somewhere in the room. I can't hear Verkor, but there's a distinct whimper of a wounded animal. The tangy scent of copper fills the air. Someone is bloody, and it's bad.

Finley yells my name. I need to get to her. I turn my bear head toward her screams and see some huge ass dude carrying her away. I release the loudest roar I can.

"How dare he touch what is ours,", my essence seethes in my mind. I'm in complete agreement.

"We will make him pay. He will die slowly and painfully,", I respond. My essence rumbles his approval.

"We will make sure he doesn't get away with it."

"No, he won't." If he hurts her in any way, and I mean even a single scratch, and I'll make what I'm planning to do to him even more painful.

Fire erupts along my arm. I turn back to Breaker and look at my arm. He used my momentary distraction to get in a cheap shot. He raked his claws down my arm. Blood oozes from the wounds and mats my fur. I growl, low and deep.

"Remember, we must not kill him. But we can maim him to within an inch of his life," my essence reminds me. It's a good thing he does because I would love nothing more than to end his life. But I don't have the time to waste on him. I need to get to my mate.

I wait for him to charge me. Luckily, it doesn't take long. He rushes forward, and I rise on my hind legs. Breaker leaps in the air, claws extended. He's aiming for my chest, but he won't make it. I use my front paws to slam him into the ground. He lands on his stomach. I need to make sure he doesn't get up. I pounce, landing all of my weight on his lower back. I feel and hear the crack of his spine. The agonizing wail that comes from Breaker is like music to my ears.

"Obsidian, we have to go. We have to get to Finley," Verkor's voice comes from beside me.

I don't want to leave Breaker behind. I don't want to give someone the chance to come and take him to safety. I swing my head back and forth between Verkor and Breaker. It takes Verkor a moment, but he gets what I want. He uses his shadows to wrap Breaker's body up.

"He'll be with us. He's not going to get away," Verkor says. I nod my bear head and take off after the guy that has Finley.

The smell of sulfur assaults my nose and I know Stolas is nearby. With the pounding footsteps behind me, I know Verkor is following. I turn my nose to the air and inhale deeply. I pick

S. DALAMBAKIS

up Finley's scent, strawberry with a hint of brimstone. I let the scent guide me.

We end up in front of the door. The door I know all too well. I don't have to wallow in my own thoughts. My mate and baby need me. I have to be strong for them. I charge straight for the door, using my strength to ram through it. I quickly scan the room, and see Finley posed and ready to attack with knives in her hand. It's a beautiful sight.

CHAPTER 23

FINLEY

"It's about time you guys showed up," I smile at them.

It gives me the perfect opportunity to do what I need to. The guys who took me are distracted by my mates coming through the door that they forgot about me. I flip the knives in my hand and fling them, one right after the other. Both of them land right where I want them too... in my kidnappers' chests. They drop to the floor.

Stolas shifts back into his human form, immediately coming to me. He drops down on his knees in front of me. His hands go to my hips and his ear to my belly.

"Are you alright? Are both of you alright?" he asks, peppering my belly with kisses. I smile down at him and run my fingers through his hair.

"We're both fine, I promise. They didn't hurt me," I reply.

It seems like my words calmed Obsidian enough for him to shift back. He stomps over to me, running a gentle finger down the side of my face.

"Are you sure you're both alright?" he asks, cupping the side of my face. I nod against his hand.

"Don't forget we have an appointment when we get back with the doctor. We'll tell him what happened and have him double check." Obsidian nods before placing a gentle kiss on my lips.

"Who's that?" Stolas questions. Pointing to the shifter that is still tied to the table.

"I don't know, but he was in here when those two dipshits brought me here. I will give you one guess why he's in here though," I state.

"Breaker was torturing him and was more than likely going to kill him," Stolas responds with a sigh. Stolas walks over to the wall with the knives and pulls one off the wall. He strides over to the table and the shifter starts to aggressively pull at the straps. "Whoa," Stolas says, holding his hands up. The guy settles down. "I'm not here to continue whatever they were doing to you. I'm just going to cut the straps so you can go, I promise."

Tentatively, Stolas closes the distance, and makes it a point to let the shifter see his every move as he cuts the straps. Once the last strap is done, the shifter rolls off the table and lands on his hands and knees. None of us take a step toward him. We wait for him to gather his strength. It takes a few minutes, but he rises to his feet.

"Thank you," he says. He meets each of our eyes before limping out of the room. None of us tries to stop him.

I look over to Verkor, who has moved closer. I notice a black floating blob behind him.

"Whatcha got there?" I nod my head toward whatever is behind him. He turns to see what I motioned too.

"Oh, that's Breaker," he replies.

"Is he dead?" I question. Verkor shakes his head.

"Not yet."

Stolas stands and takes my hand, interlacing our fingers. I turn my attention toward Obsidian.

"You still have the map?" He pats his pockets and pulls out the last piece, the three pieces we already have together. He puts them back into his pockets. "I'm so ready to go home."

"We have one more thing to do before we leave," Obsidian states. I raise an eyebrow at him. He points to the floating mass. "Someone else needs to kill him. This region needs someone better than him running it."

"Well," I say with a sigh. "Let's go and tell the masses."

I link my other hand with Obsidian's as we follow Verkor out of the torture room, back through the house, into the backyard. A crowd of people from the beach are already waiting. It's like they could sense the change.

Verkor lowers the mass to the ground before removing the shadows that cloaked Breaker. I expected him to jump up and attack, but he doesn't. He just lays there and whimpers. Gasps fill the air when the shifters see Breaker's broken body. Obsidian steps forward and everyone turns their wide eyes to him. Not a single sound can be heard as they wait with bated breath.

"As you can see, Breaker is severely injured. I didn't kill him because I don't want to be your Packmaster. I am leaving that decision to you. And for the love of the realm pick someone better than the last few Packmasters."

I giggle, causing Obsidian to look at me. "Great speech," I say with a smile. He rolls his eyes then looks back toward the crowd. It's then that I notice his arm is bleeding. It doesn't look too bad, but I still want to check it out.

"Whoever you pick needs to come up here and finish him off," Obsidian states.

There is a hush whispering in the crowd that seemed to go on forever, when in reality it was only a few minutes. The guy we just set free, limps forward, holding an arm around his middle. The guy walks right up to Obsidian and sticks his hand out.

271

"Jonathan McClearin." Obsidian sizes him up.

"Do you have any history with abusing others?" Obsidian asks.

"No sir," Jonathan replies. He winces as he tries to stand up straight.

Obsidian crosses his arms over his chest. "What do you plan to do with the region and its shifters?"

"Anything and everything I have to, to fix this," Jonathan answers without dropping his hand. "I know what these people have been through. It's going to take time and therapy to get them through this, but I'll see they get the help they need."

Obsidian accesses him a little longer before finally shaking his hand. "Then you know what to do." Obsidian nods towards Breaker. Jonathan gives him a sharp nod.

He shuffles over to Breaker's prone body, shifting only his hand. It looks like a wolf paw. Quickly, he uses his claws to slice open Breaker's neck. It doesn't take long for Breaker to bleed out. The quiet clearing erupts into loud cheers. The once dead party comes to life. I guess they do have something to celebrate after all. Hopefully, he'll be good for this region, for these shifters, and turn things around for the better.

I eye my guys ready to leave this place behind. I'm ready to sleep in my own bed and just be home.

"One thing before we leave," Verkor says before rushing back into the pack house. He emerges a minute later with my violin and bow in hand. Thankfully, one of us remembered it. I'm going to have to inspect it for damage when we get home. Together we quietly take our leave.

We walk back toward the bed and breakfast, tired and a little bloody. Obsidian rummages through the bushes out front, grabbing our bags. Stolas and Verkor each take theirs, but Verkor opens mine, putting my violin inside. Obsidian keeps my bag and his. Stolas steps up next to me, taking my hand. Together we walk to the gateway, stopping before it.

"Magic Realm," Stolas says and we step through together.

VERKOR

"Are we going back to yours and Izzy's place?" I ask, following behind Stolas and Finley. Obsidian is walking next to me.

All I want is a shower and some sleep, but I know Finley won't rest until she puts that map together.

"Yup. Izzy should be home. I want her there when I put the final piece together," Finley replies. "We can crash there if you like, then go home tomorrow."

I love that she thinks of mine and the guy's place as home, because it is. She belongs with us.

"Sounds like a plan," Stolas says.

We don't speak as we walk through the busy streets of the Magic Realm to Finley's place. The second she opens the door she yells.

"Iz, you up?"

"Of course, I am. You didn't need to yell; I'm just in the kitchen," Izzy says. "Besides, it's not actually that late."

Finley shrugs and smiles as she walks toward her friend. "Sorry, it's hard to tell when you come from a place with only four hours of daylight."

Izzy sets her cup down on the counter, before gathering Finley in her arms.

"I've missed you, Mama."

"I've missed you too, Iz."

Finley pulls back and Izzy does a once over, making sure that she's unharmed. I'm grateful they have each other. You can see the love and the bond that they share.

"Woah, look at you." Izzy places a hand on Finley's belly. She giggles, and from the corner of my eye, I see Stolas puff up his chest.

"I know right. I feel like I've doubled in size." Finley smiles at Izzy. So much joy is radiating from Fin. She's absolutely gorgeous, and I get to call her mine.

"Pregnancy suits you. You're glowing, girl."

"Thanks," Finley whispers.

Finley places her hands next to Izzy's. Moments later, Izzy's eyes widened. I know the baby must have kicked. The girls look at each other and start to giggle.

"You got a strong one in there," Izzy teases.

"Don't I know it."

Stolas would be preening right now if he was in his hell-hound form. Finley looks over to Stolas and winks. Izzy moves her hands, taking a step back from Finley.

"I take it since you're home you retrieved the last piece of the map?"

"Hell yeah we did." Finley turns a blinding smile in mine and the guys' direction. Izzy turns her attention to us, finally realizing that we're in the room too.

"Hey guys," Izzy says with a smile.

"Hi," we all say at once.

"I found the spell I was looking for. I put it up around this place and yours. If anyone wishing to do you harm comes anywhere close to here, they'll forget why they're here, turn around, and leave."

"Thank you, Izzy," Finley says.

"No problem. I want all of us to stay safe." It's then that Izzy really takes a look at us. She raises an eyebrow. "I take it from the blood, it didn't go that smoothly?"

"When does it ever," Finley says with exasperation. "Speaking of," Finley walks over to Obsidian, looking at his arm. "Don't think I didn't notice."

"I'm fine. My shifting ability has already started to heal me, and the bleeding has stopped," he replies.

"Yeah, yeah. I don't care. I'm still going to look," Finley says, inspecting his arm. Obsidian huffs but lets her continue until she's satisfied. She looks up at him and crooks her finger. He leans down. "Thanks for being a good sport," she says before kissing him.

When they pull apart, Obsidian runs a gentle finger down the side of her face. She stares at him lovingly. It's funny how fast your life can change. Who would have thought this would be my life? I found my mate, she's agreed to marry me, and we have a baby on the way. I can definitely say that I wouldn't change a thing.

"As sweet as this is, can we put the map together? I want to know where we're headed next," Stolas says bouncing on his toes.

Finley rolls her eyes but puts out her hand, palm up, toward Obsidian. Luckily, the magic that comes with being a shifter allows them to shift with clothes, and they reappear when they shift back. Otherwise, we would have lost the map.

Obsidian pulls the last piece of the map and the three pieces that are already together and hands them to Finley. She walks over to the coffee table, dropping down to her knees. The rest of us gather around her. Finley looks up, meeting each of us in the eyes. I give her a nod. She looks back down to the map, lining up the pieces. The familiar bluish white light flares, sealing the last piece together. This time as the lines appear on the map, they don't fade. I suck in a sharp breath from the rippling waves I feel in the air. By the sounds around me, I'm not the only one. I lean in closer to see mountains, lakes, forests, and bridges. I focus on the names of the places and my eyes widen.

"I know where we're going," I say. Everyone turns towards me, waiting for me to answer their unspoken question. "We're going to Heaven."

EPILOGUE

LUCIFER- HELL REALM

A wave of magic ripples across my skin, as I sit behind my desk, staring at the violin Finley left on the ground. Goosebumps pebble my flesh. I sit up straight in my chair. What the hell was that? What could have caused such a release of energy? My eyes drift back to the violin. The light bulb goes off, and a thunderous laugh escapes me.

"Oh, that little minx. She actually did it." I throw my head back and laugh more.

The door to my office opens and one of my guards rushes in. His eyes dart around the room, looking for a threat.

"You okay, boss?"

"I'm fine. You can leave." I wave him away with my hand. "Close the door behind you."

I wait until I hear the click before standing. I walk over to the violin, running my fingers along it.

"You are full of surprises. I can't wait to see what you do next."

It's about time all the realms are on equal footing. I, for one, can't wait to see the outcome.

. . .

PRESIDENT- EARTH REALM

A shiver runs through my body. The air feels different. I look around to my aides and staff, but they don't seem to notice.

Something is happening and I don't know what it is. Let's just hope it's nothing bad.

CIRRO- FAERIE REALM

"How's the progress on retribution for those Kellan wrongfully imprisoned?" I ask my assistant. He flips through a couple of pages before answering.

"Good. We only have a few more..."

I don't hear the rest of what he says because a wave of energy flows over me. It's strong. What could have caused something like this? I go on alert, waiting to see if someone attacks. Only someone with strong magic could cause this kind of effect. Minutes tick by, but nothing happens. I relax in my seat.

My assistant is still talking like he felt nothing. My gaze shifts around the room, glancing over the painting that hides the safe. I stop, bringing my eyes back to it. No, there's no way. Could they actually have all the pieces? I mean, if anyone could do it, it would be them.

I whip my head toward my assistant. "I'm sorry, but can we finish this later? There's something I need to do."

I usher him out of the room, closing and locking the door behind him. I need to call my cousin. I need to know if they did it.

GUARDIAN- HEAVEN REALM

"What's so urgent that you had to call me here?" Finley's mother questions as she walks up to me. I meet her gray eyes. I try to keep my face clear of emotions, but I fail. "What is it? Has something happened to Finley?" she questions frantically.

"He's found her," I whisper. I don't need to elaborate because she knows what I'm talking about.

"No, no, no." Finley's mother starts to pace around the room. "What am I going to do now?"

"I don't think there's anything you can do. If he's as bad as you say, he won't stop until he has her." Finley's mother lets out a whimper. "There's more." She stops pacing to look at me. "Did you feel that wave of energy?"

"Yes, but I don't know what it's from."

"I do. It was from the last piece of the map being assembled." Finley's mother sucks in a breath. "She has it. Finley has the map."

"Yes." My eyes bounce back and forth between hers. "Your daughter is on her way here."

Finley's Father

"Sir, Sir, we've found her," one of my minions says bursting through my office door. I look up from the files in front of me.

"Where?" I ask.

"The Magic Realm," he responds.

A smile spreads across my face. I knew I'd find her. Her mother hid her well, but I knew it was only a matter of time.

"There's more sir." I wave my hand for him to continue. "She has the map."

The grin on my face widens. This is better than I could have hoped for. "Well, I think it's time I met my daughter."

The End

To Be Continued in Book 4 of the Gypsy Notes Series, Stolen Treasure

THE MAP

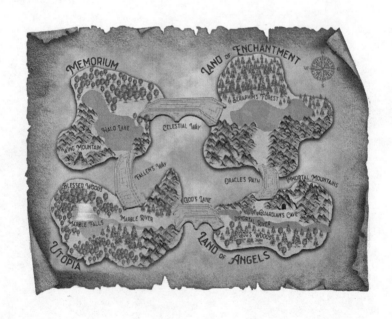

AUTHOR NOTE

First, I want to thank all of you for bearing with me. I know it's been a while since the release of Stolen Fire. I have to admit, I wasn't feeling like myself. I was having a tough time mentally, then the quarantine happened. Recently, I have been feeling more like myself. I'm sorry it took so long to get this book out to you. I hope you enjoyed Obsidian's story and are looking forward to the conclusion of the Gypsy Notes Series.

If you liked Stolen Twilight, please consider leaving a review. They help indie authors like me.

I'd like to thank Rachael, my editor. As always, you do such a wonderful job. I love all of your feedback.

Thank you to my beta and arc readers. You guys rock.

Consuelo Parra, thank you for the gorgeous cover.

To my readers, thank you. You give me so much encouragement to continue to do what I love.

Next up is Stolen Treasure, the epic conclusion. Be ready for a journey into heaven.

Thank you to everyone behind the scenes.

If you are reading this, I do have a newsletter and a Teespring store. The links can be found on my author on Facebook. I'm still trying to figure out the best way to sell signed copies of my books and for swag packs. If you have any suggestions, I'm happy to hear them.

I hope everyone is staying safe during this pandemic.

Much love,

S. Dalambakis

Playlist
"Moon Trance"- Lindsey Sterling
"Darkside"- Lindsey Sterling
"Under Control"- Ellie Goulding
"Take What You Want From Me"- Post Malone & Ozzy
"Got What I Got"- Jason Aldean
"Right Now"- Korn
"Today I Decided"- Sno Tha Product
"Candy"- Doja Cat
"Neon Moon"- Brooks and Dunn
"Can't Fight The Moonlight"- Leann Rimes
"With Or WIthout You"- Dope
"My Heart Is Lost To You"- Brooks and Dunn
"Save Me"- My Darkest Days
"Get It On The Floor"- DMX
"Tonight Looks Good On You"- Jason Aldean
"Truth To The Weak"- Fire From The Gods
"Right Now"- Fire From The Gods
"Dance Money"- Tones & I

MORE BOOKS BY S. DALAMBAKIS

Shifter Royalty Trilogy (Complete)
Royals
Queen's Guard
Alpha Queen
Reign (novella)

Gypsy Notes Series
Stolen Warriors
Stolen Fire
Stolen Twilight
Stolen Treasure (2020)

ABOUT THE AUTHOR

Hi! I am S. Dalambakis. I am a thirty-something mother of twins and a native Ohioan, who just recently moved to Florida. I have been married for 10+ years, to a loving and supportive husband. I graduated from Youngstown State University, with a degree in Criminal Justice and Biology. I have been an inspiring writing for years and finally have the courage to release my writing to the world. I have a love for books and all things Harry Potter and "nerdy". I also have an unhealthy obsession with planners and pens.

Come and stop by my social media.
http://www.facebook.com/s.dalambakis/
https://instagram.com/s.dalambakis
www.facebook.com/groups/Theroyalpack/
www.twitter.com/s.dalambakis
www.pinterest.com/sdalambakis

Happy reading!

Made in the USA
Columbia, SC
31 January 2022

54674452R00174